BLUE  THIRD
CHASING TIME

BLUE THIRD
CHASING TIME

TATE PUBLISHING
AND ENTERPRISES, LLC

BRAD BLAKE

Published by Tate Publishing & Enterprises, LLC
127 E. Trade Center Terrace | Mustang, Oklahoma 73064 USA
1.888.361.9473 | www.tatepublishing.com

Tate Publishing is committed to excellence in the publishing industry. The company reflects the philosophy established by the founders, based on Psalm 68:11,
"The Lord gave the word and great was the company of those who published it."

Book design copyright © 2013 by Tate Publishing, LLC. All rights reserved.

Published in the United States of America

ISBN: 978-1-62746-141-2
1. Fiction / Science Fiction / Action and Adventure
2. Fiction / Fantasy / Epic
13.10.30

For
Janice and Leonard

Mom was a teacher and librarian,
opening a lifetime joy of reading and writing,
and would've loved the Blue Third books.
Dad opened a love of history and made some too,
surviving the Japanese attack on Darwin, Feb. 1942,
serving in World War II from start to finish.

To each of them this book is lovingly dedicated.

MAIN CHARACTERS

HUMANS

Citlalli
Heather
David
Lupe
Tyson
Maddy
Estrella
Lisa
Gilad
Jamila
Mary
Lucy (Honorary Human)

ALIENS

Gelzain: Sklizz, Wizza
Trixian: Tarayon, Summahon
Plinn: Humley
Okyrick: Kikikik
Doozy: Supreme Doozy, Kriner, Kahpoo, Rooq, Stauffa, Waima
Fiberian: Thrix
Uppsalians: Llarke, Vomisa, Einlen, Vorwin
Bull: Hinge
Celery: Jak-toll
Meemer: Prince Zed
Lizard: Yore
Anemone: Vivvy
Weevles: ???
Watcher: Theal

The Anahuac universe was born of Light and Dark.

The Mother of all Gods, Coatlique,
first gave birth to the Goddess of the Moon,
Coyolxanuhqui,
and then to male Gods who became the stars.

When Coatlique learned they all plotted to kill her,
she brought Dark to the cosmos,
giving birth to the God of War,
Huitzilopochtli.

He destroyed his brothers and sister,
and the heavens crumbled to pieces.

PART ONE

AWAKEN

Magnified bug eyes peering through curved glass; uncaring, emotionless, scientific stares; and then nothing. Perhaps she slept. Maybe she was dead. There was no sensation of time; weightless, drifting, floating.

And then in the blink of an eye, her Anahuac village lay just below. Citlalli knew she'd made it home!

A ridiculously smart man from Citlalli's planet once said, "Put your hand on a hot stove for a minute, and it seems like an hour. Sit with a pretty girl for an hour, and it seems like a minute. That's relativity."

Citlalli sailed on air currents for hours searching for her family, but time being relative it seemed like minutes.

The Okyricks had sent her five thousand years into the past, to the land of Cemanahuac on planet Earth. It seemed she'd made it back but could only float, unable find her family. In addition, there was no sound. She tried to yell, to scream, to shatter the quiet, but couldn't even make a squeak. Her joy was turning into a nightmare.

Was she really home? What was going on?

Drifting over a cluster of theobroma trees she heard a faint noise, like the padding of furry feet on a floor.

Citlalli realized she was waking up. She stayed in her dream-state, eyes closed, lying on something solid and cool. She focused on the tip-toeing, pretending to be asleep, wondering who was there. Was she still on planet Scradle? Did she make it back to Earth with her family? She remained frozen, holding her breath, listening intently.

The touch of a soft hand on her cheek jolted both eyes open to what she hoped was her world of five thousand years ago. Instead, she found herself staring up into the yellow eyes of a black-haired jaguar-like alien she knew as Tarayon.

Tarayon had been delivering supplies to planet Uppsala, still grieving over his lost mate Summahon, when his spacecraft was instantly teleported into orbit around an unknown planet. Invisible beings called Watchers then telepathically shared an amazing story and sent him down to a cave inside the planet. He was shocked to find an alien; a Human being he knew as Citlalli.

Dressed in a dirty and torn camo-suit, she had many cuts and scrapes turning into scabs. She'd obviously been in a brutal fight. Citlalli's pure white hair was spread around her bronze face like a beautiful snowy fan.

What had happened to this brave young Human?

Tarayon kneeled next to Citlalli, then reached down and gently touched her cheek.

Citlalli opened her eyes.

SUMMAHON

Several months earlier, two small spacecraft had crossed into a dangerously unstable area of space ruled by beings called the Watchers. It was widely known that entering this Watcher territory was tempting fate. Most who did never returned and no one knew what happened.

Tarayon piloted one spacecraft and his Trixian life-mate, Summahon, flew the other. Both were expert pilots and knew the deadly risks and possible rewards of entering Watcher space. They hoped the Watchers would provide a miracle in their losing battle with the galaxy-devouring evil entity known as the Destroyer.

Not only were these Watchers unpredictable, but this area of outer space was riddled with dark matter, tiny black holes, and other unknowns.

These two Trixians were braving the incredibly dangerous journey when Summahon's spacecraft hit an invisible tachyon space fracture and began to vibrate.

Tarayon heard Summahon scream his name, glanced over, and saw her spacecraft vanish. Then he blacked out.

When Tarayon awoke he remembered nothing after Summahon's disappearance. He found himself far from Watcher space, and on his controls were two mysterious necklace amulets. These amulets did indeed perform miracles for Citlalli and another Human named David in helping defeat the Destroyer.

Since losing Summahon and helping Citlalli defeat this Destroyer, Tarayon had grieved and wondered what happened to his life-mate. He knew no one ever returned from space fractures, so he had to accept that Summahon was gone forever.

But Summahon was not dead.

It had been several months since Summahon screamed Tarayon's name and found herself instantly teleported to a world of insanity. After vanishing, she'd reappeared still inside her spacecraft, flung to some miserable corner of the universe.

Upon arrival, Summahon had to call upon all her flying skills to escape a gargantuan black hole, then maneuver through areas of space riddled with ancient debris, and finally enter the atmosphere of a huge planet, only to have her spacecraft inexplicably lose all power, forcing her to parachute to safety as her spacecraft smashed into the ground.

Summahon had no idea where she was.

It was easy to lose track of time on this crazy world, but she knew it'd been at least a few months. On this particular afternoon the insanity continued, as she found herself inside a hollowed-out tree trunk, hiding from a large, eight-legged insect-monster. She could hear the monstrous beast thrashing in the surrounding forest of alien trees. The sound seemed to be moving away, which was good because Summahon was exhausted. What little sleep she'd gotten had been laced with nightmares.

She wasn't sure what happened to Hinge, Jak-toll, and Vivvy, her new alien friends. They'd been trying to find a town located somewhere in this area when the insect-monster attacked. After fleeing in all directions, she'd screamed at the enormous thing to chase her. Summahon knew Vivvy and Jak-toll would've been easy prey for this monster, and when it turned to pursue her, the others were able to escape.

As she sat in the cool tree trunk, her mind returned again to those last seconds with Tarayon as they approached the Watchers, wanting to look in her life-mate's deep yellow eyes one more time.

They'd fled their Trixian home world after deadly gamma rays wiped out their planet's evolutionary food-chain vital for survival. Rather than relocating, Tarayon and Summahon headed out into the universe.

Like Tarayon, Summahon resembled a two-legged walking jaguar without a tail. However, instead of black hair, hers was a reddish copper color along with a white-haired chest and face. She had pointy feline ears and four-fingered hands with retractable claws, and her dirty once-white camo-suit was getting frayed rapidly.

Relaxing inside this tree trunk Summahon began dozing. It was quiet in the forest and she was so tired. Perhaps the beast had finally given up. Just a little nap...

Suddenly the trunk was yanked violently into the air, Summahon's claws digging into the rotting wood to keep from flying out. The monster gripped the tree trunk in its pincer mouth and she heard the wood crackling, ready to snap in two. As the beast swept the trunk back and forth in swinging arcs, Summahon saw its large purple torso below. The trunk started to shatter and as the torso swung back into view she leaped out just as it splintered in half. Landing hard on the beast, Summahon's foot smashed through its exoskeleton into its body. The monster shrieked as she pulled out her yellow gore-covered boot. Wasting no time, she pounced onto its rear body part and then hit the ground running. The thing turned with a hideous clacking and shrieking sound, knocking over trees and smashing through bushes.

She zigzagged through the forest growth, barely staying ahead of the monster. Exhaustion was close to overtaking Summahon as she reached open ground next to a high plateau. The forest ended as she entered a rubble-strewn canyon that cut through two steep plateau walls. The monster was closing fast and Summahon ran deeper into the narrow canyon. She quickly found herself trapped against a tall rock pile. There was no way around, no time to climb, and she didn't stand a chance against this killing machine. As razor-sharp pincers moved in to tear her apart, she thought of Tarayon one last time.

Boom!

The earth seemed to leap in the air, knocking Summahon and the monster off their feet. A powerful earthquake began raining boulders down into the canyon. She crawled and rolled on the rippling earth. A rock smashed into the ground next to her, shattering and pelting her with shards, one gashing the back of her head. She plastered herself against the canyon wall, watching as the shrieking purple creature was crushed beneath a shower of pulverizing boulders, its yellowish insides splattering everywhere.

Finally the shaking stopped. Since her arrival Summahon had survived dozens of these quakes. She'd also seen volcanoes spewing out flames, rock, smoke, and lava.

She sat up, feeling the slight gash underneath the tan fur on the back of her head. It wasn't too bad. She looked over at the monster's crushed and oozing carcass. It was buried under boulders now blocking the entrance. She was stuck between two piles of huge rocks. She could either climb the goo-splattered boulders on one side or goo-free boulders on the other side.

Reaching the top of the clean boulder pile, she saw the motley alien threesome of Hinge, Jak-toll, and Vivvy waiting at the bottom.

"I thought we heard you pizzing about over there," said Hinge, "and figured you were a goner."

"Did your fight cause that quake?" said Vivvy.

Jak-toll just buzzed and shook his leafy blue head.

Summahon smiled with her new friends, all very different races of aliens, and like her stranded on this strangest of planets in a forgotten corner of the universe.

If only Tarayon could see her now.

CRASHING

Summahon would've been shocked to learn how close she was to friends of Tarayon's.

After surviving the U.N. kidnapping, horrible Doozies, a death arena battle, and leaving time-traveling Citlalli behind, the spacecraft piloted by Sklizz and Einlen was returning to Earth when it vanished while exiting a zip. They found themselves teleported somewhere unknown and captured in the gravitational death grip of a huge black hole. After barely escaping its clutches, they evaded bizarre space debris, only to have their saucer-shaped spacecraft lose power as they entered the atmosphere of an enormous planet.

Heather, Estrella, Tyson, and Lisa watched helplessly as they plummeted toward the surface. Einlen was piloting their speeding spacecraft toward a high plateau at the edge of a forest. It was the only possible landing area, though covered with rocks and trees.

Heather and Estrella could see they were going to smash into the plateau wall. Bravely they closed their eyes, held their breath, and waited for impact.

BAM!

The saucer-bottom slammed into the edge of the plateau, bouncing crazily and skidding on the ground at incredible speed. Trees, bushes, and churned-up dirt were flying past. Everyone gripped their seats, tense, waiting to smash into something. Then, thankfully, they gradually slowed as the front end of the ship dug into the ground.

Einlen was such a good pilot she'd found a tiny gap between trees and other obstacles, helping them slow down before the front end finally slammed into a large rock. Everyone felt the collision as the saucer flipped forward over the boulder, doing a slow-motion somersault and stopping pointed straight up at the sky. The saucer rear-end had dug into the soft earth next to the boulder. They were in one piece, but stuck in the ground like an alien Ferris wheel.

Everyone caught their breath, lying on their backs and looking up into a pinkish gray sky outside the front window.

"You okay back there?" asked Sklizz.

The shaken passengers saw everyone still in one piece.

"Yeah," said Lisa, "seem to be."

Sklizz leaned back and reached for the emergency exit. It opened easily, but was too far away for passengers to reach from the rear seats.

"I have a space cord. We'll pull you up. Wrap it around you and under your arms. You first Estrella."

The tricky exiting went smoothly, and in moments she was outside into a humid and overcast day. Once on the boulder's edge she removed the cord, slid down a few feet, and hopped to the surface. Estrella shook her long red hair with its white streak, happy to be back on solid ground—though not necessarily *this* planet's solid ground. "*Mi Dios,*" she muttered. "Where the heck are we now?"

Far in the distance a snarling roar echoed across the plateau, causing Estrella and her heart rate to jump. She scanned the area in all directions, seeing nothing except strange alien trees and plants. She also looked at the odd sight of their spacecraft stuck sideways in the ground like an enormous saucer. How would it ever fly again?

Minutes later, Heather, Tyson, Lisa, Einlen, and Sklizz had exited, bringing as many supplies as possible. Estrella told them about the terrifying roar. At least they knew the planet was inhabited, but by what?

At that moment an earthquake threw everyone to the ground. Undulating waves rippled across the terrain, and in moments their spacecraft began rocking. Just before the shaking stopped, it toppled forward onto its belly.

"The ground should've shook twenty minutes ago," said Sklizz, "and saved us from having to climb out."

"Do you have any idea where we are?" asked Lisa.

Sklizz could only shake his head.

"As we approach, do quick check," said Einlen. "Wherever we are, space area is strangest I've seen."

"That black hole was unbelievable," said Sklizz.

"I see deformed stars, weird darkness, blurry space, and time bands: destruction, violence, and chaos."

"It's a space madhouse," Sklizz agreed.

"I think we're near ultimate singularity."

Sklizz looked at Einlen with surprise. "It would explain a lot..."

"Time's beginning."

Everyone thought about these comments. Finally Tyson broke the silence.

"Do you mean the Big Bang?"

"Uh, yes, Tyson your Earth name also applies," said Sklizz. "If true, the zip sent us to infinity; your Big Bang—the place where all time began."

Heather looked at Tyson, impressed. She noticed the shock of white in his curly black hair; their ancestral link to a five-thousand-year-old cousin named Citlalli. She wondered for the zillionth time if Citlalli had made it home.

Heather had long, straight black hair with its own distinctive white streak, topped off by her well-worn powder-blue softball cap.

"If we're near the universal core, it would explain why no one returns after disappearing from a zip," said Sklizz.

"Will the spacecraft fly again?" asked Lisa.

"Good question. There was no reason for it to lose power in the first place. It went dead the moment we neared this planet's atmosphere."

"Food and shelter first," said Einlen.

"Not that way," said Estrella, pointing in the direction she'd heard the roar.

AWAKENING

Citlalli had been dreaming of her village and home, so waking up to Tarayon's yellow eyes was shocking.

"Citlalli," said Tarayon, "it's good to see you. I'm supposed to welcome you on behalf of the Watchers."

Still groggy, it took a moment for Tarayon's comment to make sense. When it did she leaped to her feet, dizzy as she staggered against the cave wall.

"The Watchers?"

"Yes, they gave us the amulet you used against the Destroyer. They brought us here."

Citlalli could only shake her head with confusion.

"Citlalli," a Watcher's deep rumbling voice echoed through the cave. "Do not be afraid. We've teleported you and Tarayon to our birth planet to ask for your help."

Citlalli's dream of traveling to her ancient village and family still lingered.

"I was going back in time. The Okyricks were sending me home," said Citlalli.

"The Okyricks offer no such time travel," said the Watcher. "Had we not taken you when we did...had we not intervened to bring you here, your atoms would've been rearranged and you'd have been killed. The Okyricks play with time in ways that will spell their doom."

Citlalli's heart fluttered at this devastating news.

"Do not despair. We know of a way to return you back in time to your family. But this cannot happen unless we reverse terrible processes now in motion. Time itself and the entire universe will end as we know it. Your and Sklizz's latent power and time signatures are our best hope. Alas, we cannot find Sklizz."

The Watchers told of an expanding and evolving universe of Light skidding to a stop, a halt that would kill all life everywhere. The Watchers had discovered an unknown force interconnected with zips that seemed to be reeling in the universal zip network. This mysterious Dark force was yanking the fabric of space and time.

"Why Citlalli and Sklizz?" said Tarayon.

"They come outside of our time, making them uniquely valuable in the struggle against the Dark. The Dark's power seems limitless. We are running out of options."

"Is this power...this Darkness...a god?" asked Citlalli.

"Dark and Light are the universe's two ultimate opposing powers. You may have other names for them. They represent good and evil in the cosmos."

"Well then," she said, "where is Sklizz?"

"We have no idea. His spacecraft vanished inside a zip. There is no return from a zip disappearance."

Citlalli gasped.

She'd been on board with Sklizz, Heather, Estrella, Tyson, Lisa, and Einlen when they'd escaped the Doozies. She'd chosen to remain on planet Scradle with the Okyricks, to time-travel back to her family. She last remembered watching Sklizz's spacecraft as it accelerated away from the planet.

Citlalli couldn't believe her friends were dead. She knew they were alive, somewhere. Her Anahuac inner spirit wouldn't lie. But that same inner spirit seemed to tell her not everyone would survive.

"Tell me what we must do," said Citlalli.

The Watchers began to tell Citlalli and Tarayon of a journey that would take them and a crew of fourteen others to the end of the universe and back again.

When finished, the Watchers shared secret thoughts.

"Why not tell them that Summahon, Sklizz and the others ended up in this place?"

"They mustn't be distracted. Besides, we have no control. Their friends are probably all dead."

SCHANZE

Far back across the universe on the Doozy world of Yerti, galaxy-shaking plans were in motion. The Supreme Doozy was more determined than ever to get his greedy four-fingered hands on zooey—what Humans called cocoa. However, the Human race and its new alien allies still stood in the way. He planned to solve this problem once and for all by destroying Mars and exterminating humanity.

However, there was a young and seemingly innocent agent of change at work.

Waima was a fifteen-year-old Doozy, the only daughter of a widowed male named Stauffa, a leader in Space Command. She was excited to be with him at this historic meeting inside a mountain hideaway called the Schanze. She was proud to deliver a special footstool to the empty meeting room, nervously placing it under the Supreme Doozy's main planning table.

This secret meeting focused on sending a suicidal spaceship to Scradle, the legendary Okyrick time-travel planet. Disguised as a Doozy peace-ship, it would unleash mind-boggling planetary destruction, turning Scradle into a burned-out hulk and killing anything on, around, or inside the planet.

It was a prototype planet-killer spacecraft and the Supreme Doozy named it Exterminator. It would end the Okyrick time-altering threat and open their solar system to conquest and enslavement. He hated Okyricks.

The Supreme Doozy was already building Exterminator II to be used on Mars. Once the first Exterminator proved itself, they could go after juicier prey: the Humans and their allies in that distant solar system. He'd start with the Red Planet they called Mars with its infestation of Fiberians. They would wipe out the surviving Fiberian vermin before they began breeding. He'd have revenge for his previous defeat on Mars, as well as the death arena humiliation and knife in his eye from the Gelzian named Arizza. His nightmares were horrible, seeing Arizza's rage-filled eyes, hearing her berserk scream, and feeling the plunging knife over and over again.

On this fateful day the Supreme Doozy returned from a nourishment break, surprised to find there were three missing staff members.

"Where are Stauffa, Garz, and Lemmor?"

No one had an answer.

"They better have a good excuse for wasting my time."

In reality, Garz, Lemmor, Stauffa, and young Waima were already on the run. Waima's footstool was a cleverly disguised bomb that would kill everyone in the meeting room, and it was ready to detonate in moments. Waima was working with her father and the other conspirators to stop the Supreme Doozy from leading their entire civilization to its destruction.

However, as ticking death stared him in the face, the Supreme Doozy said, "I leave the next task to you. When I return from my cleansing, I want Earth invasion details."

And thus with dumb luck he twisted fate and headed for the exit, entering the doorway just as the footstool exploded. All those around the table were killed, while the Supreme Doozy felt heat and jagged shrapnel slamming into his back as he was blown out the door and away from the table of death. Badly wounded, he screeched at shocked guards to find the traitorous Stauffa, Garz, and Lemmor immediately.

Waima and Stauffa heard from Lemmor that the Supreme Doozy survived. This was devastating news and meant they all needed to flee immediately. Lemmor was quite old and refused to run, saying heartfelt goodbyes. He knew his time was short.

Stauffa had hoped for the best and prepared for the worst. He and Waima quickly sped away from the Doozy solar system in his private spacecraft. Father and daughter were on a zip path to distant Earth and Mars. The Humans and Fiberians needed to be warned about the coming War of Armageddon. They must be made aware of Exterminator II.

Lemmor took his own life, painlessly, which enraged the Supreme Doozy. The other would-be assassins were rounded up, tortured, and executed, their ashes flushed down a rectalizer. An empire-wide death notice was issued for Stauffa and Waima, and the Supreme Doozy sent his finest tracker-killer, named Kriner, after the two traitors.

The Supreme Doozy's stabbed eye was already hideously sunken, and now this footstool bomb left him hunched over with bubbly gray burn scars covering his head and back. He wore a perpetual scar-faced sneer on his pasty-white pumpkin face with forever-leaking yellow drool oozing out one side of his deformed and crooked mouth.

PLATEAU

The crash-landed castaways had been walking for hours on the plateau, the forest getting denser and the sky growing dark. Stumbling upon a stream, Sklizz tested the water and found it safe to drink.

Lisa was still limping from the serious bite wound she'd gotten in the death arena on Yerti.

Heather's cracked ribs, caused by the grip of that death arena monster's tentacle, were feeling better. She remembered Citlalli's Anahuac war cry and flying leap onto the monster's huge eyeball, arms and legs sinking into the gooey eye. She sure hoped Citlalli made it back to her Anahuac family.

"Let's follow this stream and see where it leads," said Sklizz. "At least it should take us downhill."

A loud animal roar came from somewhere across the stream inside the forest.

"Quickly," said Einlen.

Everyone followed Einlen in a rapid walk alongside the shoreline. Occasional glances revealed nothing following.

"Let's find some kind of shelter, or at least a defensible position," said Sklizz.

A loud screech came from the opposite side of the stream, somewhere in the dense foliage. They stopped and stared. Einlen had a blinger drawn and ready. Nothing appeared, and after a minute they continued on their way.

Within an hour it was nearly dark and they decided to camp on a mossy area between tall trees. Lisa sat against one tree while the rest gathered branches and brush for a campfire.

Food from the spacecraft was distributed and it was clear this would be one of their last meals unless they found edible food on this alien world. The oxygen atmosphere and water gave them hope of success.

"Tomorrow we'll continue downstream. It should either lead us off this plateau or show us the edge," said Sklizz.

"How could that zip send us so far?" asked Estrella.

"And why here?" added Heather.

Sklizz and Einlen started to speak at the same time. "You first," said Sklizz, and Einlen nodded.

"All zips interconnected," said Einlen, "some unstable. Unlucky travelers like us are sent to place all zips begin."

"And neither of us know why we ended up here," said Sklizz.

"If near place time began, maybe all zips lead here."

"This means we're never going home, right?" said Lisa.

"I don't know," said Sklizz. "Only if we can teleport again, somehow."

Eventually they tried to sleep, lying around the campfire. The surrounding forest was surprisingly quiet; the only sounds were the crackling fire and rippling of the mountain stream. Soon everyone was asleep.

Not far away in the forest a hungry predator slowly approached the fire, its eyes not used to seeing this kind of bright light at night. Standing on two legs, it looked down from thirty feet at the sleeping prey, its long, sharp teeth white in the fire light.

It was very hungry.

TARTARUS

After crash-landing, Summahon had been alone for several days, scrounging for food and water. She'd begun to think the planet was empty of sentient life and she was marooned, all alone.

She first heard shrieking metal and then saw the smoking trail of a doomed spacecraft. Rushing to the crash site, she was surprised when a plant root tripped her. Then the bluish plant held her down with strong branches, vibrating and shaking a leafy head that sat atop a tall celery stalk body.

Summahon knew it wanted to communicate, but the universal translator was useless. Frustrated, the plant lifted Summahon to her feet and they ran to the crashed spacecraft. Keeping out of sight, they saw a four-eyed bull creature trying to crawl from the wreckage. Rushing forward, they helped their new friend—who subsequently introduced himself as Hinge—get away from the growing flames.

Later that same day they stumbled across a shaking and quivering anemone-like creature named Vivvy.

Summahon had gone from being all alone to being a member of a group of four friends in less than a day: bull-like four-eyed Hinge, walking anemone Vivvy, and a giant blue celery stalk named Jak-toll.

All this time later they were still a team, finding the town of Tartarus and hoping for a sound sleep behind its hybrid barrier of rocks, boulders, trees, dirt, and the wreckage of many spacecraft. They'd been hunting for this rumored "town" for days and approached its makeshift wall several hours ago.

Arriving at the entrance, they each had to convince the inhabitants to let them in. An amazingly diverse collection of bizarre aliens peered over the wall and asked questions.

"What species are you?" "What do you eat?" "Do you taste good?" "Show us your teeth." "What are those tentacles for?" "Are you a plant?" "How did you find us?" "What do you want?" "What can you give?" "When will you leave?" "Why shouldn't we kill you?"

Since this crazy planet seemed populated by lost space travelers from every corner of the universe, you never knew who or what might show up next. Friend, foe, big, small, nice, mean, strong, weak, hunter, prey...the list was endless.

Summahon, Hinge, Jak-toll, and Vivvy were examples of this diversity. Summahon presented her jaguar-like appearance; Hinge had a bull-like head without horns, four eyes, two arms, and three-fingered hands; Vivvy was a mobile land anemone with multiple legs, tentacle arms, antennae eyes, tiny mouth, and a sweet personality; and Jak-toll was a ten-foot-tall, two-legged walking blue celery with two red eyes and seven powerful branch-like arms randomly scattered around its circumference. Jak-toll had no mouth and communicated by buzzing, a kind of Jak-code they were learning.

Tartarus residents were a strange and ever-changing mix of aliens who'd banded together, just trying to survive inside a defensive wall built with whatever they could find. Dirt, rock, crashed spaceship parts, bones, logs, and lots more. At least it kept out unwanted castaways and anything else that might come knocking.

Summahon and her friends were allowed to spend the night, but asked to move on unless they were willing to build their own walled extension to Tartarus. This is how the makeshift town had grown to a current population of more than one hundred different aliens.

Once inside, things seemed fine, but Jak-toll didn't like the way a couple of larger plant-eating aliens were staring. If they touched a single leaf on his head, he'd turn them into fertilizer.

URGLE

Back up on the dark plateau the Urgle was tired of staring at the campfire and sleeping prey. With a massive dinosaur-like head-bone, terrifying three-eyed face, and T-Rex teeth atop a six-legged dinosaur body, the hungry Urgle started moving toward the creek. In moments it would be feasting on the snoozing adventurers.

Urgles were nearly extinct in their own solar system, the remaining survivors in zoos. This Urgle was a young baby from one planet's zoo. While being transported its spacecraft had vanished, crashing here and killing the entire zookeeper crew. The sedated Urgle's secure cage broke open during the crash, leaving it to wake up in this strange place.

As a large starving carnivore it knew speed and surprise were critical, since this small two-legged prey would scatter quickly. It moved faster.

The Urgle's tree-trunk legs shook the ground, and everyone woke up thinking it was another earthquake. The snapping of trees and branches as the Urgle crossed the creek got them to their feet.

Einlen and Sklizz grabbed for their blingers, unable to take aim as a thick tree branch flew into them. The kids and Lisa dove underneath, but it hit Einlen and Sklizz as they raised their weapons. Einlen fired fast, missing the Urgle while being knocked thirty feet and smashing her blinger. Sklizz ducked, the branch glancing off his head as his blinger fell in the fire.

As Heather, Estrella, and Tyson ran for their lives, Lisa remained riveted, disbelief on her face as the monstrous Urgle bore down on her.

The Urgle's mad charge ended when its feet tripped, sending it face first into the ground, smashing and sliding through the campfire and snapping at Lisa as it ran her over. Confused, the Urgle spotted Heather. It was starving and needed to devour one of these tiny creatures.

Heather had taken the stream route. Her mending ribs were making it hard to breath. She hadn't gone far when the Urgle turned to give chase. The sound of pounding earth and forest destruction was rapidly getting closer. She cut across the stream, cold water splashing in every direction, the crescendo of Urgle noise growing. It was dark and getting harder to see. The monster was closing fast.

The stream was deeper now with a quicker current as she stepped awkwardly on a rock and fell headlong into the cold water. Coming up for air, she saw the Urgle's massive black shadow move past, obscuring the forest and stars, its roar seemingly endless.

The Urgle smelled its prey and turned, nocturnal eyes easily spotting a dripping wet Heather. It moved into the stream, jaws opening wide to strike.

Time slowed for Heather; thoughts of never seeing her family again filling her with regret. She tensed, watching it move closer and closer. She dove to one side as the beast lunged, deadly jaws snapping and grazing her arm, slamming her against the stream bottom. She came up gasping for air, amazed to still be alive. Heather saw the monster's dark shadow moving past, then turning with three hungry, gleaming eyes. This time Heather was boxed in, still short of breath with nowhere to hide. It could easily scoop her up with one swallow. She felt strangely calm now that death was at hand.

The Urgle let out a loud screech, shining eyes focused on her as it zeroed in for the kill. Its large feet moved quickly, skidding on the slimy stream bottom, and Heather saw the massive black silhouette vanish into the ground. It took a few seconds of stunned amazement before Heather realized the Urgle had plunged over a waterfall at the plateau's edge.

SHANGHAING

Back on the Watchers' planet, Citlalli and Tarayon learned about the threat to the universe. The clues as to what was pulling the zips all led back to the place where eternity began.

Over many eons the Watchers learned a little about the birthplace of time and space—the Big Bang. They discovered it was a mess. There were ancient stars with planetary cesspools of deviant interbred species, evolutionary dead ends, widespread insanity, and the home of whatever terrible force now threatened the Light.

For many years the Watchers had felt something pulling on the intergalactic zip network. Eventually this would lead to a dead stop and the end of all life. Unless the slowing ended, the process would become unstoppable.

The Watchers' only option was sending a secret group to find the cause of this slowing. It was so far away the Watchers could only teleport four spacecraft carrying four passengers each, all sent to the outskirts of this deranged center of the universe. The energy expended would nearly end the Watchers' existence.

Fourteen individuals would join Citlalli and Tarayon on this epic journey, first teleported to the Watchers' world and told of this universal doomsday threat.

The Watchers kept one big secret from Tarayon and Citlalli: They could only return a single spacecraft. Most of these carefully selected aliens would be making a one-way, no-return trip.

DEFECTION

Fleeing Yerti en route to Earth and Mars, Waima and Stauffa exited the same zip where Sklizz had vanished. They were immediately surrounded by a Gelzian fighter patrol. After warnings, they were escorted toward interrogation on Mars. Any threatening moves and the fighters would blast Stauffa's tiny ship to pieces. Thankfully this peaceful capture was what Stauffa hoped would happen.

"Papa," said Waima, "I've been thinking."

"Uh oh, now we're in trouble, Waima's thinking." He was proud of his daughter and smiled at her.

"I know the planet killer's wrong, but how can we stop the Supreme Doozy? You said Doozies have better spacecraft and armies than these Humans and their friends."

"That's true, but we have to try. We tried with the footstool bomb, but somehow the maniac survived. This was always our backup plan, to make the Humans and their friends understand the threat. We have to try and do the right thing, otherwise nothing matters."

Waima thought about this as they headed toward Mars, deciding her papa was right. As the daughter of this brave and honorable Doozy she'd stand by his side no matter what.

Approaching Mars, Waima loved the stark rust-colored landscape. She marveled as they descended into the largest, deepest canyon she could imagine. When they got out, she looked up at impossibly high canyon walls.

They were escorted to a secure facility at the base of Valles Marineris, the Great Canyon of Mars. After a few minutes alone with her papa, the door opened and Waima saw a big blue alien hop in. The creature seemed to be missing two of its four arms. At first it just stared at them, both eyes boring in and making Waima very uncomfortable.

"My name is Thrix."

Both Doozies stood, Stauffa holding his four-fingered hand up in friendship. "I am Stauffa and this is my daughter, Waima. We come in peace hoping to make a new life with you. We also bring news of a planet-killing weapon and vast army being sent to end your existence."

Thrix listened as Stauffa described the Supreme Doozy's terrible plans. This Doozy seemed to speak the truth, but after what Doozies had done to his remaining Fiberians in attacking Mars, instinct said to kill them.

"Assuming you're not lying," Thrix said, "please explain why two Gelzian patrol fighters were vaporized shortly after you came through the zip?"

Thrix noted surprise on their pasty-white pumpkin faces when he delivered this news.

Kriner was the Doozy assassin sent after Stauffa and Waima, and exiting the zip he'd been surprised by two Gelzian fighters. He opened fire and destroyed them, then took a secret route behind asteroid belts and gas clouds. He wanted to stay hidden as he approached Mars, the place he expected to find Stauffa and his daughter spawn. Kriner would find a way to end their existence. He never failed.

DESCENT

The sun was rising as Heather struggled upstream, limping slightly on a sprained ankle. The Urgle had shattered vegetation all along the shoreline, and as Heather reached their devastated camp she saw Tyson and Estrella kneeling over a body. Hobbling closer she saw it was Lisa. Einlen was sitting against one tree, while Sklizz sat against another, unable to remember the attack.

The only witness had been Tyson, having leaped behind a bush. Apparently the tree branch that hit Einlen and Sklizz had wrecked both blingers had thus been their undoing.

"I saw the monster try to bite Lisa," said Tyson. "It missed, but she couldn't get out of the way."

Heather told them about her lucky escape as the monster fell over the waterfall. She'd also found a pathway heading down one side of the plateau.

"Space cord in pack," said Einlen, rubbing her crocodile head. "We climb down."

"What about Lisa?" asked Heather.

"We'll make a stretcher," said Sklizz, "and rig up a pulley system."

Estrella was sitting with Lisa. She looked over to the others with tears and grief-stricken eyes. "She's g-gone."

After a minute of stunned silence, they found some material to wrap Lisa in, preparing her for burial.

Of the original group taken from the U.N., only Heather and Estrella remained. Sklizz, Einlen, and Tyson were rescuers, while Citlalli stayed with the Okyricks, her fate unknown. Lisa joined Arizza, the vice president, and all the others who'd died along the way. This universe was not a safe place.

They picked out a peaceful location next to a large boulder overlooking the stream. Tyson and Sklizz took turns digging in the soft earth, while Estrella used a hammer to hack out a sad-looking cross on the boulder. In no time Lisa had been buried, a few words said, a few tears shed, and they continued on their way, each deep in their own thoughts.

OBADDON

Not far away from Lisa's final resting place, Summahon and Hinge were finishing the last of their dried meat, remnants of some alien they'd killed last week. By now they'd gotten used to seeing Jak-toll lean back, stretching his branches wide in the morning sun. As long as he got sunshine and water, Jak-toll was fine. Hinge and Summahon called Jak-toll "him" although they weren't sure what he was. If Jak-toll understood the male and female concept, he wasn't telling. Vivvy was always eating, her tentacles capturing molecular matter from the air. Like Jak-toll, Vivvy seemed genderless; to balance things out she thus became a she.

They were preparing to leave Tartarus town and speaking with a purple-colored lizard who told them this planet was named Obaddon. Apparently Obaddon's original meaning was a place where all hope is lost. Everyone agreed this was a perfect name. The purple lizard, whose name was unpronounceable, claimed to be the oldest alien still alive in Tartarus, and maybe on all of Obaddon.

"But of course," said the smiling lizard, "who can say for sure in this here place."

"We've heard of an ocean beyond the mountains," said Summahon. "Do you know if it's true?"

"You bet. I crashed near the shoreline," said the lizard. "I been told many have tried sailing, but only one returned. And this lucky sailor woulda been eaten by sea monsters, but had some kinda wings and made it back alive. Claimed he'd seen terrible ocean creatures and new land over the horizon. Told of strange lights in the sky over this land he named Pith."

"Did he land on Pith?" asked Hinge.

"Funny thing...said he did, but he sure didn't want to talk none. Something made him turn around and try comin' back."

"How could anything be worse than here?"

The lizard shook his head. "Never said, at least not to me. Same night we heard bad yells. The kind of yells that didn't sound right. Never found a body."

"Something ate him?"

"There's some believe that. I think he just up and walked into the jungle. Something made him give up."

Hours later the four alien friends were marching down a well-trodden pathway through the forest. They decided that if death was their destiny on Obaddon, they'd keep exploring and try to find answers. Passing a distant mountain and reaching the ocean were their first goals. They'd build a sturdy and weapon-ready boat for a sailing journey. Hinge had been a master boat builder on his water-based world. This dangerous sea voyage to the unknown land of Pith seemed like a grand adventure.

Vivvy was slowest and walked in front. Since Vivvy's species had no males or females, Hinge was pestering Vivvy about how they reproduced. No matter how hard Hinge tried, Vivvy didn't answer. As they walked, Hinge speculated with Summahon that it had to be pollination.

"Yep," said Hinge, "I'll bet it's horny bugs."

Summahon just smiled. Hinge's bull-like head, large upper body, powerful lower legs, and four horizontal eyes made him one of the most frightening creatures she'd ever seen. When you realized he was a softy inside and funny too, the scary looks faded away.

"Hey Vivvy," shouted Hinge, "you gotta reproduce somehow; I know you're not immortal. I'm sticking with pollination. It's my final answer."

As always, Vivvy ignored Hinge's kidding. Summahon wasn't sure if Vivvy even had a sense of humor. Jak-toll, however, could break into hysterical plant laughter, which meant its seven branches waved spastically as its leafy head shook. At least she thought it was laughter.

Summahon and Hinge each carried thick branches carved into deadly spears. Hinge had a jagged chunk of crashed spacecraft tied to the end of his spear. Jak-toll used his strong branch-arms to carry their food in a rubbery bag made from the stomach of an unknown alien carcass. Vivvy had hundreds of poison-tipped tentacles, but unless its prey was close by, they were useless.

Wind was blowing smoke from the distant volcano in a sideways direction. They were making good time on a heavily used path through the forest, still a day from the mountain and keeping a sharp lookout for attacks by other aliens. On this insane planet, you never knew what might spring out.

Several weeks back, they'd been five alien friends including a tiny and feisty centaur-like female named Rork. Rork had walked into their camp and introduced herself. She'd crashed a week earlier and survived this long.

Days later as they hiked up a hill, Rork was midway through a dirty joke when she was caught on the sticky end of an enormous tongue, yanked in the air, and swallowed in one gulp by a slimy froggish monstrosity. Rork never had a chance. The eldritch frog horror escaped with several leaps, never to be seen again.

They were sad, but since no one expected to live long on Obaddon, they had a morbid laugh later, remembering Rork hadn't been able to deliver the dirty joke's punch line. You never knew how or when death might strike on this insane world, or if you'd even get to finish telling your joke.

And now it happened again.

Summahon watched from the rear as a silent shadow struck from above, talons ripping Vivvy off the ground. The thing resembled a leathery Earth-like condor and scaly dragon.

Hinge leaped, getting a three-fingered grip on the monster's left foot. His weight kept it struggling to gain altitude. Hinge stabbed wildly, sticking his spear into the beast's side.

Vivvy was helpless, making a high-pitched keening sound as Summahon charged with her spear. The beast swiped at Hinge, ripping his arm open and dropping him to the ground. It shot upward just out of Summahon's reach. She threw her spear, but it deflected off the right wing. Hinge's spear fell out of the beast's side, not doing much damage. Without a single squawk or shriek, the flying creature carried Vivvy over the treetops and out of sight.

For the second time one of their friends was here one minute, gone the next.

After stitching up his slashed arm, Hinge was ready to go. Keeping angry thoughts to themselves, they continued onward, now watching the skies.

CRIMINALS

As the new day's sun dawned on Mars, it was still dark and shadowy inside the deep canyon. Thrix was escorting Stauffa and Waima on the floor of Valles Marineris. Morning mists floated, hovering just off the ground and burning off as the temperature rose.

Stauffa saw massive terraforming systems, giving Mars an oxygen-based atmosphere. He noted that Fiberian technology was far beyond Doozies in making planets habitable, while Doozy technology was far better at destroying planets.

Waima remained wide-eyed by his side, her four fingers holding tightly to his hand.

Thrix wanted to learn if these two Doozies were honest escapees or very clever spies. Upon entering a building, he observed the reaction of seven Doozy prisoners behind a secure force field. They were war criminals and awaiting execution. One was Kahpoo, supreme commander of the Doozy attack on Mars.

Thrix noticed surprise on Kahpoo's face as he said, "Stauffa, the last Doozy I'd expect to see."

"Out of so many, you survive?" said Stauffa.

Kahpoo glanced between Stauffa and Thrix, clearly confused.

"I'm warning the Fiberians and Humans about your insane friend's Exterminator," said Stauffa. "He's rushing it into use at the Okyrick planet Scradle."

Thrix saw Kahpoo turning pale green as he screeched, "What a monstrous betrayal!"

Waima surprised her father and everyone by shouting back, "My father is not a traitor. He's trying to save us all. If our footstool bomb killed the Supreme Doozy, you'd be sorry."

The Doozy prisoners were all shocked, but then Kahpoo smiled at Waima and said, "You are a very brave and very foolish little spawn. And my, my, my, you've been up to no good back on Yerti." He squatted down behind the force field, staring straight into Waima's eyes. "You and your father will surely die for this betrayal." He leaned even closer, almost touching the humming energy field. "Yes, I'm certain of it. I already see death in your eyes."

Thrix had watched this exchange, now convinced of Stauffa and Waima's sincerity. He stepped forward and used a Human phrase he liked, "Shut your trap, Doozy! The only ones with death in their eyes are all of you. Today you'll pay for your crimes. We'll have you murderers spaced and dying horribly by midday."

They looked defiantly at Thrix, whose blue kangaroo-like face smiled in return.

"I'll personally push the spacing button and enjoy watching you die."

UNAGI

Back on Obaddon, Heather led the group downstream to the pathway by the waterfall. She shuddered, remembering how close she'd come to being devoured right here.

The pathway did lead off the plateau and seemed quite treacherous. Heather and Tyson would have to battle their fear of heights. It was a harrowing fifteen-minute descent, with Sklizz staying close and keeping them focused on the path. Finally reaching a ledge still a hundred feet from the bottom, Sklizz tied the space cord around a secure boulder and they began climbing down, Einlen going first.

"Just concentrate on the cord, nice and slow, hand over hand," said Sklizz to the kids.

Heather and Tyson sat nervously awaiting their turns, hoping they could do this.

Einlen made it seem easy, dropping the final ten feet where the cord ended, landing safely. Tyson was next. Before he could chicken out, he grabbed the cord and started down, moving even faster than Einlen, making the entire climb in a minute.

Tyson's go-for-it attitude made it easier for Heather, and she didn't hesitate, moving slowly, hand over hand.

Meanwhile, inside a dark crevice halfway down the cliff, hungry eyes had watched Einlen and Tyson. Looking like a dry-land eel, this creature had one black eye in its broad forehead and clawed feet that anchored it in the crevice. The eel usually ate insects, rarely having anything larger within range of its vice-like jaws and razor teeth.

As Heather moved closer the eel crept stealthily, peering out. *If it stops*, thought the eel, *I attack.*

Heather was so focused on the cord that she glided past without noticing the eel or its gleaming teeth. The timid eel decided if another showed up, this time it would strike for sure.

Once Heather finished, sweating profusely and proud of herself, Estrella began climbing down. She always enjoyed rope climbing in school and scaling rock walls in amusement parks. She was rapidly nearing the crevice.

The excited eel began drooling in anticipation, its bone-crunching jaws opening and closing. It coiled like a taut spring, ready to shoot out and strike.

Estrella was focused on the cord as something darted out of the rock wall. She jerked away as the eel's jaws snapped closed, missing her arm by millimeters and tearing her camo-suit sleeve. This caused Estrella to slide down the rope, the camo-suit sleeve clamped tightly in the eel's mouth jerking her to a stop. She flopped on the rope, nearly falling with the eel flailing about, tearing and ripping off Estrella's entire sleeve. Estrella screamed as the last threads tore free, her hands getting rope burn as she fell the final twenty feet, falling into Einlen's waiting arms. The collision knocked both to the ground.

Meanwhile the eel was even more tangled in a knot of space cord and camo-suit sleeve. Its whine sounded like a woman's high-pitched scream and it was thrashing about as Sklizz started down. He was prepared to kick the thing off, but as he got closer had a better idea. He maneuvered carefully around the hysterical eel and in one swift motion yanked it out of the crevice. In moments the eel was untangled and screeching as it plummeted down to the ground.

A few hours later they were all enjoying grilled native Obaddon eel for lunch.

RECRUITS

The Watchers knew Tarayon required Trixian nourishment, just like Citlalli needed Human food and water. The Watchers provided these in a room whose side wall was a one-way mirror to see their fourteen recruits and fellow adventurers.

"Our visions of the Light have shown us who will join you, whether young or old, good or evil, strong or weak."

"Visions of the Light?" asked Tarayon.

"The power of eternity, evolution, and spiritual good that is present throughout the universe."

"I've never heard of such a thing," said Tarayon.

"And yet the Light is there."

"Our Anahuac gods were everywhere and in everything," said Citlalli, "like the Light." Then she asked something she had been wondering for a while: "How did you make the amulets to help us fight the Destroyer?"

"We rarely offer such things. Incredible power is required. For the amulets our energies focused on creating objects of the Light; the same principle that spawned your Destroyer from the Dark so long ago."

"The Destroyer was a terror that had to be stopped," said another Watcher, "and yet it was a close thing. The Destroyer almost prevailed, if not for you, Citlalli."

"But I wasn't alone."

"Your friend Maddy didn't have the strength to do what you did with the amulet. She would have failed. When David used his amulet the strength required was a fraction of what you needed to vanquish the Destroyer. Once we saw your power, we saw a glimmer of hope for the task ahead."

"But I don't know what I did. I still would have failed if not for Lucy."

"Your Earth Basset hound was meant to be there and played her innocent part to perfection. And now she and your other friends also carry the gift."

"The gift?"

"The Light becomes one with those who touch it, especially you. Since it is strongest in you Citlalli, the Light will draw you toward your destiny. It will seem almost magical the way it brings you together with others on this journey."

Citlalli didn't know what they were talking about. "What about the Destroyer? I used to feel it searching for me, but when I awoke here the feeling was gone."

"It no longer exists."

Citlalli felt dizzy relief wash over her, the threat lifted from her mind. She almost felt giddy.

"Oh," said a Watcher, "the first arrivals are coming. It's time to watch them and learn. Once they've all arrived, the visions tell us you will assign the teams of four to each spacecraft."

A flickering light came from the other room and two Uppsalians appeared, each with the same crocodile-duck features as Einlen. One was asleep while the other must've been sitting because they fell on their backside. Hopping to his feet, the Uppsalian tensed ready to defend himself.

"That's Llarke," said Citlalli.

"Yes," said a Watcher, "and the other's name is Vomisa, the most wanted Uppsalian on their planet for killing hundreds during Uppsala's recent troubles."

Vomisa awoke, leaping to his webbed feet ready to attack Llarke. Then both froze, listening to the Watchers.

EXECUTION

The Supreme Doozy's hunter-killer Kriner had secretly circled the Earth solar system and was now approaching Mars totally undetected. He'd picked up the two life signatures of traitorous Stauffa and his rotten little assassin daughter Waima. They were inside a shuttle approaching stationary orbit around Mars. Killing them would be all too easy.

More surprising was detecting other Doozies on board. He found one match: Kahpoo, the Earth/Mars invasion leader. What perfect timing. He could kill the two traitors and the disgraced survivor of the lost battle for Mars, Earth, and of course zooey.

He rapidly closed on the shuttle, preparing his laser cannons to vaporize it in one surgical shot. When that mission was complete, he would then easily escape pursuit back the way he came.

In the shuttle, Thrix stood with Stauffa and Waima, still guarded by two armed Fiberians. Thrix let them witness the executions, but was taking no chances. He was surprised Stauffa wanted his daughter to watch the spacing of these Doozy war criminals, but felt it wasn't his place to say anything. Spacing was an ugly way to die. The condemned Doozies were already inside the airlock, awaiting their release into the deadly vacuum of space. It would be a painful death.

"Any last words for these Doozy scum?" asked Thrix. Stauffa shook his head. He wanted Kahpoo and these other Supreme Doozy zealots dead too.

"As mass murderers and war criminals," said Thrix over the intercom, "before your last painful nanoseconds of life, any final pathetic words?"

"I do," said Kahpoo, "and—"

"Silence!" shouted Thrix, cutting him off with a nasty smile on his blue kangaroo head. "Shut your trap!" He did so love that Human phrase. Then turning to Stauffa and Waima, he said with a smile, "Did he think I was serious?"

His blue hand hovered over the airlock venting switch as he turned to Waima. "You might want to close your eyes."

Without hesitation he opened the airlock.

To Thrix's surprise Stauffa and Waima vanished seconds later. Checking the controls, Thrix confirmed the prisoners were dying in the space vacuum. Counting the floating bodies, he realized one was missing.

"Commander," a frantic voice shouted over the intercom, "a Doozy spaceship materialized in weapons range, laser cannon locked on you."

Thrix flinched, expecting to die.

"But Sir, I detect no life forms on board."

Far, far away, teleporting into the waiting room, were four shocked Doozies: Kahpoo, Kriner, Stauffa, and Waima.

Stauffa instinctively shoved Waima behind him.

Kahpoo collapsed in pain from the effects of being spaced moments ago.

Kriner remained motionless, thinking hard and staring at Stauffa and Waima, his two assassination targets. He decided whatever had happened didn't matter; he would turn it to his advantage and kill them all.

Citlalli and Tarayon were closely watching this drama unfold, seeing the one called Kahpoo groggily sitting up. As before, whatever violence might have transpired was interrupted by the Watchers. All four Doozies and two Uppsalians listened intently, gradual shock spreading across their faces.

HOMOSAPIENS

Back on Earth, three Humans were about to be teleported to the Watchers' planet.

Lupe's mom ladled out more menudo.

"Mom," said Lupe, "I'm stuffed, plus David and Maddy are waiting online."

Lupe was enjoying her first day without the famous cast on her leg, signed by an amazing collection of people and aliens. Yesterday had been quite special as news media from around the world joined Lupe as she donated her priceless cast to a museum in Costa Rica.

During the past unbelievable couple of months, Lupe had separated her shoulder while bike riding, broken her leg while climbing Mt. Torpur, helped defeat the Destroyer, met the President of the United States, survived Simi the killer who got squashed by Princess Pat, fought Doozies in a spaceship around Mars, and received a hero's welcome in San Jose, Costa Rica. The grateful people of Costa Rica had granted Lupe and her mom income for life. It was like winning the lottery.

And yet Lupe was worried sick about her missing friends. Were they still alive somewhere out in space? Did Citlalli make it back home to her family and Cemanahuac of five thousand years ago?

On the other side of Earth, two unsuspecting enemies were about to join Lupe.

Gilad was a member of Mossad, Israel's Institute for Intelligence and Operations. Mostly it was an information gathering service, but its members also directed assassinations around the world. After many years Gilad was acknowledged as one of their top agents. If a special job needed doing, he was the person called.

Jamila was a Palestinian who fought against everything western civilization stood for. She had lost many family and friends to the endless fighting, and her hatred of Mossad ran deep. To her people, she was one of their many heroes, but to others she was a terrorist. There were no known pictures of Jamila, so no one in Mossad knew what she looked like.

On this day Gilad was moments from bursting into a basement room where the deadly terrorist called Jamila was supposed to be hiding. Silenced pistol drawn, Gilad kicked in the door and put three quick bullets into the woman seated in a chair against the far wall.

Stepping into the room, Gilad felt a sharp gun barrel jab hard into his back, followed by a woman's voice, "Drop the weapon and turn around Mossad."

Gilad realized he'd been tricked. His three shots had nailed a mannequin. He dropped the gun and slowly turned, seeing a nice looking woman with short black hair, western jeans and a San Jose Sharks teal colored tee shirt.

"So, you are the one called Jamila."

"I've waited a long time to avenge those you've killed. It's time to meet your God Mossad."

She raised the gun toward his head...but never got off a shot as both enemies flickered and disappeared, Jamila's gun falling to the floor.

Back inside the Watchers' planet all three freshly teleported and flabbergasted Humans appeared: Lupe, Gilad, and Jamila.

Gilad felt for his missing gun and Jamila did the same, but both weapons had vanished. Along with Lupe, they stood in shock, transfixed as the voice of the Watchers came from all around.

"Lupe," Citlalli shrieked, leaping into the air. Of course Lupe couldn't hear Citlalli through the soundproof wall.

Tarayon also knew Lupe, but merely growled, the black hair on his jaguar head tingling. What could these Watchers be thinking bringing back these Human kids?

Jamila and Gilad were as freaked out as two Humans could be, only moments before trying to kill one another, then instantly appearing here, surrounded by terrifying aliens and hearing voices tell them about the end of the universe. All they could do was back away from each other and find open places against the wall. As they glared from across the room, they couldn't help shift their gaze to the bizarre aliens, their minds spinning with fear and confusion.

TRAIL

It had been hours since the rock eel attack. No one had gotten sick from eating the eel, at least not yet. It was now later in the afternoon and the group was hiking though an alien forest toward drifting smoke they'd seen far in the distance.

Wobble!

This time the earthquake felt like standing on jelly, the ground quivering and wiggling. No one could stay on their feet and the shaking continued for nearly a minute.

When it finally stopped they heard voices in the distance where the smoke had been. They soon reached the edge of the forest, and stood for a moment looking across an open meadow of bluish grass and tree stumps at a motley group of aliens who were frantically trying to repair a crumbled wall of dirt and metal. No two of the aliens seemed alike.

"Do you recognize any of these species?" asked Sklizz.

"No," Einlen said. "Six-legged creature with tail looks like Watu, but it's not Watu."

Heather's sprained ankle from the Urgle chase was throbbing, and falling during the quake had caused sharp pain in her ribs. She gritted her teeth through the pain, looking at the strange aliens and their collapsed wall.

Since first leaving Earth, Tyson's view of girls had changed dramatically. He used to think they were soft, weak, manipulative, and full of themselves. What he'd seen from Citlalli, Heather, and Estrella had forever changed his opinion. In fact these girls were tougher than any boys he knew.

He saw the pain on Heather's face. "Do you need any help?"

"No thanks, I'm fine," she said, grimacing as she got to her feet.

"Do you think they're friendly?" asked Estrella.

"Good question. They seem to have quite a defensive wall," said Sklizz, "presumably to keep out hungry and dangerous aliens like us."

The group cautiously approached the quasi-town, holding out empty arms, their multi-fingered hands opened in the universal sign of peace.

The aliens scampered, hopped, ran, climbed, and slithered back behind the enclosure, only a large purple lizard remaining. It sat unmoving on two crossed legs, both arms resting in its lap as it stared at them, a long tail acting as a counterbalance to keep it upright. It was ten feet long from its lizard head to the tip of its tail. To Estrella this reptile with a Mona Lisa smile looked like a skinny lizard Buddha.

"Stop, frien's. State yer business."

The group halted, everyone facing the frozen, smiling, and unblinking purple lizard.

"We mean you no harm," said Sklizz. "Our spacecraft came down on the distant plateau. We're just trying to find friends and figure out how leave this planet."

The lizard's golden-eyed stare was getting on Sklizz's nerves as he watched its skin color gradually change from purple to dark blue.

"There is no escape from Obaddon," said Lizard—or so the others had named him in their minds. He spoke in a slow drawl. Its tongue flicked out once as its smile vanished.

Estrella swore she'd heard the lizard's voice before.

"Obaddon," said Sklizz, "this planet's name?"

"Yup," said Lizard, "Tartarus is our town, though it ain't much. And there's no room so you gotta move on."

"Can we just spend one night?" asked Sklizz.

The lizard cocked its head ever so slightly and smiled. "Ya'll sound like the crazy aliens here last night. But ya seem harmless. To some ya might even look like a meal. We'll let ya spend one night inside Tartarus, and even promise not to eat ya, at least for tonight."

The lizard's chuckle sounded like a donkey braying.

"Musta been some flyin' to land on yonder plateau."

He peered at Heather with beady lizard eyes, focusing on her well-worn blue softball cap, and said, "I'll be wantin' that thing."

Heather stared at the others with horror, "No. My cap's been with me everywhere. No, I can't—"

"Stop," sighed Lizard, "don't need it none."

This last forlorn comment helped Estrella realize that Lizard sounded like her favorite Pooh character, Eeyore. Lizard dropped to four feet and led the adventurers inside Tartarus. Estrella noted that lizard's long tail seemed to be permanently attached.

NEST

As the group took shelter behind the walls of Tartarus, not too far away Summahon, Hinge, and Jak-toll were studying rocky hills that seemed to offer good shelter for another dangerous night. A cave between some rocks caught their attention.

"Back home I snuck into a cave once," said Hinge. "The beast I surprised wasn't happy at all."

Jak-toll buzzed in code, "U kills it?"

Hinge snorted like a four-eyed bull. "No, I ran like a mochee wind."

"Mochee?" asked Summahon.

"A terrible wind that carries screaming mochees, demons that will tear the soul from your body."

"So, you ran like a newborn spawn," said Summahon.

"I ran until I turned and blasted that stinking cave beast back to the mochee fire it sprang from."

Summahon laughed and Jak-toll buzzed.

"Well, we can't wait forever. It's getting dark. Let's go, kittens," said Summahon, "follow me."

She charged up the short hillside to the edge of the dark cave, the other two following close behind. Without waiting, she thrust her spear in front and ran into the cave screaming like a crazed Trixian she-beast.

Hinge glanced over with a look that said, "She's crazy," and Jak-toll shook his leafy head, agreeing.

They waited, not hearing a sound. Then Summahon sped past, running out of the cave and disappearing around a large rock. Jak-toll and Hinge could take a hint, diving down with Summahon into a secluded crevice. Turning to peek, they watched a swarm of flying things dart out into the early evening sky. Their black silhouettes looked like man-sized wasps with the heads of demonic vampire monkeys.

ASSAULT

Back inside Tartarus, everyone was relaxing near the entrance, talking about tomorrow. A steady drone of noisy insects came from the surrounding forest, although the sound was more like a thousand tiny woodpeckers.

"We have to keep searching," said Sklizz, "and find energy to get our spacecraft working again."

"Agree," said Einlen, "but where?"

Lizard, who had now turned dark green, said, "Why don't ya follow yesterday's visitors, past the mountain of fire?"

Heather smiled at Estrella, who'd told her how Lizard sounded like that blue donkey with a tacked-on tail.

"Perhaps," said Sklizz, "as good a direction as any."

"Well frien's, the great sea lies beyond the closest mountain. That's where Summahon said they were headed."

It took a few moments for Summahon's name to click, but then Estrella and Heather said in stereo, "Summahon?"

Lizard cocked his head to one side again.

"Said she was Trixian. Had three frien's, one with horns, another leafy, and a third with tentacles. They was an odd group, even for this crazy planet."

"And headed to this ocean, past the mountain?" said Sklizz.

"Some calls it the mountain of madness. I've heard about sounds, chanting, and strange creatures; things older than time; things not meant for the light of day; things worse than any alien that ever crashed here."

Lizard had turned dark black as he talked.

Heather felt like she was around a campfire hearing scary stories. A craving for s'mores popped in her head—roasted marshmallows and a layer of chocolate between two graham crackers. The memory of biting into a crunchy, gooey, chocolaty s'more was so vivid she could taste it.

"Yer frien's had lotsa questions about sailing across this sea to the land of Pith. A journey I recommended they skip by the way, but they were a determined bunch, and who was I to tell them no."

"They left yesterday morning?" asked Einlen.

"Uh huh," nodded Lizard. "Like I told'em, ya got two eyes to see both sides of things; so use yer third eye to see everything at the same time and yet not see anything."

Everyone looked at Lizard like he was crazy.

"But the bull creature had four eyes," said Heather.

"Ya see, it don't matter how many eyes ya got if ya can only see two sides of things. But it doesn't matter. Yer friends will be sea monster snacks for sure."

"Tarayon said Summahon hit a space fracture on their way to the Watchers," said Sklizz. "If so, this place must be the dumping ground for disappearances across the universe."

"Yup," said Lizard, "we should be wall-to-wall strange critters, considering how many crash here. Heard from an old-timer, who'd heard from another old-timer, the place creatures used to appear was inside Obaddon's atmosphere. Visitors zipped straight from their own planets. Maybe even Earth, since spacecraft weren't needed."

They all thought about what Lizard had said.

"Flight 19," said Heather.

Everyone looked at her questioningly.

"A bunch of planes that disappeared from the Bermuda Triangle could've crashed here if they didn't have to be in outer space."

"What about Amelia Earhart," said Estrella, "or Percy Fawcett?"

"Yeah, even Jimmy Hoffa," said Tyson.

"Earhart?" said Lizard. "Frien' named Fred? I think maybe I heard—"

"Look, gang," said Sklizz, "I don't know about Earth history, but in the morning we'll go after Summahon."

All around Tartarus town the strange alien insect noise suddenly went silent.

Out of the quiet came a humming sound, a drone-like buzzing. Everyone inside the twenty-foot-high walls of Tartarus stared toward whatever approached. The freakish noise grew closer, coming from beyond the back wall where most of the town's population lived. Homemade weapons were in every alien's grasp. Several carried burning torches that created flickering shadows.

The five adventurers looked toward the far wall where the buzzing noise rapidly approached.

Like dive bombers, dozens of the wasp-monkey horrors from Summahon's cave skimmed over the wall and started attacking anything that moved. Smaller aliens were stabbed by the flying demon-monkeys' three lethal stingers. One flyer impaled a torch carrier, both catching fire. The torch bearer collapsed in a ball of flames as the burning wasp-monkey tried flying away, spinning wildly in midair before crashing in flames onto the huts. Tartarus aliens were fighting back with spears, knives, rocks, trunks, tails, tentacles, paws, anything and everything they could find. By now all five adventurers and Lizard were fleeing out the front entrance and running to the nearby forest. They stopped near the edge and watched the ongoing horror.

Every alien scream imaginable and sound of a raging battle continued from inside the town. Flames were growing and a few other aliens fled out the gate, but most remained inside, where fire and swarming death had come to call.

Rising above the burning town, three of the flying horrors began hovering, fire glittering in their demon eyes. One took off after an alien on the far side, while the other two spotted the adventurers and began swooping toward them.

"Go quickly," shouted Lizard. "I know what to do."

There was no time to argue and they ran into the forest.

Lizard calmly assumed his natural Mona Lisa smile as he moved into the open, drawing the wasp-monkeys. He wasn't sure why the urge to be a hero came over him, but decided those young alien Humans were worth it. Their natural friendliness and curiosity was refreshing. Besides, he was tired of the struggle on this insane planet. At long last it was time for a final stand.

Lizard shifted to his native purple color, wanting to exit life the same shade as he'd entered it.

The three stingers on each flying demon were ready to rip him apart. He waited until the last moment, using lightning lizard reflexes to scoot away. Their buzzing squeals of rage were loud as they sped past. He felt the breeze of frantically beating wings as they U-turned. He thought of fleeing, but his lizard energy was nearly gone. They had him dead to rights and he knew it. The crazy planet of death had finally caught up with him. It had been a good run. He smiled, flicked his tongue one last time, and closed his eyes, breathing deep and humming a childhood song.

Thwack!

One of the wasp-monkeys was plucked out of the air by the long sticky tongue of the same froggish monstrosity that had eaten little Rork weeks before. The thing was whiplashed into the froggish monster's enormous mouth and swallowed.

Hearing the strange sound of a shrieking, whiplashed wasp-monkey, Lizard opened one wary eye and saw the other demon-thing dancing in the air, confused and alarmed. Without warning the tongue struck again and the flying horror vanished in the blink of a lizard eye. Recognizing unbelievable good luck when he saw it, Lizard scooted into the forest hoping to find the adventurers.

Suddenly he felt life was worth living again.

However, the frantic escape had separated everyone, with Tyson and Heather running one way, while Estrella dashed with Sklizz and Einlen in the opposite direction. Each quickly realized they'd lost the others, but it was too late now as they'd already begun a long and dangerous night.

FIFTEEN

Citlalli and Tarayon saw more new arrivals into the crowded room of aliens, starting with someone Citlalli had met only once: Wizza.

Wizza had arrived on Earth after Citlalli's kidnapping by the Doozies, learning about Citlalli's heroics in defeating the Destroyer. As the ambassador from Gelz, Wizza had been a driving force in forging a diplomatic partnership between Gelz, Meemer, Plinn, Earth, and the emerging Human/Fiberian world on Mars. Together they would straddle both galaxies and rebuild slowly from the ashes left behind by the Destroyer.

Wizza was packing for a return trip to Gelz when her comm buzzed. On the video screen was her friend and Mars Fiberian leader, Thrix.

"I bid you a safe journey home," said Thrix.

"Thanks, you big blue thing," smiled Wizza. She'd gotten to know Thrix well since their miraculous victory over the Doozies on Mars. Each had played a major role in the combined air and ground battle, overcoming incredible odds to destroy the powerful Doozy armies.

"I heard about Kahpoo and the other Doozies. What happened?" said Wizza.

"They just vanished, leaving no trace. Strangest of all was finding the empty Doozy spacecraft, laser cannon ready to fire and vaporize our shuttle."

"Could Doozies have some kind of long-range teleporter?"

"I seriously doubt it."

"What's the latest on Mars colonization?"

"Humans will be able to survive here in weeks. Radiation shielding remains the big challenge."

"Well," said Wizza, "I'll—"

As Thrix watched in amazement, Wizza flickered and vanished.

Wizza materialized, as confused and frightened as all the rest when first appearing. And moments before Wizza's arrival, everyone had watched two other aliens appear.

The first was a bat-creature from Plinn named Humley. He was the genius behind their invisibility technology, and since arriving had cowered in one corner.

The second was Prince Zed, a fast-growing newborn son of Princess Pat on Meemer. The Watchers told Citlalli that Princess Pat was now Queen Pat. Prince Zed was one of her snake-creature children who'd helped defeat the Doozies in the first battle for Mars. Prince Zed slithered to one side, quietly watching the other aliens.

Citlalli had been through a lot with Princess Pat, and she smiled through misty eyes at the sight of her son.

Into the midst of these staring aliens, Wizza materialized. As she slowly scanned the room she felt a tap on her shoulder. She saw a very upset Lupe with tears in her eyes. Wizza barely had time to be surprised when Lupe dove into her arms with a fierce hug. Wizza helped a sobbing Lupe over to a side wall as the Watchers began retelling their story.

Inside Citlalli and Tarayon's room a Watcher spoke, "There will be two more. You must begin deciding which four will be together in each spacecraft. Let instinct guide you. Do not tarry as time is critical."

SCRADLE

Back on planet Scradle, the time-travel experiment Kikikik had done with Citlalli, including lying about traveling back in time to rejoin her family on Earth, had ended in confusion. Citlalli should've reappeared, hideously deformed, another casualty of Okyrick science.

But she vanished and never reappeared. They had no idea why or what happened to her.

Since then Kikikik and his fellow bug-eyed, praying mantis–like Okyrick scientists had been scouring the data deep inside their underground facilities.

A few days earlier on planet Yerti, the Supreme Doozy had limped up to the planet-killing spacecraft he'd named Exterminator and spoken to its doomed pilots.

"You have eternal honor," he said to the four Doozies flying Exterminator to Scradle. "Your names will go down in history on this glorious mission."

The Doozies who'd volunteered for this suicide mission nodded reverently to their Supreme Leader.

And now Exterminator was entering Okyrick space near Scradle, its target. They were on final approach.

Kikikik learned of the unidentified vessel and was back on the planet's surface. All communications attempts were ignored. The mystery ship sent its own message claiming it carried technology gifts as a friendly gesture from their ancient Doozy enemies. The Okyricks let it approach the planet, all defenses poised to fire if it tried anything funny. It drifted slowly closer as a voice spoke over the intercom, "We carry a special message for all Okyricks. It is our great honor to deliver this on behalf of our Supreme Doozy."

At that moment the Doozies detonated Exterminator, just as Kikikik vanished.

The immense explosion was directed at Scradle, a speeding shockwave of planetary annihilation. The planet barely remained in one piece, its surface scoured and vaporized. Every opening and crevice to its interior was seared and bubbling with incredible heat and unstoppable radon particles. Within minutes the planet was a burned-out hulk, devoid of all life.

Exterminator had worked better than even the Supreme Doozy's wildest dreams.

While Scradle was exterminated, Kikikik made his miraculous arrival into the Watchers' room.

Citlalli recognized Kikikik instantly and felt incredible rage and pity wash over her.

"We know of Kikikik's deception," said a voice. Citlalli and Tarayon spun around, seeing a Human-looking woman dressed in a white camo-suit with short brown hair and an athletic build.

"I am Theal. I am your final team member."

"Who are you?" said Tarayon. "How did you get here?"

"I am a Watcher turned into Human form."

She gave a nod to Citlalli.

"On behalf of all Watchers, I am honored to meet your physical presence, Citlalli."

Citlalli still felt like the daughter of Mecatl, a young woman living with her family as part of the Anahuac people; her home was the land of ancient Mexico. It was hard to think of herself as an intergalactic hero.

"I'll remove the barrier to the others," said Theal, "but first tell me how you'll assign our sixteen team members into four spacecraft. Time is short and we must begin our journeys."

NIGHT

Since the horrific sight of wasp-monkeys flying out of the cave, Summahon, Hinge and Jak-toll kept pushing on in the dark. It wasn't long before they'd scaled several hills, finding shelter in a narrow, hidden crevice.

They heard distant rumbles from the mountain.

Miles away two others walked through a forest that was almost pitch black. Heather and Tyson moved slowly, staying next to one another, brushing away invisible branches and tripping over unseen roots. Far in the distance they heard a nasty snarl. Heather grabbed Tyson's hand.

"I still can't believe we lost them," said Heather.

"It just happened so fast," said Tyson.

Heather had been thinking about surviving this night. She said thoughtfully, "We have a Shumard red oak in our backyard. Dad built a tree house for my brothers and me. Ever climb trees?"

Tyson first shook his head, then realizing Heather couldn't see him in the dark, said, "Uh, not really."

"It's easy if we can find a good tree."

"They all looked pretty gnarly before it got dark."

"Big and gnarly is the kind of tree we want."

"We can't see a thing, so we might as well try."

Shortly thereafter they found a promising tree. Tyson gave Heather a lift to the first branch and minutes later they'd both shimmied out on a thick branch to a fairly secure spot twenty feet above the ground.

"Think we should try yelling for the others?" asked Heather.

"Uh, probably not a good idea right now."

"Yeah, guess you're right."

"Let's try to get some rest, wait for morning, and head toward the mountains."

Sklizz, Einlen, and Estrella had also stopped, finding shelter between jagged boulders. They could defend from one direction while resting against the rocks. Einlen and Sklizz both made sure Estrella was safe and snug between them.

"They know we're heading toward the mountains," said Sklizz. "We'll keep looking until we find them."

"Night forest very dangerous," said Einlen.

"Back at the town," asked Estrella, "what happened to Lizard?"

No one said anything for a moment.

"It was an act of bravery and sacrifice," said Sklizz.

Estrella sniffled, thinking about her lost friends and Lizard giving his life for them. She crossed herself and said a prayer for all three, then wondered if God knew of Lizard. After all, Lizard wasn't Human. *Well, of course God watched over Lizard. God knew everything, existing everywhere, right? God had to know about Lizard, didn't He? But the bible said God made man from the dust of the earth, breathing into him the breath of life: and man became a living soul. Did that mean God made Lizard's race from the dust of their earth, breathing life into them?*

Estrella fell asleep having a serious theological debate with herself.

LIZARD

A wise Human named Mark, who used to be called Samuel, once said, "...the report of my death was an exaggeration." This was certainly true for Lizard. He remained very much alive, and on the trail of Tyson and Heather.

Lizard had followed the two young aliens deep into the forest. His nocturnal eyes worked well in the darkness as he cautiously followed their trail. Earth military would call his current skin color army-camouflage green.

He began to hear something that sounded like soft rainfall on the sand of his home world. He moved toward the sound, stumbling upon a long, albino-white creature moving atop a fallen log. The snaky thing didn't slither, but crawled on thousands of tiny legs like a huge caterpillar. Lizard saw that it had black eyes and fangs, and it hadn't seen him yet.

As it climbed a tall, twisted tree, Lizard kept his distance. Glancing up he was surprised to see the two sleeping kids, and he realized the beast was after them. It was nearly upon them when Lizard yelled, "Humans! Awaken!"

The shout jerked both kids awake. The creature froze on the tree, stunned by the sudden noise.

Heather peered down at the writhing white-fanged nightmare, its eerie black eyes staring hungrily.

"Oh crap, move!" said Heather, scrambling against Tyson. He started moving forward, but the creature had already wrapped itself around Heather's ankle. The tiny legs were needles dancing on her skin. It yanked downward and Heather grasped the branch as her legs slid off.

Tyson turned and saw Heather hanging on when the monster pulled again. He lunged forward and grabbed one of her wrists as the thing jerked Heather clear off the branch. Tyson looked in Heather's frantic eyes, trying to pull her back up. A final yank ripped Heather from Tyson's grasp. He watched her fall, helpless with anguish and despair as she bounced on the ground far below.

Lizard had been unable to help and now saw the alien almost upon the girl, fangs and rows of sharp teeth ready to strike. Lizard had one chance; he darted toward its head. The white creature was so focused on devouring Heather that Lizard easily clamped his reptilian jaws around its entire head, chomping down. The skull cracked once and then caved in like a shattered egg. Spitting out the foul-tasting mess, Lizard saw Tyson landing on two feet next to Heather.

"Get frien' out of this tangled beast fast."

He and Tyson pulled the dead creature off Heather. She was breathing and seemed okay. The undergrowth had helped cushion her landing. When she opened her eyes and sat up, Tyson breathed a sigh of relief.

"Mr. Lizard!" said Heather. "You're alive!"

"The hand of luck arrived just in time."

"Yeah, what the heck were those flying-monkey things?" asked Tyson.

"And what was this thing?" Heather said, backing away from the white corpse with the squashed head.

"The flyers attacked Tartarus before, but never so many at once...must've been their entire nest. The most vicious creatures I've come across. And as for this," he spat on the white creature, the taste in his mouth nearly unbearable, "I have no idea."

"Have you seen the others?" asked Tyson.

"Yer frien's? No, just followed yer trail."

"I'm sure glad you did," said Heather.

"Headin' past the mountain of madness toward the sea?"

"That's where everyone was going before we got lost."

"Mind if I join ya?"

"Are you kidding?" said Heather. "We'd love to have you join us."

"Thank ya, ma'am. How're ya feeling...after that fall?

Heather stood and said, "I'm ready to get outta here."

"What're ya both called?"

"I'm Heather." She turned to Tyson, waiting.

"Oh, uh, my name's Tyson."

"Well, ya can't pronounce my name."

"You kind of look like an Earth lizard," said Heather. Then she remembered the Hundred Acre Wood and Pooh's blue friend. "How about Yore?"

"Is that a good name?"

"It's the perfect name for you," smiled Heather.

"I like it," said the newly christened lizard. "You all can call me Yore."

As they turned to follow Yore, the ground began shaking again, knocking the kids down. As Heather fell she could feel her ankle tightening and hurting.

"Shakes been gettin' worse since I got here," said Yore.

Seconds later an ear-shattering sonic boom shook the air. A fireball passed overhead and crashed with a huge explosion up ahead in the forest. When they got there nothing was left but blasted forest and burning wreckage.

"I see all kinda ships slam into this planet. I bet lots get sucked into this galaxy's black hole. Only us lucky survivors get to see how long we can stay alive on Obaddon."

AVARICE

Meanwhile, no one was lucky enough to stay alive on Scradle. They never stood a chance against Exterminator.

Deep underground on Yerti and checking the status of Exterminator II, the Supreme Doozy learned that Scradle had been utterly destroyed. Opening one good eye, a crooked smile stretched his warped and scarred pumpkin face as yellow drool oozed down his nonexistent chin.

Turning to his master weapons builder, he said, "Finish Exterminator II. I want it ready to go now."

As he spoke, flecks of sticky yellow saliva sprayed outward, several landing on the weapon builder's face. He dared not wipe them off, nodding obediently.

Turning to the roomful of new military leaders—the old ones having been killed by the footstool bomb—the Supreme Doozy said, "Time for a Rooq lightning strike. No prisoners and no survivors."

"What if Earth offers to surrender?"

The Supreme Doozy wiped his yellow drool, peering at the questioner with the withered and disfigured eye that Arizza had stabbed.

"Earthlings had their chance. I want Mars scorched into oblivion and Earth's Human species exterminated."

Meanwhile Thrix spoke via video link with Earth's leaders about Mars terraforming and construction of a protective radiation shield. Lastly he opened up the topic of the recent disappearances.

"The Doozy father and daughter named Stauffa and Waima claimed to be fleeing their assassination attempt of the Doozy leader, the one they call the Supreme Doozy. What you don't know is that Stauffa mentioned a planet killer called Exterminator. It was being tested on a planet called Scradle, part of the Okyrick civilization."

"The Okyricks from Sklizz's last message?" said the U.S. President. "Isn't the planet Scradle where they left Citlalli?"

"That's correct," said Thrix, "she is most likely dead. And according to Stauffa the Doozies' next target...is Mars and Earth."

HOBGOBLINS

During the night Summahon and her friends felt several earthquakes, and this morning they'd been knocked off their feline, hoof, and leafy feet twice. They were moving rapidly past the volcanic mountain.

"Obaddon's trees not good for boat-building," growled Hinge. "I hope things change closer to shore."

Rounding a corner they came upon Vivvy and the flying creature lying on the ground. The flying thing was dead and Vivvy barely alive as they gathered around.

"Vivvy, what happened?" said Summahon.

"My arms, poisoned...the thing," whispered Vivvy. "Listen, time short...must hear...."

Vivvy's dying words described horrors that had visited during the night. "Wings...starry eyes...feelers..."

Vivvy shuddered one last time and died.

The three remaining friends looked down at their comrade.

"Vivvy was a tough little gal," said Hinge, "but way over her tentacle head on this planet."

Jak-toll quivered, shook, and buzzed frantically.

"Slow down," said Summahon, "we can't understand."

Jak-toll took a photosynthetic deep breath from his ten-foot height and began buzzing slowly in veggie-code.

"Vivvy spoke of old ones. We have legends winged, starry-eyed monsters."

"Come on, Jak-o, these can't be the same things," said Summahon, "especially not on this planet."

"Vivvy's picture precise."

"I've never heard of these old ones," said Hinge, "and besides, why would that matter on this crazy place?"

"In my cosmos," buzzed Jak-toll, "believe universal Armageddon. End of everything...Galaxy Wraiths and the Dark."

"Wow," said Summahon, "even I've heard of the Wraiths. But they're just fairytales...hobgoblins to keep the young quiet. They're supposed to be bringers of interstellar doom."

"Superstitious nonsense," snorted Hinge.

They all looked down at their dead friend.

It was tough making friends on Obaddon since everyone died, usually soon and almost always violently. They each said private goodbyes to Vivvy, continuing past the fiery mountain. Happily, they felt the ground and landscape begin a downward slope and moments later could see a pinkish-purple sea far in the distance.

Watching from stinking hot lairs and dark noxious caverns inside the mountain, the five-pointed red eyes of degenerate elder beings glared down at them.

Not too far behind, Einlen, Sklizz, and Estrella kept to the rocky hills, watching for Tyson and Heather as they marched toward the left side of the mountain.

Simultaneously, Tyson, Heather, and Yore hiked through dense forest, heading toward the right side of the mountain, just hours behind Summahon.

LAUNCH

Inside the Watchers' cavern, Citlalli and Tarayon were trying to assign the four spacecraft teams, letting instinct and gut feelings dictate their decisions. It didn't help. Nothing seemed right.

Theal mysteriously reentered the room.

"Thank you," said Theal, "Your minds have spoken."

"They have?" said Citlalli.

"All are ready," said Theal. "Each understands the threat and importance of our mission. Shall we remove the barrier and begin?"

They nodded and saw the wall shimmer and disappear. The Doozies, Uppsalians, Plinn, Meemerian, Gelzian, Okyrick, and Humans stood, staring at the three new faces.

Citlalli smiled at Lupe, who beamed back. They were both wiping shining wet eyes as Theal spoke.

"You've been told about Tarayon and Citlalli, and the vital nature of your journeys. We don't know what you'll find, but we must stop whatever is slowing the universe. If we fail, all life will end."

As Theal debriefed them one final time, thoughts were swirling among the chosen travelers.

Waima marveled at Citlalli's long white hair. She saw the smile between Citlalli and Lupe, jealous of their bond. She wanted to know these Humans, to understand these beings that her Supreme Doozy leader wanted to exterminate.

Stauffa was worried sick about Waima. The hated Kahpoo and the mysterious Doozy called Kriner just made things worse.

Prince Zed knew about Citlalli and Lupe from his mom. How they'd defeated the Destroyer and then the Doozies. He was in awe, seeing the famous Citlalli in person.

Wizza thought Citlalli looked the same, but there was something in her eyes, something new. This young Human had changed since her stowaway arrival on Gelz.

Learning Citlalli's fate had Kikikik in a tizzy. She knew he and his fellow Okyrick scientists had lied about traveling in time back to her family. He'd been quietly grinding his mandibles since arriving.

Jamila had been trying to understand why she was here. How could she help save the universe? And why was Mossad here? The urge to kill him was strong.

Gilad was just as confused, surprised at the irony that he and Jamila were on this joint mission to save everything. It didn't matter; he still wanted her dead.

Lupe had loved being home and pampered by her mom. And now here she was again, thrust into insanity. She was feeling overwhelmed and scared to death.

"This is our last message," said a Watcher, "Theal or Citlalli will know when it's time to return. You must keep both of them safe if you are to return. We don't know where you'll arrive in space. Your spacecraft are programmed to find the universal core. Look for your spacecraft ion trails as you near the core and you should find each other. Be prepared for anything."

There was a brief moment of silence, the entire group hanging on every word.

"May the Light shine through you."

Before anyone could ask any questions or even say goodbye, the Watchers had teleported all four spacecraft and their diverse collection of passengers to the place where time began.

"We're nearly done," said a Watcher.

"We must save power to return one spacecraft; it's the only way we'll know what happened."

"They have so little chance of success."

"We must hope for another miracle."

"Do you think the Anahuac girl has it in her again?"

"Who can say?"

"Does she have any idea about her power?"

"Of course she has no idea. Nor do we know what it'll be; what it'll do; or how strong it'll be. We couldn't tell Citlalli or anyone else because nothing is certain. Citlalli must find out herself."

"The only thing we do know is that Citlalli carries the Light within her. A compass and magnet that should help guide her to the others, or manifest itself in other ways."

"Like the power she displayed against the Destroyer."

"Yes. And we must hope the Light still shines where time began, at least a little; our very existence rests with this group of mortal beings."

"You are overlooking the others."

"True, but what can they do?"

"Nothing yet, but the battle is not yet lost. The Dark and its terrible servants can yet be defeated."

"Saving the universe is never easy."

"The Light does work in mysterious ways."

"Indeed, and we know that better than anyone."

"A truer statement was never generated."

"I hope we survive long enough to see how it ends."

"Yes..."

PART TWO

HOMEFRONT

As Heather, Tyson, Estrella, Lupe, and Citlalli fought to stay alive across the universe, the other two kids who'd been part of Seven of the Blue Third were back on Earth with their families: David in Porcupine Plain, Saskatchewan, and Maddy in Richmond, Virginia. Both were trying to fit back into their normal kid worlds. It wasn't easy.

Each family knew that special agents were quietly protecting David and Maddy, while staying out of sight. For the moment this protection continued around the clock.

However, neither family was aware of surveillance by the Canadian and United States governments. After the mysterious disappearance of Lupe, Wizza, and four Doozies it was clear something was going on. The agents protecting David and Maddy were told of these recent vanishings, but sworn to silence. Word of the disappearances was top secret. Even Lupe's mom was now in protective custody—safe, comfortable, but not allowed to communicate with anyone.

Since returning from Mars, David, Maddy, and Lupe had talked or texted every day. They'd speculated endlessly about their Blue Third friends.

Maddy celebrated her fourteenth birthday with girlfriends and a sleepover. She shared David's private emails and texts with her girlfriends. There was much giggling and David would've been shocked to know many were jealous of Maddy. They kidded that she was robbing the cradle, since David wouldn't be fourteen for two months.

Maddy would've been mortified to know every email, text, and phone call was analyzed by intelligence personnel.

And now David and Maddy were told Lupe was on a secluded vacation, out of contact for a few weeks.

And yet something else was wrong that neither could explain; a restless energy that never seemed to go away. Doctors said they were healthy, so they said nothing.

And then the dreams began—dreams that included the heroic Basset hound named Lucy. They could never remember exactly what happened and kept the dreams to themselves. And that's when things really started to happen.

It was a bitterly cold day on the Canadian plains in Saskatoon as Agent Wanda Smithfield walked into the warm motel room. Hunched over a laptop was her partner, Wade Hamm. He looked up as the cold breeze hit him.

"Tim Horton's coffee and honey glazed," said Wanda.

"Jesus, close that door."

"You're very welcome, and don't call me Jesus."

She kicked the door shut and stood behind Hamm, staring at David on the video monitor.

David was by himself watching TV when he heard something out by their family's barn. He got up to look out the kitchen window, wanting to know what the noise was. In the blink of an eye David was standing outside the barn, whipped by the icy breeze. He saw his dad's back, working on the family tractor. His dad didn't see him, and in another blink David found himself in his bedroom.

Secretly placed micro-cameras had captured David entering the kitchen. Hamm switched to the kitchen camera and there was no David. He clicked back to the TV room, also empty.

Smithfield held out Hamm's coffee. "Where's David?"

Bored agents were watching Maddy's family at dinner when the three porcelain ducks fell off the wall. Maddy had endured those ducks from her seat at the table for years. She hated those ducks. Stabbing her Virginia ham she imagined those ducks starting to move, to escape their wall shackles. As Maddy watched, all three ducks struggled to break loose, yanking free of their hooks and plummeting down, shattering on the hardwood kitchen floor.

The rest of her family was so shocked by the crashing ducks they didn't notice the look of shock and confusion that ran across Maddy's face.

However, it wasn't until later when David and Maddy shared their experiences with one another that the radar went up at the highest levels of government.

Within the hour both kids were quietly taken away to a secret underground facility shared by the U.S. and Canada. Maddy was flown by jet since this facility resided far away under a wheat field near the home of the Royal Canadian Mounted Police in Regina, Saskatchewan. Their families were told David and Maddy needed further debriefing. Neither family was happy, but they had no choice.

The building David and Maddy entered was next to a wheat field and road. An elevator took them below ground.

Intelligence personnel allowed David and Maddy a quick hello before being locked in separate rooms. There were no electronics or ways to communicate, and neither kid knew why they'd been brought here. They were told to get a good night's sleep. *Yeah right.*

Elsewhere, interrogation plans were prepared. If these kids did have teleporting or telekinetic powers, there had to be a way to understand, master, and manipulate these capabilities. But first they had to determine if the kids were truly capable of these things.

Also in Canada on this chilly Saturday, a ten-year-old girl named Mary was walking the family Basset hound, Lucy, world-famous for helping defeat the Destroyer and saving Earth. Lucy had already forgotten most of that dreadful experience, happy to be back where she belonged with Mary and her family. She was running free, sniffing everything, and leaving her occasional territorial marker as they neared the county road.

Mom asked Mary to check for the mail and as they approached the road the mail truck just arrived; perfect timing. As the mailman stepped out and opened the mailbox, Lucy spotted him. The mailman waved and smiled.

Since the first letter carrier brought stone tablets to a dog-owning Hittite scribe, dogs have defended their territory against deliverers of mail. Lucy carried the same proud blood as her canine ancestors, and seeing this trespasser, her doggie instinct kicked into full force.

Mary heard Lucy's barks and saw her run toward the mailman, wondering why he stood there with a silly grin, not moving at all. Mary started running toward the mailbox, Lucy a few feet from the frozen man, barking up a storm. As she got closer it was obvious something was wrong with him.

"Sir?" she said, as Lucy kept up her barking. "Lucy!"

Lucy heard Mary's shout and knew she'd done something wrong. Distracted from the mailman, she trotted away.

At that instant the mailman looked down at Mary, his waving arm stopped. He looked confused, starting to say something. Then shaking his head, he jumped into the mail truck and drove away fast.

When Mary and Lucy got back to the house, she tried explaining what happened. Her mom said she imagined it, and then made Mary a piping hot cup of cocoa with extra marshmallows. Mary forgot all about the frozen mailman.

BOO

All seven Blue Third kids were once again in peril. David and Maddy were prisoners of their own governments; Citlalli and Lupe were teleporting across infinity; and on the incredibly dangerous planet called Obaddon, Heather, Estrella, and Tyson were fighting to stay alive.

Preparing to cross the sea in search of a mysterious land called Pith, Hinge finished building a wind-propelled vessel with Jak-toll and Summahon's help.

"We'll add a wooden-missile harpoon gun and a rotating scythe. That's all we can do with this wood," said Hinge.

"Let's get off this beach before dark," said Summahon, "I can't shake the feeling something's watching us."

Jak-toll agreed with a buzz.

As the trio raced to finish the boat, the others were getting closer.

"Heather! Tyson!" shouted Sklizz. They'd been calling both kids' names all day.

As darkness fell they decided to stop for the night underneath several boulders, projectiles spewed out of the volcano long ago. Building a fire was out of the question, remembering the Urgle's attack that killed poor Lisa.

Heather, Tyson, and Yore moved past the mountain on the opposite side. Following the same path as Summahon, they came upon the bodies of Vivvy and the flying thing. Yore recognized Vivvy but kept quiet, not wanting to scare the young Humans. After staring at the bizarre aliens for a few moments, they continued on.

Unholy red star-eyes watched from hidden places on the mountain, waiting for darkness.

Hinge finished installing weapons as darkness fell over the sea. The craft was twenty feet long and ten feet wide with a dark blue sail made from Summahon's saved parachute material. The sky was dark purple as they drifted off shore, where they anchored, as it felt safer than on land. All three felt the relentless presence of something watching.

Sitting in their dark campsite, Tyson, Heather, and Yore felt the same vile presence. But Heather also had another worry on her mind.

"We should keep moving," said Yore, "away from here."

"Yes," said Tyson, "there's something...not right."

"I'm sorry, I can't..." said Heather.

They turned to Heather questioningly.

"My ankle's killing me, right where that thing grabbed me. It's all swollen and I can't walk."

At that moment the final sliver of sun slipped behind Obaddon's horizon, a nightly signal for the Dark. A horrible blasphemous wail broke the silence from somewhere on the mountain, followed by the high-pitched chant of piping voices.

Heather had never felt the hair rise on the back of her neck until now. This was the scariest thing she'd ever heard: a haunted pipe-like chanting, a primordial dirge of unspeakable evil never meant for mortal ears. She felt a terrified scream rising up inside her.

"Come on," said Yore. "Climb on my back."

"Are you sure?" Heather's voice was a loud whisper.

"Yes, get on me, Human. We must leave, fast."

Tyson helped Heather climb atop their ten-foot-long friend, arms holding on tight around his neck. She was surprised how soft Yore's skin was, almost leathery. Tyson walked behind Heather and Yore, happy to be leaving this terrible place.

Black shadows moved in the darkness, silently trailing Yore and the kids.

Yore trotted fast in the cool night air. This was his time of day, out of the sunlight. He stayed low while maneuvering through the foliage, Heather keeping her head down and Tyson jogging right behind. They were making good progress, the haunted chanting becoming more distant.

Tyson's mind wandered back to the desperate battle atop Mt. Torpur. How amazingly brave Heather had been, both of them wielding swords and fighting those undead Kreyon. They'd been through so much since, and now here they were, Heather riding an alien lizard on some planet a zillion miles from home. He couldn't help but smile.

Whip-like tentacles shot out, wrapping around Tyson's mouth and ankles, silently lifting him off the ground and yanking him into the darkness. It happened so fast he couldn't make a sound. As his abductors ran through the forest all he could hear was their feverish whispering and all he could see were their glowing red star-shaped eyes. Terrified and barely able to breathe, he felt tentacle cilia exploring his body like hundreds of tiny maggots. His muffled attempts to scream ended quickly as the curious cilia maggots tried entering his mouth. He could only clamp his mouth shut and close his eyes against the horror.

Yore continued trotting with Heather on his back, oblivious to Tyson's abduction and disappearance into the dark.

BEACHHEADS

The Watchers' instantaneous teleporting of four spacecraft to the tiniest pinprick location across the vastness of infinity meant the likelihood of any two arriving together was slim.

No one even had time to say goodbye.

Each silver spacecraft was shaped like a cylinder with interstellar engines on each side. This Watcher engine technology was well beyond the knowledge of the passengers. They were armed with old weapon technology laser cannons in front and rear. The pilot sat in front, with two passengers in the middle, and one in back with the rear laser.

The first spacecraft blinked into existence near the same enormous black hole that almost got Sklizz and Summahon. Llarke was piloting with Kahpoo in the rear. Humley the Plinn and Vomisa the psycho killer stared out the passenger windows at the gigantic black hole. It stretched across their line of sight, a vast panorama of absolute darkness. Llarke turned sharply, trying to escape its gravitational pull. Kahpoo fired the laser cannon, watching the light bend, pulled horrifically by the black hole's powerful gravity toward its dark center.

Llarke knew they were doomed, but Watcher space thrusters were miracles of power, and to his amazement they began pulling free. As the thrusters roared louder and louder, struggling against the unbelievable gravity, Humley began screaming. Vomisa grabbed Humley, shaking him violently and shouting. Humley panicked even more, his bat face stretched into a single silent shriek. In the rear, Kahpoo mouthed prayers to his Supreme Doozy.

The incredible Watcher space thrusters shot them free like an interstellar cannonball, their only savior being Llarke's piloting as he dodged a minefield of space debris.

Their speed was uncontrollable as a result of the black hole's gravitational sling shot effect. In seconds a huge planet filled their windows. Llarke tried skidding to a stop on the atmosphere, but they were going way too fast.

And then they lost all spacecraft power.

As Llarke sped into Obaddon's orbit, Heather and Yore finally noticed Tyson was missing. They frantically backtracked to where Yore could sense Tyson had been taken. He was now a prisoner of whatever eldritch horrors lived on that mountain.

"If they have frien' Tyson, nothing we can do."

Heather fought back tears. "We have to find the others; they'll know what to do."

"Dawn come soon, we must hurry."

At that moment another earthquake hit, but Yore and Heather ignored it and started moving again.

Seconds later the entire area was lit up by bright light, followed by a sonic boom. Looking back they saw the bright streak of Llarke's helpless spacecraft slam into the side of the mountain, a huge explosion and fireball shooting sideways into the night sky.

"Never had a chance," said Yore.

Flames erupted as dry brush caught fire.

"I wonder who they were," said Heather.

Yore shook his head and turned, moving toward the sea.

The second spacecraft was luckier, materializing in an empty location in space. Theal piloted with Jamila and Waima as passengers and assassin Kriner in the rear.

"Coordinates okay," said Theal. "No sign of others."

Jamila was totally out of her element, sitting next to this alien kid named Waima.

Kriner's killer mind was thinking how he'd dispose of Waima easily. The question was how to kill this Human-looking Watcher called Theal, and the real Human woman called Jamila.

Waima'd been holding her dad's hand before appearing here with these strangers. She was scared but determined to fight like her dad. She could still sense his tight grip. Waima thought with pride that she was the daughter of Stauffa, a man of principal who stood up against the evil Supreme Doozy. She had to find a way to survive.

The third spacecraft arrived at the edge of a rainbow nebula, silky remnants of a supernova draped across the blackness of space like a beautiful yet dangerous translucent scarf.

Wizza piloted, with Prince Zed and Lupe as passengers and Gilad the Mossad agent at the rear laser.

Each looked around, shocked at their instant arrival.

"A moment," said Wizza, veering away from the nebula.

Lupe glanced at the large snake-creature next to her.

Prince Zed's diamond-shaped head peered down at Lupe. "Mom teaches me talk better," he said, "tells of Earth."

Gilad was a brutal Mossad agent, but the snake called Prince Zed had him speechless. He watched as Prince Zed and Lupe, the girl he knew as the hero of Costa Rica, got acquainted.

The fourth spacecraft arrived just below an endless asteroid belt with Tarayon piloting, Citlalli and Kikikik as passengers, and Stauffa at the rear laser cannon.

With long praying-mantis legs folded, Kikikik's bug eyes stared at the asteroids. He felt incredibly self-conscious and guilty next to Citlalli.

This asteroid belt was longer than any Stauffa had ever heard of, but all he could think about was Waima. One moment they'd been holding hands in that cavern, and then he was here and she was gone. Perhaps this Citlalli and Tarayon knew something. "My daughter, please where is she?"

Citlalli didn't hear him. She felt strange, jumpy, like she needed to get out of this spacecraft. Her mind was spinning and bubbling energy was making her crazy, legs bouncing up and down, her fists and teeth clenched. It was hard to focus on anything.

A tap on the shoulder made her jump. Turning, she saw Stauffa in the rear and Kikikik next to her. *Why is lying Kikikik here? Why can't I focus? What's happening?*

The tapping continued and she turned to Stauffa, yelling, "What?"

"I've been asking what happened to my daughter, Waima."

Citlalli shook her head, trying to focus and gain control over the energy surging through her.

"Waima," she said, "your daughter. I don't know."

Kikikik suddenly remembered the Doozy peace ship he'd seen explode.

"I come from Okyrick planet Scradle," he said, black eyes peering at Stauffa. "Tell me about exploding ship."

Stauffa couldn't believe Kikikik had seen Exterminator. Had the Supreme Doozy's insanity and planetary genocide already begun?

He was about to answer when a bright flash lit up the spacecraft as asteroids collided inside the belt, one enormous chunk spinning toward them, seconds from smashing into their spacecraft.

They were helpless. It would kill them.

Acceptance of death flashed in everyone's mind, and then it hit.

The huge rock vaporized into a trillion grains of space dust, washing harmlessly over their spacecraft.

They were alive! It was impossible, but they had somehow survived. At most they had a very dirty spacecraft.

Tarayon wasted no time, flying away from the asteroid belt on a direct line toward the universal core.

The passengers were all stunned.

"How did you do that?" asked Stauffa.

"I didn't...I don't know how," said Tarayon. "It must have self-destructed, somehow."

Stauffa knew better, but didn't speak further.

Kikikik was just grinding his mandibles silently.

Tarayon looked back, seeing a shocked expression on Citlalli. He suspected why the asteroid vaporized, wondering how Citlalli did this thing.

EMBARKATION

Sklizz, Einlen, and Estrella had tried sleeping, the night filled with sounds from the terrible mountain. They felt the same earthquake as Yore and Heather and decided to leave this unholy place, starting toward the coast.

On board their small wooden ship, Summahon, Hinge, and Jak-toll stared at the raging fire where Llarke's spacecraft had crashed and vaporized in an instant.

"Should we leave now?" asked Summahon.

"According to the lizard," said Hinge, "crossing to Pith takes a day and it's safer during daylight. Besides, Jak-o needs his sunlight, don't ya, big fella."

Jak-toll glowed in the dark, not bothering to reply.

"All right, but let's leave at sunrise," said Summahon.

When Yore and Heather reached the coast, Heather marveled at the water's purple color. The pink sky dawn was nearly upon them.

"Where do we go from here?" said Yore.

"Stay near the mountain and Tyson," said Heather, "so let's turn left."

Beneath her, Heather could see Yore's dark color getting lighter as they moved along the wild shoreline.

As the others reached the sea, they decided Heather and Tyson would be to the right, assuming they still lived.

With an hour until dawn, both groups were headed along the coast toward Summahon and each other.

HORRORS

Tyson awoke in a clear bubble enclosure inside a murky cavern lit by dull reddish light. He could see tunnels in every direction. He was living a nightmare with no escape.

The brightening sky shone off Estrella's red hair as they spotted something in the distance, just offshore. Approaching cautiously, they saw a strange wooden boat. A tall bluish-colored tree walked on board, along with a horned beast and smaller tan creature. It was hard to make out details from this distance.

Yore and Heather also spotted the wooden ship from the opposite direction. They were so focused on sneaking closer that they stumbled upon Sklizz, Einlen, and Estrella.

Facing Yore straight on, they saw the bizarre sight of Heather's Human head and blue softball cap sticking out of Yore's lizard head. Heather leapt from Yore's back, wincing on her painful ankle, then limped over and hugged everyone. Yore followed, approaching slowly.

Heather related Tyson's fate. Everyone wondered what to do.

A hail from the boat interrupted them. Hinge, Jak-toll, and Summahon had been watching this reunion. Before sailing, they were curious who these creatures were and why they were here. The lizard looked familiar, but was a different color than the one in Tartarus.

"Strangers, what brings you here?" said Hinge, speaking loudly from the boat deck.

"We lost a friend in the night," said Sklizz, "to the creatures on that mountain. Can you help us? Do you know anything about them?"

"Sorry about your friend," said Hinge. "We know nothing about what or who haunts that place. And now we're casting off for a sea journey to Pith."

"What's on Pith?" asked Sklizz. "Why risk crossing the water to get there?"

"We're searching for a way to leave this planet. Perhaps something's across this sea. We aim to find out."

"Well, good luck," said Sklizz. "If you come across a Trixian called Summahon, let her know there are friends searching for her."

Summahon was so surprised she nearly fainted, and it's almost impossible for a Trixian to faint. Hinge and Jak-toll stared at her, just as shocked.

"I have no idea who they are," said Summahon.

"Then how..."

"I don't know, maybe the lizard, but we'd better find out. Perhaps they can help. At the very least I think we need to delay sailing."

After a few moments her bullish friend nodded. "Maybe they have something that will help. But I hate to wait."

After securing the watercraft, they hopped off, wading toward the waiting group of strangers.

Watching from the beach, it was obvious to everyone that they had found Summahon.

KILLER

At this moment Theal's spacecraft continued speeding toward the galactic core. Their view was filled with dark streaks, mysterious star debris, gaseous clouds, and other frightening and unexplainable things.

Waima had barely moved, trying to wish everything back the way it was before. How had she ended up here? And Kriner—the way he looked at her was bizarre and scary.

Meanwhile, Kriner discovered his dagger was missing. He glared again at the Doozy brat. He'd have to find a different weapon, or perhaps use his bare hands.

"Jamila," said Theal, "a universal translator and breathing device were implanted in your head."

"What?"

"They let you communicate with almost any intelligent alien species, while also allowing you to breathe on most planets. Humans are new to space, so we had to physically prepare you."

While Jamila digested this, Kriner thought about killing all three and then taking the spacecraft. The females and kid should be no match, even without a knife.

They approached a shadowy planet, far from its dying reddish sun, and entered an atmosphere stuck in perpetual twilight. They landed in a field of fluorescent yellow moss, trying to absorb every last bit of light from its distant red sun. Kriner watched the others exit, thinking these three females would never leave this miserable twilight world alive.

An eerie red glow bathed their spacecraft as Kriner climbed down. He decided Jamila was most dangerous and should die first, but he needed a weapon.

Waima stayed close to Jamila, which in some ways annoyed Jamila, while in other ways seemed really nice. Jamila wasn't used to kids, period.

"We won't stay long," said Theal. "All four ships need to find water. As we landed I spotted a stream in that forested area."

The forest was remarkably Earth-like, and as they entered, Kriner found a thick, sharp, deadly branch—perhaps even better than his dagger. Nearing the stream he found a second excellent wooden shard. He had the two weapons he needed: one for each adult female.

The others were at the stream, filling the half dozen empty water carriers.

Kriner figured he could take Jamila from behind, and in one motion leap the stream to stab the second branch deep into Theal. Then the Doozy brat could either run away or die; her choice. It would all be over in seconds.

Once done he'd take the spacecraft and begin the long journey home.

Approaching quietly, he focused on Jamila's Human physique. As a Doozy, he knew a knife thrust into a certain spot on Humans would cause almost instant death.

Waima had been warily watching Kriner out of the corner of her eye, and she glimpsed the dagger as he prepared to strike. "Aaaauuugh!"

Waima's scream sent Jamila's warrior instinct into motion as Kriner struck. Jamila rolled aside as the dagger sliced harmlessly through the air. In one motion she spun a vicious kick, and her foot smashed into Kriner's thin legs. She felt something snap as Kriner flipped back onto the ground. Moments later she had his weapon and was kneeling on his chest, dagger at his throat. He was groaning, one leg badly broken.

Theal had watched the entire attack, while Waima stared in shock.

"Let's get this water to the ship," said Theal. "Leave him for now. He's not going anywhere."

Once the water was loaded, they returned to a very upset Kriner. One second he looked ready to cry, and the next like he wanted to strangle them. Theal took out a mystery device that bound his wrists. She used another device to cocoon his broken leg in some kind of cast.

"It seems our Human is more resourceful and stronger," said Theal, "not surprising after seeing what your Seven of the Blue Third have done."

Jamila digested this and said, "This was a test?"

"Not exactly, Jamila. On this journey we have no time for tests. Kriner showed his true self, as did you and Waima. This journey is about fate, chance, and hopefully a good deal of luck. The Light is as it should be."

Jamila turned to Waima, "Thanks for the heads up."

Waima smiled back, having no idea what "heads up" meant.

Theal marched toward the spacecraft and said, "Bring the Doozy along. He may yet be useful."

Helping a limping Kriner, they heard a distant roar and saw flickering orange light over the horizon. Not sure what was coming, they pushed Kriner to move faster. Theal climbed in her pilot seat first.

Over the hillside appeared a shadowed mass of grunting creatures charging toward them. The red twilight revealed aliens brandishing sharp weapons and flaming torches. Jamila helped Waima climb in, and together they tried pushing Kriner up as the mob got closer. Glancing over at the onrushing creatures, Waima saw bloated, two-legged Earth pigs with big black eyes and long waving antennae.

Kriner wasn't helping, lying limp like a rag doll. Jamila clambered around him into the craft and together she and Waima tried pulling him in. He was at the passenger window when the snorting mob arrived.

"Drop him, now," shouted Theal. "Toss him down. Give him to these freaks."

Waima was shocked but Jamila didn't hesitate, Kriner screaming all the way down to the deranged squealing natives. Waima watched for a moment, and then closed her eyes at the horrific sight.

Kriner had proved to be useful after all.

Theal had them airborne in moments. In the underside mirror she saw three pig creatures hanging on. Theal accelerated into the upper atmosphere, the hangers-on dropping off one by one, sure to enjoy their last seconds of life in a long free fall down to the ground.

PURSUIT

"I just picked up an ion trail," said Wizza. "It's one of our other spacecraft."

"Can you tell its passengers?" asked Prince Zed.

"No, but it's one of ours."

As Wizza began following the ion trail, Lupe changed the subject. She'd been wondering about Queen Pat's babies, wondering about their father.

"Does Queen Pat have a king?" asked Lupe.

"My Queen Mother rules all," said Prince Zed. "I know word king, but understand not. My Queen Mother and Meemer have no king."

Gilad was finally getting used to this enormous snake that called itself Prince Zed. He spoke for the first time.

"Females rule your world?" Gilad asked.

"There is always queen," said Prince Zed, "for long as our species' memory burrows."

"With women in charge, no wonder you're all so nice," said a smiling Lupe.

Wizza hadn't been listening, focused on the ion trail.

"I have them," said Wizza. "We can follow. They're on a course into the core. They've found the passage."

Tarayon followed the asteroid belt on a pathway inside energy clouds, ion storms, burnt-out suns, and other scattered garbage that littered the place where time began.

Sitting silently, Citlalli still wasn't sure she'd caused the energy burst that vaporized the huge asteroid chunk. It would've pulverized them in a nanosecond when Citlalli *wished it to be vaporized*, and it was.

Ever since then, the energy that had been driving her crazy disappeared. It seemed impossible, but her mere thought must've turned that asteroid into dust. Somehow she knew this was true. She was sure of it.

"We need to stop for water," said Tarayon. "There may be a solar system up ahead with a wet planet."

"Could our other spacecraft have passed this way?" said Stauffa, thinking of Waima and sick with worry.

"I would have detected their ion trail."

Stauffa sat back resignedly.

"Fourth planet in the second system," Citlalli said.

Tarayon turned questioningly, "Huh?"

Citlalli shook her head, feeling a little dazed, then repeated, "Fourth planet, second system."

Everyone looked at the tiny, white-haired Anahuac girl, somewhat awed by her mere presence.

"Okay," said Tarayon, "fourth planet, second system."

PROBING

Unable to move and resigned to a terrible fate, Tyson heard things moving outside his bubble. He couldn't see a thing in the gloomy light. Lying on his back, it occurred to him that during the past day—at least, as far as he could calculate—he'd turned fourteen. Happy birthday, Tyson, he thought to himself.

He opened his eyes to dark silhouettes; two octopi with long tentacles and wings. Each stared in at him with a single, glowing, blood-red star-shaped eye. They were gone in moments, leaving Tyson plastered against the bubble wall in free-falling terror.

Then he heard more piping, like gibberish talking. His bubble was picked up and carried into one of the tunnels. He couldn't see a thing, bouncing around inside. Minutes later he found himself lying on a flat surface on the side of the mountain, while the star-eyed beasts scrambled back into the cavern, piping as they went.

Tyson wondered how these things lived inside a volcano. He didn't have time to ponder as something black and enormous swooped down and enveloped the bubble, flapping huge wings and then taking off into the morning sky. Tyson was shaken and tossed sideways so he could see out the bottom. To his surprise he saw a boat and aliens down at the water's edge. His view was fleeting as whatever carried him sped across the shimmering purplish sea. In no time he could see another land mass. He couldn't help the tears when they came, as he was scared beyond belief and feeling alone, so very alone.

The thing dropped Tyson next to a waterfall that dropped into a bottomless pit of darkness inside the planet. As his bubble rolled over the edge, he glimpsed enormous wings and tentacles. A nightmare come to life.

And then he was falling into oblivion.

SHIPS

The kids were enthralled by four-eyed Hinge and the towering celery-stalk called Jak-toll. They told Summahon of their adventures with her mate Tarayon, the ultimate defeat of the Destroyer, the horrible Doozies, Citlalli, the time-traveling Okyricks, and how they'd been teleported here while exiting the zip home to Earth.

As they talked, Einlen moved over to the shade, working on something.

Suddenly a dark shadow passed overhead. Everyone could see a helpless Human carried by an enormous winged monstrosity. It headed directly toward the blinding morning sun and disappeared over the sea's distant horizon.

"Your friend?" said Summahon.

Heather and Estrella were speechless.

"Yes," said Sklizz, "Tyson. We have to try crossing this sea."

"If you sail on that sea, you will all die," said Yore, sitting in the shade.

"We'll make a second vessel," said Hinge. "I can improve on the first design and increase our chances of fighting off whatever lives under the water."

The group began gathering materials and working on a second craft. Yore figured they were doomed, but he shrugged his narrow lizard shoulders and jumped in to help.

Summahon pulled Sklizz aside and made him finish telling everything about Tarayon. She felt pride and longing for her mate. She was amazed they'd actually defeated this unstoppable being that had destroyed galaxies for more than fifty centuries.

"It was a miracle," said Sklizz, "thanks largely to the Watchers' amulets from you and Tarayon, and the Human called Citlalli."

It was midday before the second craft was ready.

"I say we leave now," said Sklizz. "I don't think Tyson has much time."

"No want be near mountain second night," buzzed Jak-toll.

"You coming, Lizard?" asked Hinge.

Yore snapped an insect out of the air with his long tongue, then swallowed and cleared his throat.

"Old-timers say no one survives this water journey, but maybe they be lousy boat-builders and crummy sailors."

Yore dropped down to all four short legs.

"What're ya waiting for? Let's sail!"

Heather gave Yore a hug around his lizard neck, much to his chagrin.

After a quick sailing and weapons lesson, they were ready to set sail for Pith. Hinge had Jak-toll, Estrella, and Einlen join him, with Sklizz, Summahon, Heather, and Yore sailing the second boat.

On board, Estrella saw something on Einlen's belt.

"Is that a blinger?"

Einlen whispered, "Don't get hopes up. Try fixing. Not sure if work."

Moments later they were sailing onto the calm Obaddon Sea. It reminded Heather of the warm waters of the Gulf of Mexico. Of course water on Earth was blue instead of purple, and the only sea monsters were imaginary.

YERTI

Back in the Milky Way Galaxy on Yerti, the Supreme Doozy was happy with the already finished Exterminator II. Sitting inside a cleansing rectifier, his scarred head poked out as he spoke to a junior commander named Oophak.

"Your father was loyal," he said, "but Kahpoo failed. We should own Earth, Mars, and zooey. You have command of Exterminator II in his name. You will reclaim family honor, Oophak, and be revered for all time as a great Doozy."

Oophak nodded reverently.

"Prepare for your sacred journey. The greatest army in history will accompany you, led by Commander Rooq. You have the exalted honor of delivering holy cleansing to Mars. Your name will reign as legend across the galaxies and your mystical aura will rise to a seat at the heroic table of Doozy immortals."

The Supreme Doozy nodded to a worshipful Oophak and added, "I've been honored to know you."

Commander Oophak was led from the room as the Supreme Doozy smiled with smug satisfaction. It was so easy to manipulate the weak minds of blindly loyal followers.

Back on Mars the number of Fiberians was increasing.

"Both newborns are hopping," said Stilla.

Thrix looked up from construction plans with a big Fiberian smile on his blue kangaroo head.

"Wonderful news, Stilla, thank you. We Fiberians may yet survive."

"Anything further about the disappearances?"

"No. Let's hope Wizza's okay and those Doozy scum are rotting. It's so strange. I can make no link between Wizza and these Doozies. The vanishings make no sense."

Stilla had been friends with Thrix's family. Both their families had been killed along with nearly the entire Fiberian race by the Destroyer. Her heart was breaking to see how hard Thrix was working, but she left him alone.

Thrix was finishing defensive shielding designs that would deflect radiation away from Mars so Humans could live safely. Planning was done. It was time to build.

"Hey you, big blue two-armed dog hot!" a voice jumped out of the intercom.

"Vorwin! The only person I know who'd mangle a Human term like hot dog."

"My government is back in place, so it was time to see how our multi-galaxy defense is working," said Vorwin.

"Where are you?"

"Final approach to Mars. I've been looking at your specs for the miserable place these Humans call Venus. I think your modified terraforming may work."

"It won't be easy, but at least it's worth a try, right? Mars isn't that big, and we'll need room to expand in a few decades."

Back again on Yerti, the Exterminator II's main construction manager groveled before the drooling Supreme Doozy.

"I'm pleased with your fast building of these holy vessels," said the Supreme Doozy, spraying yellow drool.

The spacecraft builder bowed even lower.

"Oophak is ready. Send Exterminator II on its way to Mars. I want more Exterminators. We'll expand to worlds like Meemer and Gelz. I want no one left to threaten our right to galactic domination, and zooey."

The speech caused a grating cough and vile splattering of yellow drool all over the builder. Without flinching and keeping his eyes down, the builder said, "This means even more scouring of nearby systems and civilizations for raw materials."

"I don't care what aliens or planets you pillage. I want more Exterminators and I want them soon!"

"Yes, your holiness," said the bowing builder. He knew when it was time to leave.

DANGER

As a new day dawned over the vast Canadian prairie, Maddy hadn't slept well in their underground facility, still sensing danger. She couldn't explain this feeling to David over breakfast, but Maddy knew something was very wrong.

Later in separate rooms they were asked to demonstrate their powers. David and Maddy held nothing back, sharing their experiences, but unable to duplicate their feats. It became clear to their investigators that neither was quite sure how they'd performed these mental miracles in the first place.

As the day dragged on, Maddy still sensed unknown danger. At one point they left her locked in the room and to her amazement she heard voices in her mind, "One way or another we'll extract this information. There's too much at stake. These kids are expendable."

Now I'm hearing things, she thought, still trying to remain rational when her mind was saying *FLEE!*

David was starting to think he'd imagined teleporting.

After lunch they were each locked in their rooms while the government people debriefed.

David worried about letting these people down. Maddy, however, was sure they were up to no good—but what to do?

The investigators decided drastic action was needed. The threat from extraterrestrials was too great. Perhaps the use of drugs would get some answers.

Maddy knew they had to escape, and fast. But how? They were kids locked in a secure underground facility. Even if they got to the surface, they were in the middle of the Canadian prairie. What hope did they have?

Maddy sat quietly and thought about the impossible. She stared at the lock on her door and wished the tumblers would fall in place so it would open.

CECILIA

As the midday breeze filled their sail, the shoreline and terrible mountain shrinking behind them, Hinge asked Estrella to christen their boat. Growing up in Buenos Aires, Estrella loved an old cartoon called Beany and Cecil. Cecil was a friendly sea serpent and Beany Boy's boat was named Leakin' Lena, which Estrella bestowed upon their wooden craft. Hinge and Jak-toll shrugged, while Einlen felt a twinge of motherly pride, quickly shaking her crocodile head to get rid of this strange feeling.

When Sklizz asked the same question of Heather, she didn't hesitate to name it "Jenny" after her favorite movie hero, Forrest Gump and his Galveston shrimp boat.

And so, the Leakin' Lena and the Jenny were moving fast, with a strong afternoon breeze filling their parachute sails, skimming across the purplish waters of planet Obaddon on their way to the mysterious land of Pith.

On board Leakin' Lena, Hinge manned the tiller at the rear with Estrella at his side. The blue sail was placed in the middle of each ship. Jak-toll stood in the front right corner prepared to use a twenty-foot-long, sharply carved wooden scythe. Jak-toll held it straight up, ready to sweep down toward any sea monsters. Einlen stood on the opposite corner, a loaded crossbow with wooden harpoons ready to fire. Einlen also had the badly damaged blinger in her camo-suit, just in case.

On the Jenny, Sklizz sailed with Heather next to him, Summahon holding the crossbow and Yore practicing with the scythe, taking long arcing swipes and imaging horrible sea monsters' heads being lopped off. By now Yore had turned dark black, same as the black wood boats. Yore realized he was having more fun than he could ever remember on this horrible planet.

The sea was calm, with nothing but shimmering deep purple sea before them.

Heather turned her cap around in the breeze and kept thinking about the awful image of Tyson, helpless in the clutches of that flying monster. She couldn't shake the miserable feeling in the pit of her stomach.

Estrella undid her ponytail, her red hair whipping in the breeze. She kept wondering what lay ahead for Tyson and them all. Her bemused alien shipmates heard Estrella begin whistling the *Beany and Cecil* theme song.

Far beneath the two wooden ships, merciless eyes were watching. They belonged to an eighty-foot-long carnivorous creature resembling Cecil the Sea Serpent. However, this serpent was female and would've appreciated being called Cecilia. She had sharp teeth, a voracious appetite, and was no cartoon character. Fortunately for the crews of the Leakin' Lena and the Jenny, Cecilia had just eaten another large denizen of the deep and was content to swim underneath, prepared to wait another hour or so.

SLUGS

Wizza continued sending messages ahead as they followed the ion trail of the other spacecraft. She didn't expect replies, and she got none. The crew of Lupe, Prince Zed, and Gilad sat quietly as the hours passed.

Up ahead, Tarayon was too far away to receive Wizza's messages. He'd just entered the first solar system, looking for the second solar system and fourth planet Citlalli had mentioned. To his surprise another small star and solar system were not far away. Two stars and gravitational orbits so close together seemed impossible. Then again, nothing seemed impossible in this crazy part of the universe.

Clearly Citlalli was in tune with some higher power, and thus he headed straight toward the system's fourth planet.

Approaching from the opposite side of the longest asteroid belt in the universe, Theal, Waima, and Jamila had detected an unbelievable gravitational force.

"That gravity comes from the ultimate singularity," said Theal, "what you Humans call a black hole."

"Is that where you're taking us?" asked Jamila.

"If we got anywhere near it we'd never escape. We're searching for the place all interconnected zips in the universe begin. It's there the Light has pointed us."

"What about the other ships?" said Waima.

"Like us, they're on their own."

They were between shimmering nebulas. On the left it was purple, red, and blue; the right was green and gold. Waima had never seen anything so beautiful, and Jamila stared with undisguised awe.

Theal interrupted, "We have company."

Blips in attack formation had appeared on her screen.

Theal veered right into the green and gold nebula's dangerous gases, space dust, magnetic fields, and other unknowns. No two nebulas were alike, and there were no guarantees they could lose the chasing aliens. Six of them were in a W-shaped attack vector and gaining rapidly. One of them tried firing a weapon of some kind, but they were still too far away.

"We have one chance as I pass that thick purple cloud on the right," said Theal, pointing it out for Jamila. "After we pass, try shooting a few beams into its center."

Waima was on her knees, peering out at the unfolding action in front and rear.

Speeding around the purple cloud, Theal turned hard right. The chasing aliens disappeared behind the cloud.

"Don't shoot yet, wait a moment" she said. "Now!"

Jamila fired the laser into the dense purple chemical cloud and the volatile gases exploded in an electrical firestorm that obliterated the alien pursuers.

The shock wave of energy rocked their spacecraft and spun them crazily out of the nebula. Firing thrusters, Theal was able to regain control, but something was wrong.

"Hopefully we can find a planet in that solar system up ahead to fix things and figure out what to do next."

Several tense minutes passed before they found an appropriate planet. Theal took her time during the descent, gently landing their damaged spacecraft on an open meadow of bluish grass close to a running stream and next to rocky hills. It was quite beautiful.

"Stick together and fill these two water containers," said Theal. "Stay alert while I inspect the spacecraft."

As they walked down to the stream, Jamila asked Waima about her Yerti home world.

"My dad's a military commander," said Waima. She told Jamila of their assassination attempt, describing the footstool bomb and their escape to Mars.

Jamila looked at this tiny pale alien with surprise and respect.

"I fight on Earth," said Jamila, "for my people. We also use bombs. Things often go wrong, but it's the best way to fight an enemy that's too big and powerful."

They reached the creek.

"But here in space," Jamila continued, "on this mission, our righteous holy war on Earth seems quite trivial."

Theal peered at the damaged thruster. Thankfully it didn't seem to be serious. Once the other two returned they'd leave this planet.

A strange shuffling noise from behind interrupted her thoughts as several large, multi-legged, pale white slug-beasts grabbed her. Each had tentacle arms that easily wrapped around Theal's body. She got off a loud shout before being whisked inside the darkness of the hillside.

Jamila and Waima were on their way back when they heard Theal's cry. In moments they caught a glimpse of white things dragging Theal into the mountainside.

Following Citlalli's instinct, Tarayon entered the atmosphere of the planet she'd picked. To everyone's amazement they detected rapidly dispersing ions from another Watcher spacecraft. The trail was hard to pinpoint so he landed as close as possible to where it led.

Grabbing the Watchers' blingers, Tarayon, Citlalli, and Stauffa armed themselves. Kikikik's appendages couldn't hold blingers, so he'd use his razor mandibles if necessary.

"The ion trail was centered on these hills," said Tarayon. "Let's split up and head in both directions."

"We have no way to communicate," said Stauffa.

"These hills are not far around, so just keep moving until we run into one another again."

"And hope we find the other ship," said Stauffa, thinking as always of Waima.

Tarayon and Citlalli headed one way, Stauffa and Kikikik moving in the opposite direction.

DESPERATION

Preparing to rescue Theal, Waima showed Jamila how to use a blinger, blasting a chunk from a nearby boulder.

"I watched my dad practice with Doozy blingers."

"If my people had these blingers on Earth, things would change fast."

They were ready to enter the crevice where the slugs had taken Theal. It was only a few feet wide and led them directly into the hillside.

"Can you fly that spacecraft?" said Jamila.

Waima shook her head no.

"Well then, we'd better find Theal, and fast."

Jamila led the way, a flashlight helping them move down the narrow trail. Doozies are partly nocturnal, but Waima still felt the darkness, imagining the touch of that white thing's feelers. She stayed close behind Jamila.

The trail grew steeper and split into two tunnels.

"Right or left?" whispered Jamila.

Waima had no idea, but blurted out, "Right." Her voice echoed inside the tunnel. "Sorry."

Jamila patted her shoulder as they entered the right tunnel. Moments later the flashlight illuminated a bloated white slug rearing up, blocking their path and making a chattering noise. Jamila fired the blinger and the slug exploded backward in a grayish splatter-cloud all over the tunnel walls.

"Holy Mother," said Jamila.

Several more white shapes began moving toward them from below, and Jamila calmly demolished each of them. Waima just watched, wide-eyed. They continued slowly downhill, carefully walking through the slippery remains of slug goo.

Without warning, Waima felt several feelers grasping and yanking her back into the darkness. She screamed.

Jamila turned, unable to shoot without hitting Waima. Before she could move, a feeler wrapped around her ankle, dropping her face first into slug goo as she dropped the flashlight and blinger. The tentacle started pulling her downhill. She ran her hands through white slime, frantically searching for the blinger. Her fingers wrapped around something; the flashlight. She rolled over and turned the light on a glistening wet slug that was reeling her in like a fish. Luckily the blinger was right next to her and in one quick move she blasted the slug into splattered oblivion.

Back up the tunnel in utter darkness, Waima struggled to wrap the blinger around her side to shoot her captor. She fired and it felt like falling backward onto an exploding water bed. She was covered in lukewarm greasy slug juices. Waima began crawling downhill toward a faint flickering light. The liquid slug remains trickled downhill with her.

Jamila finally ran out of slugs to burst and turned to run after Waima. On the floor of the tunnel moved another white thing and she raised the blinger.

"It's me!" shouted Waima.

Jamila pulled back, seeing Waima stand up soaked in white goo and covered with mud.

"I must look just as bad, huh?" said Jamila.

For the first time she saw Waima smile. The Doozy's teeth were surprisingly sharp, but her smile was worth it.

"Come on," said Jamila, "let's go find Theal."

They continued down, blingers drawn and ready.

Back on the surface, Stauffa and Kikikik walked through a meandering stream that flowed down the hillside. Tiny creatures were swimming inside the brownish water as it slid easily around Kikikik's exoskeleton and Stauffa's waterproof camo-suit. Upon climbing up the creek bank, they came out of dense foliage into an open meadow. And there sat the other spacecraft next to a rocky outcropping.

They quickly searched the area around and inside the spacecraft, but found no trace of its passengers. There was charring underneath, as though it had been hit with bolts of energy. On the passenger side there was evidence of a struggle, with deep scratches and perhaps blood.

"What can we do?" said Stauffa.

"Wait for others," said Kikikik, "Tarayon's orders."

"I can't sit here waiting. One might be Waima."

Kikikik sat in the shade of the craft while Stauffa searched. Okyricks were used to obeying orders, and Kikikik wasn't moving until Tarayon arrived. Finally Stauffa found scuffed dirt leading into the dark crevice.

"You have no searchlight," said Kikikik.

"Doozies are nocturnal."

"As you wish, it's your life. I'll wait here."

Stauffa checked his blinger and entered the hillside.

Coming from the opposite direction, Tarayon and Citlalli had seen smaller creatures scurry into the shadows, but little else. However, a stealthy carnivore had been stalking them from high on the hillside, waiting for the right moment to strike from above.

RESCUE

Incredibly tense minutes passed for Jamila and Waima, who were creeping ever deeper underground. They heard echoes of squishing, oozing, and squirting that made their skin crawl, and it was growing louder. They took another turn left and began passing cocooned aliens attached to the walls. They were every size and shape imaginable, and it was hard to tell if they were dead. They certainly looked dead.

Rounding another corner they looked down on a gargantuan cavern filled with slugs. There were thousands across the cavern floor, like writhing white maggots. Jamila and Waima were hidden on a ledge, gagging at this nauseous sight.

"Help," said a weak voice. Up ahead they found Theal inside a wall cocoon. A tube stuck out the bottom, running down until it disappeared into the wriggling death.

"Pull it out," said Theal, a pleading look in her eyes. "It's killing me."

Jamila immediately grasped and yanked the tube. After a couple of tries it ripped free, also tearing the front of the cocoon. Theal fell forward into Jamila's arms.

Seconds later, Jamila carried Theal over her shoulder and back into the tunnels, Waima at her side. From below came the deafening roar of thousands of angry slugs, now in crazed pursuit. One wrong turn and they'd be buried.

Waima carried the flashlight, leading them up as fast as Jamila could go. Theal was getting heavier by the minute. The pursuit was getting ever closer.

Waima came to a fork. Left or right? No time to think. She chose left. Moments later a wall of slugs confronted them. Waima and Jamila let loose devastating blinger blasts, which held them back momentarily. Then the Doozy-Human team turned and ran the opposite direction.

They recognized landmarks, but the slugs were gaining fast. There were just too many. Suddenly a slug dropped from a ceiling opening atop Waima. Jamila dropped Theal, ripped the slug off Waima, and hurtled it back down the tunnel. But it was too late; the pursuers had caught them. It was only a question of how many they could splatter before being absorbed. Below them were three separate tunnels filled with slugs, writhing rivers of unstoppable doom. It was time for a final stand.

Jamila and Waima started firing. As she blasted slugs, Waima thought about her father. With time running out, she began fantasizing she heard his voice. There wasn't time for that! She shook her head and fired again.

"Waima!"

Jamila saw Stauffa scooping Waima into his arms. There'd be time for reunions later, if they lived.

Stauffa put Waima down and picked up Theal, then leading the way as they fled toward the surface, the frenzied slugs only meters behind.

Jamila kept up a rear fire. The slugs kept coming, crawling through the glistening goo of their comrades. Jamila had an absurd flashback to her time spent hiding in tunnels and caves on Earth. She smiled grimly and fired again.

Back on the surface, Citlalli and Tarayon had just spotted Theal's parked spacecraft in the distance. Unbeknownst to them, a third set of hungry eyes spotted the same thing.

The carnivore had cut across the hilltops, keeping a wary eye on the two small creatures. Now there was another alien up ahead that looked even more appetizing. After it finished with these two, the stick-like, big-eyed alien would offer a crunchy dessert. This hungry meat-eater was like nothing on Earth, at least not modern Earth. It closely resembled a terrifying Velociraptor dinosaur with four arms, two strong legs, and a mouthful of sharp three-inch teeth.

Kikikik's telescopic eyes spotted a moving shadow on the hill, its skin camouflaged. He could see it crouching, poised to leap. Looking below he noticed its prey—Tarayon and Citlalli!

As much as a ten-foot-tall praying mantis can leap to its feet, Kikikik did just that, his spear-like legs quivering. He started toward Citlalli and Tarayon, keeping a close eye on the tensed predator.

Tarayon and Citlalli stopped when they saw Kikikik, wondering what was going on. He was walking toward them and waving his front mandibles. When Kikikik started a giant insect gallop, Tarayon's senses went on full alert. He chanced a peek up the hill and saw a silent shadow launch itself off the cliff. He grabbed Citlalli and rolled just out of reach of the attacker's slashing claws.

Kikikik was now close enough to take a killing leap toward their attacker. Citlalli saw Kikikik slicing through the air, razor mandibles ready to strike, landing on a fifteen-foot-long, four-armed vicious lizard demon. Her Anahuac people had never heard of dinosaurs or Velociraptors. Kikikik drove his mandibles deep, but the dino-creature had long claws and terrifying teeth, and could use its tail like a snake. In moments the tail pulled Kikikik close and the monster's teeth dug into his thin neck. Kikikik raised a mandible and took a desperate swipe, nearly severing the creature's head. This caused its mouth to clamp shut like a vise, snapping Kikikik's neck. Both fell to the ground, the attacker dead and Kikikik nearly so.

Citlalli ran to the Okyrick alien who had nearly killed her in the time-travel experiment.

"Kikikik," said Citlalli as she kneeled and looked into his six-inch-wide eyes. Her own tears began to flow, falling on the dying Okyrick scientist.

Kikikik couldn't move. His neck was broken and he was fatally wounded. He whispered, "My people...I wronged you. Time travel would've failed...would've killed you."

"I know," said Citlalli, "the Watchers told me."

Kikikik shuddered, near death.

"I forgive you, Kikikik. Go to your Gods knowing Citlalli of the Anahuac absolves you of all wrongs."

Kikikik's last image was of Citlalli, his last thoughts marveling at the compassion and understanding in this tiny Human. He truly hoped this Earth alien would find her way home. He shook one last time and died.

As Kikikik breathed his last, Tarayon yanked Citlalli into the air and tossed her into the spacecraft. From the hillside came the sound of a desperate battle.

"Stay inside," said Tarayon, closing the cockpit and leaping down.

Stauffa staggered out the crevice entrance with Theal over his shoulder, followed by a filthy white creature. Tarayon almost fired, then stopped, realizing it was Waima. The little Doozy turned, pointing her blinger at the entrance.

"Waima," shouted Tarayon, "move away."

"But Jamila," she shrieked.

Tarayon ran for the entrance as Jamila charged out, bumping into him, both stumbling on the ground. Tarayon whirled around as the first wave of hideous white slugs slithered out.

"Move back," he shouted, firing his blinger at the large rock overhang. He concentrated his fire at the weakest point, and as the first bloodthirsty slugs plowed into him, a massive wall of rock collapsed and blocked the exit, crushing dozens of slugs and trapping the rest.

Waima and Jamila were firing like crazy at slugs that made it out, turning one after another into explosions of vile slime piles.

Tarayon wrestled with four slugs blanketing him. He'd dropped his blinger and the slug's touch was starting to immobilize him. He was fading fast, losing consciousness.

Minutes later he opened his eyes, finding Waima and Citlalli kneeling by his side brushing and petting his fur. It felt nice, but he sat up surveying the surroundings.

"What happened," he asked.

"Theal was kidnapped by those things," said Jamila. "We were lucky to rescue her."

Tarayon saw the death embrace of Kikikik and the dino-carnivore.

"Didn't you have one other passenger?" he asked.

"Kriner? Tried to kill us. Ended up as dinner for a bunch of alien swine on another planet," said Jamila.

"Speaking of planets, let's get off this one," said Theal.

Theal had no feeling in her legs but could still pilot, joined by Stauffa and Waima. Tarayon would take Citlalli and Jamila.

Within minutes both ships were on their way.

AMBUSH

An hour later Wizza arrived, tracking the ion trails and blinger residue, smoothly landing right where Theal had taken off. All four passengers climbed out.

"What were these things?" said Gilad, looking at the splattered remains of the slug beasts.

"Apparently they were no match for blingers," said Wizza.

"Should I burrow and investigate?" asked Prince Zed.

"No time. I caught their trail as we landed. I think we just missed them."

From the opposite side of the spacecraft, Lupe shrieked. Everyone ran over and saw Kikikik.

The carnivore that battled Kikikik had been part of a clan, and two of its angry brethren were approaching, hidden in dense foliage and watching these unknown aliens. They moved to opposite sides, planning to strike from both directions.

As Wizza inspected the spacecraft and Gilad studied the strange alien trees, Prince Zed and Lupe wandered toward purple foliage where one of the creatures prepared to strike. It figured the little one was no threat, so it would go for the large slithering thing first. Surprise was the key.

On the other side of the blue meadow, the carnivore's sister watched Gilad, wishing he'd wander closer. Since the creatures communicated telepathically, she knew her brother was about to strike the big crawler. So, without waiting, she leaped out and ran across the meadow toward Gilad.

Sensing his sister's charge, her brother sprang upon Prince Zed with a snarling fury. The attacker landed on Prince Zed's back, sharp teeth trying to bite into his front torso. This was a common mistake when attacking a Meemer. Prince Zed's retractable head was in the rear part of his snake body; while his front torso was built to drive through solid rock and dirt. Two of the creature's teeth shattered as it chomped Prince Zed's diamond-hard front. In pain and furious, it turned and spotted its prey's defenseless head. Twisted awkwardly and unable to burrow, there was nothing Prince Zed could do.

Ready to lunge for the kill, the attacker's head suddenly vanished. The headless body wavered motionless for a moment before toppling over and falling sideways like a chopped tree.

Prince Zed saw Lupe; hands on her blinger just like Sklizz had taught her weeks before. She was shaking badly.

As all this happened, the creature's sister sprinted the distance to Gilad, leaping with razor claws extended to tear him to pieces. A single blast from Wizza's blinger knocked her sideways in midair, momentum carrying her into Gilad. Staggering to her feet, she saw another small alien running toward her.

How had it done this? Who were these tiny preys? Why wasn't she sensing her brother anymore?

Terrified and confused, the wounded alien hobbled back into the surrounding foliage.

Wizza helped Gilad to his feet. He was groggy and feeling the pain of a separated left shoulder. There was no time to try fixing it, and a sling could wait. He tried keeping his arm still in the passenger seat alongside Prince Zed. Lupe manned the laser cannon as Wizza lifted off the planet in pursuit of the other two ships.

BREAKOUT

Still locked inside her underground room, Maddy was very frustrated. She had focused and concentrated over and over again, attempting to move the tumblers and unlock her door. Had she really made those ducks fall? Relaxing, she kicked off her sneakers and absentmindedly tried again.

To her amazement the door clicked open.

Maddy stared at the door crack for a few moments, her head spinning. She quickly put back on her sneakers and peered down the white hallway, seeing no one. She knew David's room and moved next to it. Breathing deeply, she relaxed again and the tumblers clicked, opening the door. She slipped inside.

David was lying on his couch, looking over at Maddy with wide-eyed surprise.

"We need to get out of here," said Maddy, "now."

David sat up quizzically.

"They're going to start giving us drugs or other stuff."

David stood and said, "I tried to show them, but nothing works."

"It doesn't matter. They're not going to let us leave. We gotta find a way out. We have to get away."

Somehow David knew Maddy was right.

"Okay, but how?"

"I can unlock doors."

David was confused for a moment, and then he understood. He smiled. "Oh."

Following the empty hallway they headed toward an exit sign. The door opened to stairs and they began climbing. Perhaps they could get away without anyone noticing.

They'd gone up at least four floors when a loud siren erupted, echoing loudly in the stairwell. Upon reaching the next floor they opened the door and saw a heavily guarded building entrance. One guard blew a whistle and ran toward the door.

They turned and continued scampering up more stairs. There was nowhere else to go. After four stories they reached the top. Pounding boots were close behind as David and Maddy ran onto the flat roof of this plain gray building planted in the midst of shimmering wheat fields. They closed and locked the door.

The prairie wind was strong on the roof as they ran to the far side. Amazingly there was a one-person zip line attached to the building corner, leading across the dirt road to what looked like a stream flanked by trees.

"I guess these guards have a little fun," said David.

Banging started on the door. The only other way down was a long drop to solid concrete.

"Quick, go, David," said Maddy.

David looked at the zip line, then back to Maddy.

"I'm not leaving you behind."

"David, please."

He put his hands on Maddy's shoulders and stared into her eyes. "I'm not leaving you."

Maybe it was emotion, perhaps just the wind, but Maddy's eyes shone back at David. They turned toward the exit, waiting for their pursuers.

The door burst open, guards and government types running onto the roof, stopping in a semi-circle around David and Maddy.

One of Maddy's woman interrogators spoke.

"Listen, guys, no worries. We're here to help you."

The kids stared back, hair bristling in the wind, Maddy's white streak shining in the afternoon sun.

"Why are you running?" the woman continued. "We mean you no harm."

"That's not true," said Maddy.

A guard inched slowly to one side, close enough to make a grab for the kids. The woman gave a slight nod. The kids saw him lunge and they both jerked backward. Tripping, they fell over the edge, holding one another tightly.

Everyone watched in horror as the kids fell out of sight, plummeting toward almost certain death on the pavement four stories below. Rushing to the edge, they stared down at empty concrete.

The kids had vanished without a trace.

SERPENTS

Back on the purple sea both ships made good time in the afternoon breeze. Hinge was the better sailor, so he had Sklizz take the lead in case of any problems. Sklizz wasn't as fast as Hinge, but safety first.

They'd seen bountiful sea life during the voyage. Some resembled Earth fish, while others defied description. A school of little winged things shaped like bells swam and hopped out of the water near Heather, one accidentally landing on board. She had a fleeting glimpse of several red eyes, four beautiful translucent wings, and it was gone back into the sea. Nothing seemed dangerous so far and Hinge was hoping Yore's sea monster stories were exaggerations.

Far below, Cecilia the sea serpent was hungry again. She would attack the front creature first and then capsize both quickly. Experience showed that frightening the surface creatures created panic, and they became even easier to gobble at leisure. Plus it was more fun and Cecilia enjoyed playing with her food. She sped ahead, using a seafloor volcanic plume as her warm rendezvous spot for the surprise attack. Her sea monster tummy growled with anticipation.

Just as she got comfortable in her warm spot, Cecilia heard the sound of approaching male sea serpents. Males had two heads and larger appetites. Even though males had two heads, Cecilia thought they had half the intelligence. But the dumb brutes were cute. Fortunately they were an hour away, leaving more than enough time for her to devour the alien surface critters. She didn't want to share, and she certainly didn't want the two-header's amorous attentions distracting her.

With Sklizz in the lead, the Jenny took forever to reach the spot where Cecilia prowled. By now the lady serpent was impatient and ready to eat.

On the Jenny, Heather spotted something on the horizon. "Look...land!" she shouted, pointing ahead.

Sklizz altered course toward the distant spec.

Hinge was fifty yards behind, turning to follow. As Hinge and his fellow passengers watched, a long-necked sea-dragon burst from the dark purple ocean in front of the Jenny, rivers of water cascading off a massive head filled with razor teeth. A savage roar rolled over the boats as Cecilia's red-streaked eyes bore into them.

Summahon scrambled to turn and aim her harpoon crossbow.

Yore had been practicing for this moment since learning how to sail. The helpless Jenny was about to be smashed to pieces as Yore swept the scythe down in a blur, its edge catching Cecilia on her exposed neck. Summahon fired a harpoon just as Yore's scythe drove into Cecilia's neck. The harpoon would've hit Cecilia right between surprised eyes, but Yore's scythe snapped her head sideways, the harpoon sailing harmlessly past. Summahon winced, but then saw the monster flop sideways. Yore's powerful swipe had smashed bone and cartilage in her neck and they watched as Cecilia sank, her death shriek silenced beneath the waves.

Hinge was almost alongside Sklizz by now.

"Nice work, Yore!" shouted Hinge.

Heather saw Yore's head turn a shade of orange. She wondered if Yore was blushing. The slayer of sea monsters took a bow, looking remarkably Human.

"Let's keep moving," said Hinge, looking at the nearly setting sun. "Hopefully there's no more of those things. We need reach land before dark."

Taking the lead, Hinge set a rapid pace.

The pack of two-headed male sea serpents gained rapidly, intent upon revenging the death of Cecilia, whose cries they'd heard as she sank to her watery grave.

ASSIMILATION

Tyson awoke in darkness, still inside the bubble enclosure. He'd given up trying to figure out how he could breathe, how the bubble supplied oxygen. Closing his eyes against the dark, the only sound was the beating of his own heart. He last remembered being rolled over the waterfall's edge into a bottomless pit of blackness. He'd screamed and screamed as the bubble seemed to be falling for hours...but could remember nothing more.

And then from out of the smothering blackness he heard something—a disembodied voice coming from inside his head. It spoke an ancient, strange, unknown language, and yet as he listened to the whispered primeval words he understood! His heart raced, sensing that this was a terrible presence. He waded through a mental fog, waiting for something to jump out with a razor sharp-scalpel. The mysterious mist enveloped him, leaving him helpless as it probed his mind. Then the fog began to fade into spectral visions, the presence in his mind lifting the dark shroud and allowing him to see what it saw. It continued to speak of things that were impossible for Tyson's feeble Human mind to comprehend. And yet he felt connected to something timeless, eternal, and filled with the knowledge of sentient life across the universe. He found himself floating amongst an endless menagerie of galaxies, stars, planets, bizarre alien civilizations, and things far beyond Human understanding.

Far across the universe stretched Tyson's link. He was defenseless against the Dark and its all-powerful Galaxy Wraiths. They digested the knowledge inside Tyson's brain in a nanosecond, confident that everything was going according to plan.

MAYHEM

Eerie purple clouds blanketed the horizon, reflecting on a dark and menacing sea. The wind grew, turning the water into a choppy, wavy mess and slowing progress for the Leakin' Lena and the Jenny. Far in the distance lightning flashed, making everything even spookier. The shoreline and its alien vegetation were now much closer. The setting sun peeked through, lighting up this ominous twilight scene.

Heather's ankle had grown worse, and she sat next to Sklizz. They were now sailing behind Hinge's boat.

Estrella stood next to Hinge on the other boat as they scanned the sea. Lightning flashed again far in the distance, briefly illuminating the water ahead when the attack began.

Two enormous sea monsters erupted through the purple waves in front of Hinge's boat, water streaming down four snarling, razor-toothed heads. Each head sat atop its own long neck, connected to a twenty-foot-long body.

Jak-toll swung his scythe into one neck, snapping it sideways. The second head lunged toward Jak-toll, slamming into the weapon and knocking Jak-toll into the water. The monster flopped sideways, its jaws snapping at Jak-toll. Everyone saw their friend yanked in the air by branch arms clamped in the monster's mouth. The monster shook its head violently, Jak-tolls arms ripping from his body as he flew into the distance, out of sight in the waves. The monster then disappeared under the water, dragged down by the other head's broken neck.

Lightning from the distant ocean tempest was now flashing every few seconds, turning the horrific sea battle into something even more frightening.

As Jak-toll was lost, Einlen whirled around and fired a harpoon into the second monster, scoring a direct hit into its torso. Blood poured from the harpoon's deep puncture wound. As it shrieked in pain, a third monster rose from the depths and towered over Einlen. She could only look up, helpless. And then to everyone's surprise the beast veered sideways and lunged at its badly bleeding fellow sea monster. The sea exploded into crazed violence as dozens of sea monsters began tearing their bleeding brother to pieces, just like a shark feeding frenzy on Earth.

Hinge frantically searched the ever worsening waves for Jak-toll, but he was nowhere to be seen, probably dragged down by the sea monsters.

And then with a massive crunch, the middle of Hinge's boat exploded, splintering upward as a sea monster head smashed through the bottom. Wood shattered everywhere as its snarling head and neck shot high above the boat, then making a dive for Einlen. She scooted away, just out of reach. The beast turned, Hinge quickly lifting Estrella onto the ship's mast shouting, "Higher!"

The boat was rolling wildly and Estrella had to carefully move higher on the couple of wooden pegs. The mast hadn't been designed or built for climbing.

As she glanced down she saw the monster head swinging toward her. She closed her eyes and raised both feet as the snapping mouth missed by centimeters then smashed down near Hinge. He darted forward and rammed his makeshift spear into its red eye. It pulled back shrieking through the splintered hole into the water, only to be replaced as its vicious partner head shot through the same hole. Einlen had reloaded the crossbow and fired a point-blank harpoon into the beast's skull, killing it instantly. Unfortunately the monster head and long neck fell sideways, crashing into the mast and cracking it, while turning the huge carcass into a death anchor for Hinge's boat.

Estrella was atop the broken mast when it snapped and fell overboard. She was flung far away from both boats into the deadly sea. There was nothing anyone could do as another two-headed sea monster swam toward Estrella to gobble her up. The heads rose in tandem, arching for the kill. Heather looked away, unable to watch.

As they reached the peak of their arc, frozen for a split second in flash of lightning, the beasts two heads were blown away by a rapid fire blast from Einlen's repaired blinger. Amazement turned to horror as everyone saw her jury-rigged blinger had also exploded, leaving Einlen with a gaping wound where her left arm had been. She was staggering, but used her one remaining arm to climb on the railing, diving in after the distant bobbing head of Estrella. In moments both were lost in the raging ocean of sea monsters and darkness.

Sklizz had maneuvered next to the doomed boat, allowing Hinge to leap over. Then with Hinge's expertise, they sailed away from the shattered craft, trying to turn toward the last spot they'd seen Estrella and Einlen. The violent sea and wind were making it impossible.

The sea monster feeding frenzy was behind them and only choppy dark sea loomed ahead, along with the now much closer shoreline of Pith.

But they weren't done yet as another sea monster and its two heads appeared in the distance, rearing high into the darkness like an unholy "V" silhouette, and then diving beneath the water. Everyone held their breath, weapons poised to strike.

The huge two-headed beast flew out of the sea in front of them like a breaching whale, ready to smash back down. Summahon scored a direct harpoon hit to one of its heads, but the momentum carried it downward on top of Yore's scythe, ripping the corner off the boat and sending Yore sailing through the air into the water. He sank immediately.

The monster slid off the boat and into the white-capped waves, and yet another sea monster frenzy started as it was torn to pieces.

Hinge began wondering how many of these vicious creatures there were. Waves were crashing over the ship now, and up ahead the faint sound of water against rocks could be heard. As one large wave crashed over the boat, a very waterlogged Yore was flung back on board, nearly drowned, and holding on for dear life to one of the side railings.

This time a sea monster attacked from the rear, smashing upward from under the boat. Everyone frantically grabbed onto something.

As the beast rose above the boat ready for a deadly strike, Summahon swiveled the harpoon for one final shot. It sailed through the howling wind right into the beast's mouth, stabbing deep. In a rage, the second head swung down toward helpless Heather. Hinge jumped in front with his knife, but the beast easily snapped him in its jaws before anyone could react, diving beneath the waves in a heartbeat. Hinge had sacrificed himself to save Heather.

It was now almost dark on the frothing sea as the boat was lifted by a rolling wave and smashed down violently against a jagged rock. Sklizz and Summahon watched as Heather and Yore were flung outward into the darkness. The Gelzian and Trixian were now the last two aboard, each hanging on desperately. A second wave carried the shattered craft to the shoreline and another rock, obliterating what remained of the boat and tossing both soaked passengers onto a black sand beach. They pulled themselves away from the water, exhausted. Not too tired, however, to begin searching the beach, shouting names and hoping to find any survivors.

It was now pitch black except for the night stars, eerie lights in the sky, and purple pink-capped waves crashing on the beach. After finding no survivors, they could only huddle under some trees and wait for morning.

FLOTSAM

Estrella was such an excellent swimmer that her father called her his little fish. But this water was cold, the waves pounding, and sea monsters were everywhere. The toss from the boat had knocked the wind out of her. After struggling mightily to stay afloat, she began looking for the boat, unable to see it through the waves and thrashing monsters. Thankfully they seemed intent on devouring their own two-headed mate as Estrella tried to get her bearings.

Which way was land?

Panic started to creep into her mind. She began swimming away from the fighting monsters, the waves carrying her up and down, each stroke getting harder and harder. The thought of drowning hit her hard. She would never give up, but staying afloat much longer seemed impossible. She tried relaxing and floating on her back, but the insane waves plowed water up her nose and drove her under. Barely able to reach the surface, she spat out water and gasped for air, almost too weak to even tread water in this rough sea. Estrella knew the next time under would be her last, her energy gone. She couldn't believe it was her time to die. Thoughts of her family, of her mom and dad, began to creep in.

At that moment Estrella felt herself grabbed by a sea monster, yanking her hard through the waves. Like a surreal dream, death was upon her.

Then Estrella realized she was being carried by her friend Einlen. The horrifically wounded Uppsalian had used her powerful duck-like legs and webbed feet to reach Estrella, and now with her remaining strength was kicking the two of them toward land.

Neither said a word, Estrella mortified by the sight of Einlen's missing arm. Within minutes she'd kicked through the waves, reaching a secluded inlet with a tiny beach surrounded by dense undergrowth and rocks barricading each side. The shallow water allowed Estrella to help Einlen wade ashore onto dry black sand where she collapsed. The gaping wound where her arm used to be had been seared closed by the heat of the exploding blinger, saving Einlen from bleeding to death. Einlen lay very still, breathing hard.

Looking out to sea, Estrella could only see alien purple waves and darkness. She had no idea if anyone had survived. She had no idea what to do next.

Heather and Yore had been tossed away from land, their momentum carrying both further out to sea. Thankfully each managed to grab onto a piece of floating wreckage. Having no control over its path, they were carried along the shoreline away from the other survivors and sea monsters, following a mysterious current far along the coast.

Several times Yore started to say something reassuring to his young Human friend, but as they hung onto floating wreckage, drifting in a sea infested with monsters, on an alien planet at the end of the universe, floating toward a fate unknown, nothing really seemed appropriate. So he just kept quiet and watched for trouble.

Finally the strange current began pulling them toward land. They seemed to be entering a river that flowed inland. As they passed from the sea, floating up river beyond the shoreline, alien vegetation lined both sides. The river was still quite deep and at long last the current carried them close to the shore, allowing them to crawl onto a tiny spec of dry ground, exhausted and unable to stand. They lay quietly, hearing only the sound of the backward inland flowing river and their labored breathing.

When Heather finally sat up, she saw Yore looking with concern at her ankle. It had turned an ugly black and whatever was inside seemed to be spreading in dark nasty streaks up her shin.

Before Yore and Heather made the turn inland on their wreckage, a mere fifty yards further out to sea, Jak-toll was bobbing up and down on the waves. His plant-like body floated easily, but with five of his seven branches torn off by the sea monster, he could only drift helplessly. He'd been able to get occasional glimpses of the ongoing sea battle, but ultimately lost sight of everyone until moments ago he spotted Yore and Heather caught in the river current. This was one of the few times Jak-toll really wanted a strange set of alien mouth and lungs to yell for help. He could only watch silently, buzzing futilely as they floated upstream and he kept moving further away.

FUGITIVES

Instantaneous teleporting felt like blacking out for a moment. Then your eyes popped open to see wherever you'd arrived. After David and Maddy fell off the roof, their eyes opened on a blue sky. They found themselves lying on their backs in the middle of a barren dirt field.

Standing quickly they looked in every direction, seeing no one. They were a little dizzy and wobbly, which was understandable considering moments ago they'd been falling to their deaths, only to magically reappear here.

The horizon was flat in all directions, and they seemed to be in the middle of endless farm country. There was a lone farmhouse amidst trees and what looked like a small stream just a few hundred yards away.

"D-did you d-do that?" asked Maddy.

"I guess so," said David.

"That was amazing. How, I mean..."

"I don't know. When we fell," David paused, thinking, "I just wanted to be anywhere else."

"So, where are we?"

Maddy saw David look around and shrug.

"What do we do now?" she asked.

"Well, let's try to call our families. Maybe they have a phone," he said, pointing to the farmhouse. They began walking across the fallow dirt field toward help.

Minutes after the shocking vanishing of both kids from the rooftop, the tiny implants inserted into their lower backs pinpointed their location and resources were dispatched to get them. This time, however, extreme caution would be in place, with special plans to incapacitate the juvenile targets before they could teleport again.

One agent recognized the nearby farmhouse address and its famous resident. Alarm bells went off in the agent's mind, but recapture plans continued. It was critical they not fail again.

From the distance it looked like one big farmhouse, but as David and Maddy got closer it turned out to be a two-story house, several side buildings, a traditional red barn, and a short, fat grain silo.

There was a kid's voice coming from the other side of the house. They moved cautiously into the bushes and trees, tip-toeing around the yard. On an enormous back lawn was a young girl with short brown hair, perhaps ten years old. She was running around the yard in a Calgary Flames hockey jersey, jeans, and sneakers, wielding a hockey stick and maneuvering rubber balls. After a few deft moves, she'd wind up and fire off a slap shot toward a hockey net set up against one of the side buildings. They watched her take a few shots. She never missed.

"What do we do?" said Maddy.

"Come on," said David.

They stepped from the bushes into the yard, hockey girl oblivious as she fired off another slap shot.

"Ruff! Ruff-ruff!"

Standing from her quiet spot in the shade of the house, Lucy noticed these strangers first, shouting a bark of warning. Her natural defensive hackles were up, bravely standing her ground.

Mary stopped and looked in the direction Lucy was barking. She saw two familiar kids walking toward her. In moments she'd recognized the two faces from all the Blue Third news stories. These were Lucy's friends!

David and Maddy saw a young girl staring open-mouthed as they approached. They were shocked when she said, "David and Maddy! Lucy, look, it's your friends."

By now their familiar scent had reached Lucy, and she began a Basset hound trot toward them, tail wagging. Of course this increased the bizarreness for David and Maddy.

Moments later Mary's mom had come out to see what was going on, and within minutes everyone sat inside enjoying milk and chocolate chip cookies. After learning that Mary's dad had driven to the nearest town for supplies, David and Maddy took turns explaining their own crazy past few days. They left out the part about using their minds to unlock doors and teleporting.

Mary's mom was happy to let each call their parents. After lots of sniffing, Lucy lay down and thought happy Basset hound thoughts.

David went first.

Within moments of getting the call, his parents decided to contact news organizations, but just after they hung up with their son, and before they could reach anyone, their door was kicked in.

Maddy called home and got her mom, Flo.

Maddy's dad, Bryce, was over in Virginia Beach on a contractor job. When Flo had finished hearing what Maddy had to say, she called her husband's mobile phone and quickly explained what happened.

On the other end of the line, Bryce could hear commotion and thought Flo said, "Oh my God, they've broken in!" Then the line went dead. He tried calling, but got only busy signals.

Bryce then made two calls: first to the police regarding a break-in at their address and second to a national news organization. He was trying to call a television news station, thinking he was safe in this obscure parking lot in Virginia Beach, but cell phones are easy to trace, and before he could make a third call he was in custody.

However, his two calls were enough. Before the stories could be suppressed, they hit the net.

Back at the farm a virtual army of agents had moved into position. For the moment they set up and awaited further orders. Specialized sharp shooters were in position to take down the targets. There would be no escape this time.

ROOQ

From his secluded tower far above the Doozy populous, the Supreme Doozy watched his magnificent military force begin its glorious crusade to the Human solar system.

The largest invasion army ever assembled in the Milky Way galaxy was disembarking, all under the iron fist of a never defeated Commander Rooq. He was the finest leader and battle tactician the Doozies had ever known, standing toe to toe with Alexander, Napoleon, Sun Tzu, Caesar, Saladin, Patton, or any of Earth's greatest generals. Rooq commanded mercenary soldiers numbering ten million strong, being flown in fifty massive transport spacecraft, with an entire division of convoy protector-craft to escort them all the way to Earth.

The ten million were comprised of alien races conquered by the Doozies. This mercenary army gave the Doozies an unstoppable force, so overwhelming that even the largest enemy stood little chance. They annihilated planets like a swarm of army ants skeletonizing a helpless cow.

Like all mercenary soldiers forced to fight for a foreign master, most accepted their lot in life. It was either conform and serve, or die.

As the ten million began their journey, so did the Supreme Doozy's Exterminator II, bound for Mars and its utter destruction. Mars would be colder and deader than before those Fiberians arrived.

After destroying Mars, Rooq would turn his army loose upon every country on Earth. This would coincide with strategic laser strikes on Earth's defenses and armies. Nothing could stand up to this onslaught, which would end with the elimination of the Human species. Earth and the entire solar system, including zooey, would be controlled by the Doozy Empire.

But first Rooq expected stiff resistance at the Earth sector zip exit. The total might of the Doozy space fleet would go first, with more than a thousand battle cruisers, planet stingers, space blasters, and other powerful attack vessels. Any Humans or alien allies protecting this zip would be in for a big surprise.

GRAVEYARD

Having escaped the slug planet, Tarayon and Theal's two spacecraft were nearing the galactic core. This also meant they were getting closer to Obaddon, and it was here they sailed into the largest graveyard in the universe.

They were first surprised to find an occasional dead spacecraft drifting in empty space. But as they continued, the number of lifeless ships continued to grow, with every possible shape and size of alien vessel. Some were intact, many were just bits and pieces, and none of them contained life forms: at least not living. And then there were the alien bodies floating everywhere. This seemed to be a terrible unknown resting place for beings from every corner of the universe.

Theal and Tarayon carefully maneuvered through this haunted graveyard, marveling at star voyager spacecraft diversity and technology beyond their wildest imaginations. It was terrible to imagine the alien pilots and crew who'd up in this awful place to slowly perish, starving and suffocating, buried alive in space.

Lupe couldn't believe how different each alien species looked, wondering about the thousands of civilizations that had been home to these poor lost travelers.

After many hours the endless wreckage and bodies began to decrease, until finally their entire view was filled with ancient stars. Many of these stars were doing unexplainable things. Green dwarfs, double helix nebulas, triple star vortexes, dark blotches, and so much more. It was a black canvas of astronomical insanity.

All this time Citlalli's anxiety and restless power had been ebbing and flowing. She could feel her Anahuac Gods around her as they crept through the world of dead. Some of these aliens had been here for hundreds of thousands of years, perhaps even longer. As they moved away from the graveyard, the pull in a specific direction was overwhelming. She could feel something big was coming. She knew where they needed to go.

"There," she shouted, "over there past that blanket of hummingbird green."

Tarayon saw Citlalli's hand shaking as she pointed toward what might have been a nebula, or some kind of supernova, but was now only a translucent canopy of green gases hanging in space.

"That is where we must travel; Dark and Light."

Tarayon would do whatever Citlalli said. It was clear she was in tune with the cosmos, gifted by the Watchers or something. He followed Citlalli's directions and led Theal's spacecraft past this beautiful drapery of green, and down a debris-free gauntlet. As they moved by these amazing interstellar sights, all the passengers, including Prince Zed, Waima, Stauffa, Lupe, and Jamila, could only stare out in wonder.

Citlalli would have paid more attention, but her energy was growing stronger and more uncontrollable. She was starting to shake badly and her teeth were chattering.

"There's a p-planet, d-destiny waits...waits for us there. It lies on our c-c-current path. The Light t-tells me...tells me where to go."

The planet rapidly grew on Tarayon's view screen.

"It's huge. Are you sure this is the place?

Tarayon saw Citlalli nod, wide-eyed with intense concentration. They'd enter the planet atmosphere shortly and he relayed instructions to Theal. It was good he did, because seconds later everyone's power went dead.

"What happened," said Tarayon, checking controls and instruments in a panic.

In the other vessel, Theal noticed both ships' power vanish simultaneously. She'd been feeling weaker, but had to stay focused for this landing. She used a light-beamer to flash Tarayon's ship.

Tarayon beamed back, relaying Citlalli's specific instructions for crash landing.

Both sailed helplessly into the outer atmosphere, trying desperately to maneuver toward the destination picked by Citlalli. They'd only have one chance to do this right and neither spacecraft would likely survive.

INLAND

Still lying on the black sand beach, Estrella had gotten a few hours' restless sleep next to Einlen. Whatever gravity pulled at Obaddon's seas was now causing the tide to come in, and waves were starting to run over their legs. It took all her strength and every ounce of weight to dig her feet in the sand and pull a still-groggy Einlen up a few yards, just into the jungle edge.

Turning back to the beach, Estrella screamed as a sea monster head moved toward them! Water spilled between jagged teeth waiting to tear them apart. She lunged backward, stumbling over a woken up Einlen.

Nothing happened. The monster just stared at them.

Estrella and Einlen gradually realized it was a sea monster corpse being pushed toward them by the tide, head frozen in a horrible grimace. She crinkled her nose and Einlen gave a crocodile snort at the disgusting sight.

Estrella felt the strangest emotion bubbling up; laughter. She started giggling and couldn't stop. Einlen looked at her like she was crazy. Then to Estrella's amazement, Einlen started laughing. Of course an Uppsalian laugh sounds more like a sputtering motorcycle. This was the first time Estrella had ever seen or heard Einlen laugh. They shared this unique experience for a few more wonderful moments, before catching their breath.

"Here," said Einlen, handing Estrella her sharp knife, "carve sea monster steak. Start fire; have breakfast."

Within the hour steaks had been cooked and devoured. Estrella could see Einlen often grimacing, but there was nothing she could do. Her arm was gone and the wound sealed. Healing was in the hands of fate and Einlen's own Uppsalian body.

Now it was time to find everyone else.

Einlen followed Estrella, her remaining hand grasping the knife, their only weapon. She would fight to the death anything that threatened her hatchling.

Hatchling?

Einlen felt the strangest feeling wash over her, an ancient motherly instinct hitting her between the eyes. It was a good thing Estrella led, thought Einlen, not wanting this Human to see her crocodile tears.

A couple of miles up the coast, Sklizz and Summahon searched one last time for survivors. As they did so, it was apparent they'd seriously pissed off the sea monster community. There were dozens of these creatures not far off the coast, patrolling and occasionally tossing a loud screech in their direction. Returning on boats across the sea didn't seem like a good idea.

"Where do we go from here?" asked Sklizz.

"Well, good ol' Hinge—*honor upon his memory*—used to say we'd continue this crazy journey for as long as we still lived. Let's head inland and find your friend Tyson. That's where any survivors would go, don't you think?"

"As Citlalli used to say, *when Cecoatl smiles upon you, your journey should begin.* I hope she journeyed safely home and I hope Cecoatl is smiling on us now."

Of course at this very moment Citlalli was rapidly approaching, riding in Tarayon's spacecraft, trying to stay airborne as they passed across a vast, glistening swamp. Her shaking arm directed Tarayon toward distant mountains, their ultimate goal. The shakes had gotten so bad she couldn't speak. They had to reach an open area on dry ground to land their powerless ship. Time was short as they were losing altitude fast.

Not far behind came the spacecraft piloted by an exhausted Theal. Whatever those horrible slugs did to her was getting worse. If they didn't land soon, she'd pass out and finding a landing area wouldn't matter at all.

CONVERGENCE

Both spacecraft were on a direct line toward Yore and Heather.

After awakening, Yore gathered plants he believed were not poisonous and they ate a vegetarian breakfast. As they ate, Yore told Heather his tail would grow back in time. Later, as Heather rode on Yore she was thinking about Eeyore's tacked-on tail when he interrupted her thoughts.

"On yer planet," said Yore, "do rivers flow away from the sea?"

Heather hadn't been the greatest geography or science student, but she was pretty sure all rivers flowed into the ocean, not out of it. She told this to Yore and added, "The last time I was in a river was after we crashed. I was being chased by a huge monster and lucky to survive."

She could feel Yore's lizard ribs shaking as he chuckled below.

"Ain't it the truth? That's all this planet's good for—tryin' ta kill ya."

Rounding a bend they came upon a waterfall that fell straight into the earth. The hole was surrounded by tall blue grass and above the falling water a tiny rainbow shimmered in Obaddon's alien sunlight. Heather smiled at how pretty and Earthlike the rainbow seemed.

Yore carried Heather closer and as they neared the blue grass and waterfall hole, a massive ten-foot-tall, bulbous-headed, albino-white monstrosity rose from the edge of the waterfall with a terrible howl. Its lower body was like a gray horse with four short legs. Its upper torso was a huge centaur with four muscular arms and a one-eyed octopus head. Its grinning mouth, filled with sharp teeth, dared them to come closer.

Heather gulped down a scream as Yore moved carefully around the cycloptic horror, trying to reach a safer rocky area on the other side of the river. Halfway across the river, the white monster bellowed and charged. Yore scrambled, tossing Heather the last ten feet to shore and turned to face the beast. Yore waited until it was upon him, and then dove underneath. Forgetting he had no tail to swim with, Yore found himself hoisted in the air by four strong arms and thrown far uphill beyond Heather. He landed at the base of an alien tree, loaded with gnarly branches and hanging vines. Yore pulled himself up by a vine, gasping for breath.

At the shoreline he saw helpless Heather picked up by her legs like a rag doll, screaming hysterically. A horrified Yore watched the beast swing Heather around by her legs, bones snapping like firecrackers, and then heaving her limp body a hundred feet up the hillside, past Yore. He heard the body land with a sickening thud. He knew Heather was either unconscious or dead.

There was no time as the monster was charging up toward him. With no weapons, no tail, and ebbing strength, Yore thought fast. He needed a miracle.

As a young lizard back home, Yore and his friends would lasso small prey with twine. He couldn't kill this monster the same way, but perhaps...

Yore quickly ripped a vine from the tree and wrapped it around a boulder. The monster saw the purple creature toying with a tree vine and slowed to watch, allowing Yore time to finish tying it to the boulder. Yore saw a horrible grin cross its hideous face as it charged. Yore darted lizard-like to one side, deftly lassoing his knotted vine noose around the monster's hairless octo-head.

The beast turned, teeth gnashing, seeing the lizard trying to push the boulder. It let out a wheezing laugh, black saliva spraying as the noose began tightening around its thick neck. Realization of its dangerous situation dawned in its primordial eldritch brain just as Yore shook the boulder loose.

It lunged for Yore, but he'd started the boulder moving downhill. The rolling stone yanked the beast into the air then slammed it down to the ground, dragging the thing by its neck as it careened down the hillside.

From his vantage point, Yore could see the white monstrosity's neck whip back and forth, killing it before reaching the river's edge.

Yore rushed uphill to Heather, finding her babbling in painful delirium with both legs shattered. Yore could only stare at the horrific scene, unsure how or what he could do to help this poor Human girl. He knew the legs were beyond repair. She would never walk again. He tried straightening them, but that only made matters worse. The bones seemed to be broken shards, twisted in horrific positions. He searched for and found a native plant whose leaves seemed to offer slight pain relief. He'd save them for when she awoke.

Yore's species, like many sentient races throughout the cosmos, felt and showed sadness in their unique way. Yore's lizardlike race didn't cry like Humans, but shook uncontrollably. This was the way they sobbed, and Yore proceeded to lie by Heather's side, shaking for quite some time.

FANTASMAS

As Heather fought for her life, Summahon and Sklizz were getting closer. Fortunately they'd decided to follow the river to its source and were headed straight toward Yore and Heather. They couldn't shake the feeling of being watched by invisible eyes from inside the surrounding forest.

From the opposite direction Estrella and Einlen were moving through dense forest too as they climbed a steep hillside.

Odd sounds were coming from up ahead as they stealthily crested the hill into a secluded valley. Surrounded by steep walls on each side, the valley was remarkably empty of forest or jungle growth.

Walking quietly and keeping out of sight, they looked down on a village of shambling, hairless four-legged creatures with no heads—or at least none that Estrella or Einlen could see. Instead the beasts had two elephant-like trunks where a head would normally have been. Stranger still was their translucency. They didn't seem to have natural color, but rather a blurry light brown shade of paleness, almost like tan shadows. And yet they were translucent. You could see through them!

"They're like ghosts," whispered Estrella, "fantasmas."

They began walking closer, staying out of sight as they crept along the ridgeline surrounding the valley.

"Oh, look at that fantasma," Estrella saw a tiny one that had strayed away. From their vantage-point they could see a vicious creature had positioned itself on an overhang, and the helpless fantasma was clearly its target. Estrella thought the predator looked like a walking barracuda, but much larger. The little fantasma would be torn to pieces in seconds.

Estrella felt sick, knowing the little fantasma was doomed. These creatures reminded her of elephants and anteaters with their size and trunks. And they seemed so peaceful and friendly.

Einlen just stared, waiting for the inevitable hunter kill. Thus Einlen was shocked when Estrella burst from cover and charged the lurking predator, yelling and waving her arms.

Later Einlen told Estrella several things happened at once. First the predator was stunned to see this crazy alien screaming and running at it. It ran off with another half dozen of its hidden hunting pack. At that moment the entire village of translucent fantasmas turned completely invisible, but not before they'd seen Estrella scare off the deadly creatures. The tiny fantasma shrieked and ran back to its fellow beings before it too vanished.

Estrella and Einlen didn't wait around long in this strange and secluded valley. As they reached the top of the other side, Estrella turned for one last look. She saw a slight disturbance on the valley floor, almost like a blur that might have been the tribe of fantasmas. Then a hair-raising chorus of trumpeting rolled up and over their hilltop vantage point.

Einlen watched Estrella, smiling at the glow on her face and shiny red hair. She thought to herself what an amazing and contradictory species these Humans were.

Meanwhile, an exhausted and waterlogged Jak-toll finally washed ashore far away along the coast of Pith. All he could do was crawl inland and soak up as much life-giving sun as possible. He hoped no hungry plant-eating animals would discover him before he regained his strength. Happily, buds were already forming where his branches had been torn off.

Because of his location, Jak-toll was the first to see the two Watcher spacecraft. Lying on his back, Tarayon's oblong vessel sped past overhead, followed shortly by Theal's identical second speeding spacecraft. Both flew in complete silence, powerless like everyone who crashed on Obaddon. It was unheard of to have two spacecraft arrive at once, and the direction they came from was the opposite of every other powerless spacecraft that smashed into this planet. *How very strange,* Jak-toll thought. He hoped to find out who the passengers were on these vessels before being eaten.

CRASHING

"T-t-t-there," pointed Citlalli, "v-v-valley between high m-m-m..."

"Mountains," said Tarayon, "understood."

Tarayon could see her target, but their speed would make a safe landing impossible. Tarayon began air-braking, hoping to find a long landing area resembling the thing Humans called a runway. Not likely in this jungle.

Theal could see Tarayon's frantic air-braking and tried the same thing, still following at a distance. She didn't see how they were going to survive these next few minutes.

Descending rapidly they entered the valley, a large river visible below. Tarayon thought about landing in the river, but it wasn't wide enough and they'd be torn to pieces.

Sitting behind Tarayon, Citlalli was bursting with surging energy. What was she supposed to do?

In the back, Jamila wondered if it was time to die.

Tarayon was getting close to the treetops with nowhere to land. In moments they'd be pulverized and killed.

Realization came to Citlalli in a synaptic flash, how to use her power.

Shockingly, Tarayon felt power surge through the spacecraft as he grappled with the controls to try a last second dive landing into the jungle below. Reversing the engines and dropping fast, a tall tree pierced their outer hull, driving through the floor with a metallic screech, just missing Citlalli in the passenger seat, and exiting the top like a samurai sword stabbing clean through an enemy. Their forward momentum rocked the thick tree back and forth. It finally came to a stop, leaving them impaled on one of Obaddon's ancient trees, sixty feet above the ground.

Theal couldn't see Tarayon's landing, and assumed they'd been destroyed. Theal was still without power and heading to certain doom. Stauffa held Waima close, thinking to himself that no father had ever been more proud of his daughter.

Citlalli tried desperately to send energy to Theal's spacecraft, but only a fraction of this strange power got through. In moments she was completely drained, slumping in her seat with closed eyes.

Theal felt power ripple through the spacecraft and he used the brief surge to slow down. Perhaps they wouldn't die after all. The maneuver caused their rear to dip, clipping several treetops. The lopsided impact sent the spacecraft in a forward somersault, spinning like a pinwheel as they entered the jungle below. This rolling descent slowed their momentum as they snapped off branches like the slap of a baseball card on the spokes of a bike. Crashing hard to the jungle floor, the spacecraft was torn apart and severed by the impact, debris, branches, and leaves raining down on the devastating scene.

Upriver, Yore had been quietly sitting by Heather's side, utterly despondent. The thunderous sound of these two crashes echoed throughout the river valley, but he had no idea where they came from. Unwilling to leave Heather's side, Yore could only watch and wait to see who or what might appear. As the echoes died away, the only sound was the waterfall dropping into the black abyss and whatever lay below the surface of this place.

Summahon and Sklizz also heard the horrendous crashes coming from somewhere upriver. They moved even faster.

From farther away Estrella and Einlen heard the echoing booms, which provided a directional beacon to follow. They picked up their pace through the forest.

The epic journeys begun so far away across the infinite universe were finally converging.

FLYTRAP

Commander Rooq had won countless battles and conquered planets throughout the Milky Way galaxy. Many of these conquered races were now mercenaries in the Doozies' huge space army.

In all his experience, Rooq had never heard of the great Zulu nation from an Earth land mass called Africa. He would've been surprised to know his zip battle technique resembled their "horns of the bull" attack formation. Rooq would send a first strike force straight out the zip exit, right into the gut of the enemy, like a Zulu stabbing spear thrust. The enemy spacecraft would close from each side on this spear thrust of Doozy vessels. Then Rooq's four horns would slide out the zip in perfectly executed arcs, encircling and enveloping the enemy. Once surrounded and being attacked from the top, bottom, right, and left, the enemy would invariably surrender or be annihilated. It worked for the Zulus and it worked for the Doozies.

Given the spear-thrust lure and four-horned pincer attack, an observant Earthling might have called this battle tactic the Doozy Venus Flytrap.

Vorwin had recently arrived at the allied zip location, observing a flat two-dimensional defense. It resembled a gigantic letter U in space, with the open end around the zip exit. The idea was to surround whatever came through, attacking from both sides.

Vorwin expressed his concerns, but was told the allied plans could not be changed and should easily handle any Doozy invasion fleet.

When Rooq's first spear thrust lure shot out of the zip, the Doozy spacecraft were immediately surrounded by the U-shaped allied forces. Demands for surrender were fired off, the allies overjoyed at how easily the Doozies had been beaten.

However, moments later the four curved Doozy horns sped forth, enveloping the allies from all sides like that trapped fly. A seemingly easy allied victory turned into a typical Doozy slaughter. The Zulu four horns closed on allied spacecraft from all sides.

Vorwin had been stationed near the rear and saw the terrifying ambush unfold. It was just as he'd feared and obvious the allies were doomed. He and a few other spacecraft made a flanking move around the side of one horn, managing to destroy a few Doozy ships, but when five times their number of spacecraft began battling Vorwin's group, their only option was escape.

In less than an hour the battle was over, and Rooq easily brought his mercenary army through the zip, followed shortly by the innocent-looking Exterminator II. On his command bridge, the leader of so many victorious Doozy battles smiled.

He quickly coordinated his surviving sub-commanders into the attack formation that would strike a one-two punch: first blasting Mars into oblivion and then unleashing his army of Armageddon upon Humanity. They would start their short journey to the Humans' solar system in less than a day.

WRECKS

While Tarayon, Citlalli, and Jamila tried figuring out how to climb out of their impaled spacecraft, perched in a tree high above the jungle floor, Summahon and Sklizz had already reached the site of Theal's crash.

They weren't sure what kind of aliens might be around the wreck, approaching cautiously. They first found an unconscious Waima, lying on her side, battered, bruised, and bleeding Doozy green-yellow blood from cuts on her arms and head.

"Rim bling, that's a Doozy!" said Sklizz, astonished.

Summahon kneeled down to see if the tiny Doozy was alive.

"These are the beings you rescued everyone from?" said Summahon. She rolled Waima slowly on her back, a moan escaping the young Doozy.

"They killed my sister."

"But this Doozy is so small."

"It must be a Doozy child."

Another loud groan came from nearby. Sklizz ran to its source and found Stauffa underneath part of the spacecraft. He didn't look good, the heavy chunk of metal crushing him from the chest down. As Sklizz bent over, Stauffa opened his eyes.

"Hold on," Sklizz said, "we'll try and lift this off."

Summahon was by his side now and together they were barely able to move the jagged piece of wreckage off Stauffa, dropping it with a thud. They could see this Doozy had serious internal injuries and a badly bleeding cut on one leg. Sklizz tore material from some wreckage, creating an ad-hoc tourniquet which he tied around the injured leg. Stauffa had already lost a lot of green blood.

Summahon ran back over to Waima, who was now sitting up groggily.

"Can you understand me?" Summahon said.

Waima moaned as she spotted Stauffa on the ground next to another alien.

"Papa!"

She tried to stand, Summahon helping her up.

"He's your papa?"

"Yes! Is he all right?"

They walked over to Stauffa, Waima falling to her knees. Sklizz held her back.

"He's hurt bad," he said, "you mustn't move him."

Stauffa opened his eyes and saw Waima. A smile began forming.

"My daughter," he whispered, every breath difficult, "you mustn't give up. Find the others. Find your way home."

"Oh, Papa, don't leave me." Waima started to cry, surprisingly Human-like.

Summahon and Sklizz each stepped back.

"I'm sorry...this is my last journey. I'm so proud."

"No Papa, no."

"You nearly killed the Supreme Doozy." Stauffa coughed, his chest rattling, fighting for each breath.

Sklizz hadn't been paying close attention, until now. *Did he mention that she nearly killed the Supreme Doozy?*

Stauffa struggled, able to get out one last thought, "You must go on Waima...you must...survive."

Stauffa breathed his last. Then his body lay limp on the ground.

Waima remained in disbelieving shock for a few moments, then fell forward and hugged him tightly, sobbing.

"You stay with her," said Sklizz, "I'll keep looking around."

The spacecraft had apparently been sheared in two. The front half had ended up near the river's edge. Peering inside, Sklizz found Theal in the pilot's seat, unconscious. After some effort he undid her constraints and pulled her out, surprised she seemed unhurt.

Why was this Human female piloting an unknown spacecraft with two Doozy passengers? The whole situation had Sklizz terribly puzzled.

Summahon came over and observed the unconscious pilot. "Another Human?"

"So it would seem. Something very strange is going on here."

"The little female Doozy won't leave her papa's side."

"And her papa said she tried to kill the Supreme Doozy."

At that moment, stumbling onto the crash site were Einlen and Estrella. They spotted their friends and in moments there were hugs from Estrella and hellos for Einlen (Uppsalians never hug).

Waima had stopped crying by now, watching these four unknown aliens. The species looked familiar like others sent by the Watchers, and she was positive the young one was Human. *Who are all these strangers and why are they here on this planet?*

Theal had been groggily coming awake, weaker than ever. As a Watcher she sensed her Human body wasn't going to survive whatever those slugs did. She realized this journey's outcome now rested with Citlalli, if she'd survived Tarayon's crash.

"Help," she said.

Summahon and Sklizz kneeled down, Einlen and Estrella looking on.

"Who are you? And why do you have Doozy passengers?" asked Sklizz.

Theal looked closely at Sklizz and smiled.

"You're Gelzian, and you," she peered at Summahon, "are Trixian."

This left everyone speechless, an unknown Human female knowing their two alien races.

Spotting Estrella and Einlen she said, "A Human and Uppsalian too?" Theal struggled to sit up. "I'm actually a Watcher. I took this Human form to help with a mission vital to all our species future. So now, please, we must find the other crash, rescue any survivors. It's critical."

"Another crash," said Sklizz, "like this one?"

"Yes, came down shortly before us."

Standing behind everyone, Waima said, "She speaks true. The Watchers sent us all here."

Then another surprising voice came from the river's edge. Curiosity had finally forced Yore to investigate all the commotion.

"Glad to see survivors!"

Everyone looked over at a large purple lizard, sitting in his uncanny Buddha position with a Mona Lisa smile.

Yore led them, carrying the injured Theal and the body of Stauffa, up to the secluded rocky crevice where Heather still lay mercifully unconscious. Sklizz lay Stauffa's body down in a shallow depression under a nearby tree. Waima stood nearby, remaining in a state of Doozy shock. Sklizz was about to ask Waima about Doozy rituals for those who died, but decided to wait.

Summahon, Einlen, and Estrella laid Theal down next to Heather. They all looked at Heather's demolished legs, agreeing there was nothing to be done. The legs would have to be amputated soon or she would not live. Theal lay next to the shattered young Human female, looking on with compassion. As a Watcher, Theal was very aware of the important role this brave Human girl had in defeating the Destroyer. She calmly began evaluating her alternatives.

With everything settled for the moment, Sklizz, Summahon, and Einlen left to go search for the other spacecraft.

Before they left, Yore showed everyone the hideous white carcass of the waterfall guardian. No one had seen anything like it before, surprised and impressed that Yore had been able to defeat and kill this terrible thing.

ENSNARED

Half a universe away, news about David and Maddy was spreading fast. The first phone call to Mary's family farmhouse came from an independent news agency. Mary's mom was shocked at what she heard from this man.

"We need to get in the car and go for a ride," she said, not realizing their entire farm was already surrounded by federal agents.

Unlike many farmhouses, this one had a garage. Mary's mom told them to wait out front while she got the car ready.

The three kids and Lucy stepped outside onto the big lawn. A sharpshooter immediately caught them in his line of fire. David's upper body was in his crosshairs, and his finger was ready to punch him out. He was just waiting for the order to shoot.

Lucy's Basset hound senses were on full alert. Strange odors hovered in the air and her hair bristled with canine uneasiness. She walked on ahead, sniffing and trying to decide what was up. Finally a strong whiff of government agent set her off, starting to bark up a storm.

"Lucy," said Mary automatically. But she knew Lucy was good at sensing things and she started looking around. Nothing seemed out of the ordinary.

The sharpshooter got a green light and stood, carefully aiming at David to make the first shot count.

Strolling on the grass, David felt a sharp needle-like pain in his right shoulder. He instinctively grabbed and yanked out the dart, almost immediately starting to feel dizzy.

Maddy and Mary saw David stagger and fall to his knees. They both leapt to his side. Lucy spotted the distant sharpshooter silhouette, wishing it to freeze so she could watch it. Thus, the second shot intended for Maddy remained halfway out the barrel, unwittingly frozen in place by Lucy.

A man's voice over a megaphone said, "David and Maddy, we don't want to hurt you. Please, let us approach."

They knew that once David was unconscious there would be plenty of time to get the kids to a secure location before he could teleport. The dozens of government agents rose and slowly began approaching.

When all these people moved into view, Lucy forgot the sniper and froze these new things instead. Thus the second dart intended for Maddy, having lost all momentum, fell out the rifle nozzle at the confused sharpshooter's feet.

Lucy heard the garage door opening and forgot about the agents, allowing them to all unfreeze. The voice shouted, "Stop whatever you're doing. Don't make this difficult." The agents began moving faster. The frozen immobility had surprised everyone. Orders came through to shoot them all.

Mary's mom had the garage door open, hearing the voice for the first time.

Several sharpshooters now took aim, fingers squeezing triggers with tranquilizer darts aimed at everyone.

David was fading fast. The girls sat next to him, sitting ducks in the crosshairs. David was frustrated, wondering what they could do. Where on Earth could they go?

And just like that David had a wonderful idea. As several rifles fired simultaneously, the three kids and Basset hound vanished without a sound.

In his command vessel around Mars, Thrix received a message from Vorwin describing the Doozy slaughter at the zip. There were few survivors.

This was terrible news, but the remaining allied force of Plinns, Meemers, Uppsalians, Gelzians, and Fiberians was nearly a thousand ships strong. Everyone agreed that Thrix's battle plans were excellent, so now it was just a matter of waiting.

The battle for Mars and Earth would happen in space. If they failed, Earth and Mars would have no defense. The only choice was a fight to the death.

As Thrix waited with the allied armada to meet Vorwin's returning survivors, four surprise visitors blinked into existence on his bridge. He stared with blue-headed amazement at three Humans and a Basset hound. The smallest Human, Mary, stood wide-eyed and frozen, looking like she might faint. He recognized the dark-skinned Human called Maddy, and the one he knew as David smiled briefly before his eyes rolled up and he collapsed to the floor. The Basset hound he remembered as Lucy wagged her tail and walked over to a stunned Thrix, sniffing and licking him.

The battle for Earth and Mars had begun.

PART THREE

STRAGGLERS

The frozen corpses of large starfish-shaped beings were banging off Wizza's spacecraft and spinning away like pinwheels as she maneuvered through the endless space graveyard. They were moving in a narrow area between lifeless ships, filled with these starfish bodies.

"Probably mass suicide," said Wizza.

As they left the last corpse behind, Lupe realized she'd been holding her breath. She let it out with a whoosh.

Wizza was able to accelerate, still following ion trails toward a distant planet. Of course the planet was Obaddon, and as they entered its atmosphere, their spacecraft power inevitably died. Wizza was going faster than the other Watcher ships and desperately tried to slow, zigzagging in the atmosphere and skidding on air currents.

In the back seats, Lupe, Prince Zed, and Gilad nervously watched.

As Wizza sped around a mountain, the dense jungle was coming up fast and would tear them to pieces. And then out of nowhere appeared an open area up ahead on the right.

"Hold on," she shouted, banking hard right and diving down, their spacecraft slamming off the surface. They bounced once and began skidding, rattling and vibrating crazily, just starting to slow when the front-end side-swiped a tree stump, turning the spacecraft sideways and flipping it. Both side thrusters tore off with grinding explosions, the narrow craft rolling like an out of control log.

Lupe, Gilad, and Wizza were secured, while Prince Zed became a half-ton pinball. The ship careened wildly as Prince Zed slammed into Wizza's seat, and then sailed back over a ducking Lupe and delirious Gilad. Everything was spinning, flying, and tumbling as the cabin slammed into the jungle tree line, crunching to a dead stop. Prince Zed was thrown through the supposedly unbreakable cockpit window.

Except for the ominous hissing of air vents, all was quiet around the battered and broken spacecraft.

Meanwhile, Tarayon's impaled spacecraft still hung high up in its tree like a dead fish on the end of an Anahuac spear. Using a space cord, Citlalli and Jamila shimmied down to the ground. Tarayon made sure he had his blinger and followed.

"What is this place?" said Jamila.

"I have no idea," said Tarayon, "and there was no reason for our spacecraft to lose power."

"How will we get home without a spacecraft?"

"Another good question. Let's hope someone else made it intact."

They both noticed Citlalli staring into the jungle. She pointed toward a small rise in the distance.

"The path leads there," she said. "Answers lie below."

She started walking, and they both dutifully followed. It was up to Citlalli now.

Farther upriver, Sklizz, Summahon, and Einlen had heard the horrible crash and found Wizza's demolished ship. All three passengers inside and outside the broken spacecraft were badly hurt or dead. Unknown to the rescuers, a fourth passenger named Lupe was missing entirely.

Sklizz first found the large snake body of Prince Zed and called to the others.

"This grows stranger all the time," said Sklizz.

"What dead Meemer doing here?" said Einlen.

"I've never seen a Meemer," said Summahon.

Finding the spacecraft, they discovered Wizza and Gilad unconscious and bleeding.

"Wizza!" said Sklizz.

Summahon and Einlen looked over.

"She's a Gelzian like me," Sklizz explained.

"Why would she be flying a Meemer and Human?" said Summahon.

"It must have something to do with those Watchers that Waima, the little Doozy, mentioned."

"Let's get them out," said Sklizz. "We need to get back to the waterfall camp before dark."

Sklizz carried Wizza, while Einlen and Summahon brought Gilad. They all missed the small footprints leading away from the crash site into the jungle.

Lupe had awoken in her seat, confused and scared, with no idea where she was or why she was here. Her head hurt and she felt a big bump on her forehead. Her last memory was sitting on the couch with her mom, watching TV.

What the heck had happened?

Standing on wobbly legs she saw two unconscious passengers, neither of whom she recognized. She grabbed a blinger from the pilot's belt.

What was going on?

Climbing out of the wreck Lupe looked around, trying desperately to remember what happened. It seemed the answer was on the tip of her tongue. At least she knew this wasn't Earth, with bizarre plants and a pink sky.

How did she get here?

Lupe headed for a nearby hill, thinking she might get a better look around. It turned out she couldn't see a thing, and after twenty minutes Lupe returned to the crash site. To her amazement, both of the other survivors had vanished. And to make matters worse, dusk was approaching.

Where had they gone?

Serious panic started to set in as she crawled inside the cockpit and waited for dark.

Why couldn't she remember anything?

She shivered as the evening shadows crept higher and higher around her.

Not far from Lupe, Tarayon and Jamila continued to follow Citlalli in the darkness.

"Back on Earth," asked Tarayon, "what did you do?"

"Hmmm," said Jamila, wondering how to provide an answer to a jaguar alien unfamiliar with her people's long struggle. "I'm a soldier for justice and revenge, always for revenge. I fight against the unbelievers, those who do not follow the one true faith. On Earth I'm called a terrorist."

Tarayon was surprised, thinking about Jamila's comments as Citlalli stopped. She had led them to this precise spot in front of thick red bushes at the base of a small hill.

"There," she pointed, "that is where we must go."

"How do you know this?" asked Jamila.

"In my mind, the pattern is clear; we must perish in order to be born. The spiral of the serpent leads us back to where we began."

Tarayon looked at Jamila and shrugged his jaguar shoulders.

The bushes were incredibly hard to pull apart—nearly unbreakable—and so Tarayon fired a blinger dispersion ray, creating a blast path through ten feet of densely packed branches. Bending over and creeping through the seared bushes, they stood in front of a cave entrance. From somewhere deep inside came an eerie yellowish glow. They listened closely, but heard only silence.

"Oh, this is great," said Jamila, "just what I needed, another cave."

"In here, Citlalli. In this place is the enemy?" said Tarayon.

Citlalli stared into the dimly lit cave, unable to detect more.

"I can feel the face and heart within. I only know that this is where we must go."

Sitting in the dark cockpit, Lupe heard the distant buzz of Tarayon's blinger. She recognized that sound and left the cockpit and crash site to find out who fired it.

Strange memories of Watchers began creeping into her mind as she suddenly remembered being kidnapped off Earth; but why? Lupe had never been more scared in her life, all alone on an alien world in the middle of another crazy journey. She had to find someone, anyone. Her heart hammered in her chest as she crept through the dark forest.

Several minutes later she saw a faint glow in the darkness up ahead. Moving stealthily, barely breathing, she reached the blasted red foliage and cave entrance. A faint sound came from deep inside. Lupe figured it must be her two unknown fellow passengers...

Wait, she thought, *I remember...I know who. The pilot was Wizza! Wizza and Gilad!*

Her memories flooded back all at once.

She broke into sobs, leaning against the cavern wall, the reality of her desperate situation nearly overwhelming her. After a few moments it was clear she had to catch Wizza and Gilad. She was stranded on an alien planet, all alone. Pushing her fear aside, she gradually regained control, starting to move rapidly downhill inside the glowing cavern. She had to work hard to keep from giving in to blind panic.

SANCTUARY

Back on Thrix's command vessel around Mars, the kids and Lucy were being locked in a secure room, for their own protection in the coming battle.

"Stay with David until he awakens," said Thrix, "and whatever you're running from, well, if we survive the Doozies we'll deal with it then."

David was still unconscious from the tranquilizer and lying on a bunk. Maddy, Mary, and Lucy sat by his side as they watched Thrix hop from the room on his two powerful legs.

Lucy was very tired. This was the most excitement she'd had since her charge up the Destroyer's throne on Kreyon. She plopped on the ground next to Mary, pooped.

"I can't believe that was THE Thrix the Mighty," said Mary, still reeling from their teleportation. "I can't believe I'm in outer space."

Maddy suddenly felt older than her fourteen years. In the past few months she'd seen and experienced more than most people do in a lifetime. And here she was again, on the run from Earth with David and about to enter another space battle.

A moan escaped from David, who was still asleep on the bunk. Down on Mary's farm, his rapid extraction of the tranquilizer dart had reduced the amount of drug that got into his bloodstream. He was already starting to wake up.

By now Earth authorities had discovered that the kids were on Thrix's spacecraft, including innocent bystander Mary and her famous Basset hound Lucy. Requests for the return of all three kids and dog were politely declined.

It was time for the huge Doozy space fleet to disembark. Rooq's sweepers were clearing the zip battle debris first, rescuing any Doozy survivors and killing any allied survivors. The Supreme Doozy's orders were clear: No prisoners.

The first attacks on Mars would commence in a few Earth hours. The use of Exterminator II would coincide with the initial battle. If all went as planned, Exterminator II's explosive power would destroy all enemy spacecraft as well as Mars, thus securing absolute Mars victory in one fell swoop. The entire battle would be over in minutes, leaving Earth and its infestation of Humanity at their complete mercy. And of course there would be no mercy.

"Confirm orders with every ship," Rooq said to his second in command, a mercenary leader named Xox. Xox was in charge of the Earth Invasion Fleet.

Xox was originally enslaved after the Doozies conquered his home world. With reddish-brown skin, twin horns, hoofed feet, and horrifically sharp teeth, he might have been mistaken for the devil on Earth. Every mercenary soldier knew better than to cross Xox, if they valued their lives. It was rumored that Xox kept the frozen heads of those who crossed him in a secret deep-freeze back home on Yerti. Xox couldn't wait to begin the systematic extermination of Humanity.

As thousands Doozy spacecraft began the journey to Earth's solar system, rumors ran rampant among the mercenary soldiers about an unspeakable planet killer called Exterminator. Even these hardened soldiers and killers couldn't believe their Doozy masters would use something so vile.

SPELUNKING

The spaceship crash rescuers arrived with Gilad and Wizza back at the waterfall camp. Most of the surviving Watcher group was finally together. They shared their adventures as Heather remained asleep, thanks to Yore's native plants. Gilad had also used Yore's painkiller leaves to reset his shoulder.

Only Waima paid no attention, building a funeral bier for her father near the waterfall. Estrella had offered to help, but Waima politely declined. When done, Waima had Sklizz carry her father's body, laying it atop the mound of dry plants. Waima set the funeral bier on fire, then sat and watched quietly as her father's body was consumed by the flames. After a few minutes, Estrella moved over to the fire and took a seat near Waima. She felt incredible sadness for this alien, even if she was a Doozy. Neither said a word as the fire gradually died down.

Finally Waima rose and Estrella said, "I'm sorry about your father."

Waima looked at Estrella through her large black Doozy eyes, seeing a Human being and still wondering why the Supreme Doozy wanted them eliminated.

"Thank you," she said, wanting to say more, but not knowing what to say.

"How old are you?" asked Estrella.

"Old?"

"How many years old, like how long have you lived."

"Uh, I am fifteen of our Yerti cycles. Is this what you ask?"

"I guess so. I turn fourteen in a few weeks."

After a few moments of silence, Waima gave Estrella the briefest of smiles and went to her place in the shadows near some rocks.

As the group talked, Sklizz, Einlen, and Estrella learned of Citlalli and Lupe's presence. They were shocked. Estrella wanted to begin searching immediately, but the group decided to wait for morning. Estrella sat in grumpy silence.

And finally Theal revealed what she had known since crashing on Obaddon. "My energy is nearly gone. I cannot go on. You must find Citlalli and stop whatever is slowing the zips."

"If they crashed somewhere near here," said Summahon, "then we should be able to find them, assuming the pilot was able to get them down safely."

"I think Tarayon was the best pilot amongst us," said Theal.

The Trixian blood rushed from Summahon's head and she managed a desperate gasp, "Tarayon?"

"Oh yes," said Theal, "a fellow Trixian. You know him?"

Summahon looked at Estrella and said, "We leave at once."

When everyone realized Summahon would not wait, they prepared to start the search. It was decided that Waima and Yore would remain in camp to protect Heather and Theal. Theal kept Wizza's blinger as well.

Goodbyes were quickly said, and the group of Sklizz, Einlen, Estrella, Summahon, Wizza, and Gilad headed back toward Wizza's crash site.

Since Citlalli had discovered the underworld cave entrance, she, Tarayon, and Jamila had been descending for several hours. The climbing was occasionally treacherous, but in many cases the path was already widened and smoothed by a previous descent—whose descent, they couldn't guess. They found the eerie underground light was generated by some kind of natural phenomena in the planet's rocks. Several times they had to choose between different forks, and each time Citlalli made the decision based on whatever was guiding her.

After squeezing through a particularly narrow entrance, they suddenly found themselves on a rubble strewn ledge overlooking what seemed to be a bottomless drop into blackness below. The cavern wasn't huge, but they would have to carefully make their way along the treacherous pathway for about a hundred feet to the cavern exit.

Tarayon went first, clearing a path through the rocks and gravel, with Citlalli next and Jamila in the rear. Tarayon kicked some of the debris off the ledge. They waited, but never heard a sound of impact from below.

Shuffling carefully and slowly, they reached the halfway point.

Jamila could feel sweat running down her back, thinking how normal and safe her cave hideaways were on Earth, compared to this.

Boom!

The sound echoed through the cavern like a cannon shot, shaking the ledge and nearly knocking them off. Then a roar like a freight train seemed to come from the walls, the entire cavern first vibrating and then shaking back and forth.

Tarayon instinctively turned, crouching on hands and knees, pulling Citlalli down with him. Jamila backed against the wall, but quickly found herself off balance and falling toward the drop. She leaped to keep from plummeting off and twisted in midair to slam down on the edge, both arms the only thing holding her on.

Just as quickly the earthquake stopped, though the sound continued to echo and rumble in the distance.

Jamila was frantically clawing at the smooth rock pathway, trying to keep from sliding into oblivion. Tarayon squeezed past Citlalli and grasped one of Jamila's arms, then gradually took hold of her other hand and slowly pulled her up to safety.

After a minute spent regaining their breath, all three continued onward, safely exiting the dangerous cavern.

Lupe had been quietly gaining on them, not wanting to give away her presence, just in case these weren't her companions. The subterranean earthquake had shaken her just as much, but she was in a small flat cavern room and able to ride it out.

Unfortunately a few minutes after the shaking stopped, she took a wrong turn and the sounds of other climbers began fading away. Not sure what to do, but keeping her blinger at the ready, she continued bravely onward. Tackling a particularly steep descent, she heard a growing roar up ahead. She was about to turn around when her feet slipped in muddy slime created by eons of river mist, and she fell, sliding downhill; visions of falling off the cliff on Kreyon came rushing back. She frantically reached for the side walls, dropping her blinger and trying to stop, but there was nothing to grab. Princess Pat wasn't here to save her this time as she flew off the edge of a precipice into the black abyss.

Citlalli led her companions through another small rock entrance into a cathedral-like cavern. Stretching into the distance, multi-colored walls arched upward like the naves in a church, finally disappearing into the darkness of the ceiling far above. Jamila thought of the Taj Majal's magnificent interior. And right in the middle of this breathtaking rainbow cavern, a fast-rushing underground river carved a path. As they looked for an exit to this vast room, it seemed the only way out was the river.

"There's gotta be another exit hidden in here somewhere," said Tarayon.

"I don't think so," said Citlalli.

Jamila walked to the river's edge, peering at the dark and fast-moving water. She knelt down and dipped in her hand, causing ripples that reflected the colorful cavern walls. The water was surprisingly warm, almost like bathwater.

At that moment, floating downstream at high speed into the cavern was Lupe. She'd fallen off that slippery precipice thirty feet into this rushing river and been carried rapidly downhill. The river bottom and sides were slick and impossible to grasp, worn completely smooth by a river that had flowed underground for thousands of years.

She entered the cavern so quickly, no one had time to react. By now Lupe was frantic and when she saw Citlalli and the others, she screamed for all she was worth, her echoes bouncing in all directions. As she sailed past a dumbstruck Jamila and disappeared out the other exit, Lupe thought she heard Citlalli shout back. At least they'd seen her. For the moment all she could do was keep trying to grab ahold of something, doing her best to stay alive.

"We must follow Lupe," said Citlalli, "the river is our pathway now."

"Uh, I'm afraid I can't swim," said Jamila.

"And I don't do water well," said Tarayon.

"There is no time," said Citlalli, "do what you must." She leaped into the river before anyone could react, flowing out the exit in seconds.

Throwing his hands in the air with exasperation, Tarayon prepared to jump.

"Wait one full day for our return. Then...well, then it's up to you." He tossed his blinger to Jamila. "I truly despise water." Tarayon took a breath, closed his eyes and dove in after Citlalli.

CHOICES

Back on the surface it didn't take long for Summahon and the others to find Tarayon's crash site, even in the dark. Although the spacecraft was impaled in a tree, the ground was littered with shards of metal and debris. The sight of Tarayon's spacecraft stabbed straight through its midsection and dangling high up in the tree was amazing. They couldn't hold Summahon back from scaling the tree and happily confirming there were no bodies. After a brief debate the group convinced Summahon and Estrella to wait for dawn.

"Your report did reach Earth," said Wizza to Sklizz, as they rested against a tree, "and your sister was recognized for her heroic actions against the Doozies."

"I wondered if word got back before the zip sent us here. The kids told me Arizza and Stan, the U.S. Vice President, saved everyone's lives. They were both heroes and deserved to have Earth learn of their sacrifice."

"I still can't believe Tarayon got amulets from the Watchers. I can't believe that ziff-blinging Destroyer is dead."

Sklizz had never known Wizza well, but certainly admired her good looks. As they spoke about families and their recent experiences, he began to realize this Gelzian woman was something special. She reminded him of his sister Arizza.

Estrella, Einlen, and Gilad tried to sleep, while Summahon couldn't relax for a moment, counting the minutes until dawn, desperate to find Tarayon.

When first light finally arrived, they quickly found the cave and it was decided Einlen and Estrella would wait at the entrance, while the other four descended into the unknown. Estrella was torn between going and staying with her healing friend Einlen.

Being logical, she realized sending the four healthiest adults gave Citlalli and Lupe the best chance of rescue.

Sklizz, Summahon, Gilad, and Wizza began their descent, moving fast to try and catch the others.

Back in camp, Heather had come in and out of groggy consciousness, Yore trying to keep her sedated.

Waima sat quietly by herself, gradually falling into a long-overdue sleep.

Theal lay next to Heather, realizing the poor Human girl's only hope of survival was removing both legs. Theal also knew her own Watcher energy was fading. Yes, she'd been transformed into Human form, but it was meant to be temporary, and those blood-sucking slugs had shortened her time considerably. Theal knew she would transform soon and needed to act fast.

"So." she whispered, staring at her blinger, "what do I have to lose?"

FLUMING

Summers in Virginia could be murder, Chesapeake heat and humidity making life miserable. Lupe always looked forward to visiting a nearby waterpark. The rides she loved most were fully enclosed, superfast, downhill waterslides with corkscrew turns and a final drop into deep water.

Lupe was a strong swimmer and as the underworld river carried her ever deeper, she now figured this was the best waterslide in the universe. She had no idea how long it had been since falling off that precipice or glimpsing the others. It seemed like she'd fallen in minutes ago, but she knew it had been at least an hour, perhaps more. The river kept heading down, turning, twisting, flowing constantly deeper inside this underworld, and always with high walls, eerie light, and flickering shadows on each side. There was never anything to grab and it was impossible to stop on the slippery river bottom. So, Lupe quit fighting the water and rode this incredible waterslide to whatever fate awaited.

It was then she started to see nightmare things with glowing eyes on the shoreline. Not often, but as she quietly sailed along she'd catch them unaware, doing whatever it was they were doing: sinister black shapes with waving arms and glowing red star-shaped eyes. They were the scariest things she'd ever seen, even worse than Kreyons.

Once again Lupe was picking up speed, trying to peer ahead from cavern to cavern, to see what awaited her as this nocturnal river went faster and faster. It was getting darker and she could feel herself starting to tip downward, like the drop of a steep waterslide. Lupe had only an instant to notice the bottom rushing up, a millisecond to take a deep breath. As she hit, gravity pulled her under the water and she found herself spinning out of control, reaching incredible speeds inside a cave tube. The pummeling water knocked out what little air remained and she began to drown.

Citlalli wasn't far behind. The river scooted her past the same hideous underworld creatures as she searched the shoreline for Lupe. Citlalli's Anahuac senses told her the dark beings were not at all friendly.

Of course Citlalli had no waterslides in her ancient Anahuac world and the same was true for Tarayon. Like Earth cats, Trixians hated being in the water and Tarayon was miserable.

And so, like Lupe, Citlalli found herself falling, then nearly drowning in the cave tube before being ejected like a cannon-ball, spinning uncontrollably through the air and landing with a splash inside a large pond. Struggling to the surface, Citlalli gasped for air and tried to stay afloat. Getting her bearings she felt herself being carried in a circular motion around the pond. She was moving rapidly toward the center of a whirlpool, the pond water getting sucked down into darkness.

Citlalli wasn't a strong swimmer and this vortex was pulling her relentlessly toward oblivion. She began to do what all swim-mers should never do—panic.

"Citlalli!"

Glancing around frantically she spotted Lupe on a distant shore, waving something white. The big whirlpool was swing-ing and carrying her toward Lupe. If she didn't escape on this pass around, it would surely suck her under. One chance only and she kicked, trying to inch forward. Lupe had waded as close as possible to the vortex, swinging her camo-suit top like a lasso. Citlalli felt the whirlpool's suction growing stronger. Any hesita-tion would mean certain death. Lupe was ready to toss the camo-suit top like a life preserver. Unfortunately Citlalli swallowed more water, spluttering, coughing and trying to concentrate. Lupe's camo-suit fling landed near, but she missed it by inches. She kicked her legs harder. She had one last chance, head down and swimming against the current with every last bit of energy, reaching for all she was worth.

She had it!

Lupe struggled mightily, worried the camo-suit might rip, but seconds later she'd pulled Citlalli to safety on the shore of this mysterious pond. Lupe sat back, her shoulder hurting and reminding her that just a couple months ago it had been separated.

The girls sat on the shore catching their breath and gazing at water spewing out of the tunnel that delivered them here. Suddenly Tarayon spun wildly, shooting out of the same water tube, arcing across the pond as he fell. Twirling like an Earth cat to land on his feet, he did a major belly flop in front of Citlalli and Lupe, crawling out onto the solid rock shore, soaking wet, miserable, and exhausted.

PURSUIT

Far back upriver at the rainbow cavern river entrance, Jamila had found a secluded corner. Eerie light illuminated the colorful cavern like a dying campfire. Hidden by a rock formation, she'd been hearing someone or something approaching from the tunnels above. She grimly awaited their arrival with Tarayon's blinger.

From the opposite side of the cavern she heard shuffling and peeked out from behind the rocks. Moving mysteriously out of the shadowed walls were several of the star-eyed creatures. She stared in mute horror at shining reddish star-eyes, ugly sac-like heads and tentacles sprouting everywhere.

Jamila raised her blinger, ready to fire at these unholy things. It seemed they were waiting for something, facing the cavern's rock entrance. They didn't have long to wait.

Sklizz, Summahon, Wizza, and Gilad stepped into view, freezing at the sight of the creatures. Both groups stared down one another like wary gunfighters in the old West, the eternal river the only sound. No one moved...seconds dragged by...

Then the dark things started a crazed banzai charge, tentacles windmilling and piping voices screeching. Rapid-fire blinger blasts from Sklizz, and Jamila from her hiding place, turned two into puffs of ash. The other three reached the group with spinning tentacles, their razor-like fingers tearing gashes. Jamila dared not fire again, the combatants being too close together.

And then more of these things stepped from the shadows. Jamila saw her Earth enemy Gilad drive a knife through the last of the original five creatures. The beast's final dying act was tossing the hated Mossad agent toward her. The new group of monsters charged toward badly wounded Sklizz, Wizza, and Summahon. It would be a massacre.

Gilad staggered to his feet, seeing this disaster unfolding. A voice behind him screamed at the monsters, followed by rapid-fire blinger blasts. He saw the two largest creatures puff into nothingness. Gilad turned and saw Jamila, the hated terrorist he wanted dead. He hesitated only a moment before running over to her side, joining her in yelling at the monsters. The remaining creatures all turned at once, the ashes of their brothers still floating in the air. Shrieking in unison, their tentacles waving with rage and anger, the entire group charged at Jamila and Gilad.

There was no escape at the river's edge. The two Earth enemies shared a look of mutual understanding, fired one last blinger blast at the wind milling monsters, and leaped into the rushing water.

Backing out of the cavern, Sklizz watched the creatures dive in after Jamila and Gilad. But now even more monsters poured out of hidden exits in the walls.

"Run!" he screamed at Wizza and Summahon, all three staggering back up the way they'd come. Sklizz began firing intermittent bursts at the cavern entrance, trying to create a rock barrier. He managed a partial blockage, but it wouldn't hold them for long. They continued their desperate retreat back to the surface.

Sklizz was thinking about Citlalli down in this terrible place. What hope could she have even deeper inside this awful world? Well, there was nothing he or the others could do now, heavily outnumbered, badly wounded, and fleeing back to the surface.

Summahon was hurt the worst, but the thought of finding Tarayon pushed her on.

SEQUESTERED

Inside their locked room on Thrix's command ship, the three young Humans and sleeping Basset hound waited. They were anxious to know what was happening. Well, except Lucy. She hardly ever knew what was going on.

"Can I have some more water?" asked David.

Mary got another rationed cup from the water cooler. David had been thirsty since awakening, probably from the tranquilizer.

"I can't believe they shot you," said Mary, "right in my front yard!"

"Did Thrix say when we could get out of here?" asked David.

"No," said Maddy, "probably not till the battle's over."

"That's stupid. I want to see what's happening."

"How come we never heard about this battle on Earth?" said Mary.

They sat quietly; each knowing what was at stake.

Lucy continued to enjoy a relaxing nap, dreaming of dancing bones and biting horrible monsters in the foot.

The highest levels of government across Earth were in a state of shock. The failure of the allied defenses at the zip had seemed unthinkable. Within the hour most of the world knew of the imminent space battle between Earth's allies and the evil Doozy Empire.

To make matters worse, rumors of the Doozy planet-destroying weapon hit the street and panic erupted around the globe. In the face of this threat to the entire Human race, nearly all ongoing wars, terror activities, and other Earthly fighting came to a halt. If the allies lost, none of these petty earthly squabbles would matter anyway.

BELIEF

Far across the universe, Citlalli, Lupe, and Tarayon were also faced with a frightening reality. After searching the pond cavern, there seemed to be no way out except through the water's dark whirlpool.

"We'll never know without breathing deep and taking our chances," said Tarayon. "What was it you said before, Citlalli, about spirals?"

Citlalli thought for a moment.

"In my mind, the pattern is clear: we must perish in order to be born. The spiral of the serpent leads us back to where we began."

All three stared at the spiraling vortex sucking the pond water to an unknown fate.

"Perish in order to be born," said Tarayon, "and down the whirlpool?"

"The spiral of the serpent," said Lupe, "the river; the river is the serpent."

"It leads us back to where we began," finished Tarayon.

"Yes," said Citlalli, "In my mind, the pattern is clear."

Citlalli wondered how many eons water had shot from the river tube into this subterranean pond, then spun down into whatever lay below. *Were this underground river, pond and whirlpool here five thousand years ago when my family lived back home in Cemanahuac?*

"Well, there's only one way to find out where this serpent's spiral leads," said Tarayon. "I'll go first, and assuming we don't drown, I'll deal with any surprises at the other end."

As he prepared to leap into the water, and before he could react, Tarayon was receiving hugs from the two girls.

"I'll see you at the other end," said Lupe, smiling bravely.

"I don't think my visions would've brought us this far, only to drown in this terrible place," said Citlalli.

Tarayon marveled at how well these young Humans adapted to everything this crazy planet and universe was throwing at them.

"Are we ready?" said Tarayon.

Both kids stared wide-eyed and nodded. Tarayon noticed again the white streak in Lupe's dark black hair, distant evidence of her connection to Citlalli from five thousand years ago. He gave both girls as brave a Trixian smile as he could muster, then turned and ran, leaping toward the whirlpool's center. The girls saw his black jaguar head rise up, taking one deep breath as he spun around, before being sucked down into the darkness.

Citlalli was getting ready to leap.

"Citlalli," said Lupe.

Citlalli turned, her dark bronze face filled with grim Anahuac determination.

"I have no brothers or sisters. And I, well, I would be proud to call you my sister."

Citlalli saw Lupe had tears in her eyes and the two of them hugged—a fierce hug, the hug of two young women who might never see one another again.

"We must follow Tarayon to whatever waits," said Citlalli. "We must perish to be reborn. I will see you when we get there."

Citlalli smiled a dazzling smile and wiped her tears. Then before Lupe could reply, she was running and leaping for the whirlpool. With her long white hair flying behind her, Citlalli hit the water with a tiny splash and was gone in an instant.

Lupe's heart felt like it was fluttering fast as a hummingbird. She took a few shallow breaths and gazed one last time around the lonesome and ancient cavern. With one final deep breath she ran toward the pond.

She leaped.

Not too far back upstream, Jamila and Gilad were floating rapidly side by side. The current was keeping Jamila afloat, her inability to swim not really a problem, yet. Every once in a while they'd see the underworld creatures far behind, chasing them toward whatever lay ahead.

Since escaping into the river, neither had said a word. Gilad finally broke their silent stalemate.

"I wanted you dead," said Gilad.

"Ha! Well, I wanted you dead, too," said Jamila.

The two sworn Middle East enemies glared at one another.

"Truce?" said Gilad.

"Listen, Mossad, I've been through much these past few days, but that doesn't change what your people have done..." Jamila's black eyes pierced Gilad like twin lasers. "There can never be forgiveness; never. But we are far from Earth. You and I may never see home again. The eternal fight between our people seems much less important."

"We only took what was ours, defended ourselves against your unreasoning hatred. Your people should stop taking innocent lives and move on."

"Move on? Move on too where, Mossad? You stole our land." She glared at her eternal enemy. "Listen, Mossad, you and I, we will never agree. But that doesn't matter now; it doesn't matter here. We must work together if we're going to survive. I will honor a truce between you and me."

The two eternal enemies stared at one another, finally both nodding their heads with grim smiles. They both looked upriver toward the underworld monsters, their terrifying shadows still following.

It was good they didn't wait much longer, since the cave tube and subterranean pond were minutes away.

EREBUS

The pond vortex was strong, sucking Tarayon into another narrow cave tube, accelerating him like a bullet projectile and shooting him out the side of a high cave wall. Swallowing water and gasping, Tarayon flew through empty air and dropped thirty feet into calm, deep water. Struggling to the surface, he saw a shoreline nearby and moments later had crawled onto a slippery limestone beach.

Citlalli came next and her poor swimming ability was a problem. She'd already swallowed water in the cave tube, and the hard landing caused her to panic. She might've drowned if Lupe hadn't been following. Lupe's lifeguard training at her neighborhood pool taught her to wrap one arm over Citlalli's shoulder, across her chest, holding onto her opposite side armpit, then to swim with Citlalli face up out of the water.

Tarayon observed this rescue with fascination, helping Lupe pull Citlalli up onto the solid rock beach. He watched as Lupe pressed several times on Citlalli's chest, then pinched her nose and blew air into her mouth. After a couple times doing this, Citlalli was coughing and breathing again. Tarayon was supremely impressed.

As Citlalli sat up, taking deep breaths, they all looked around for the first time.

The water stretched to a distant gray horizon. The rock ceiling also faded into a gray blur overhead.

They had truly entered another world.

To their left, water gushed out of a cliff bordering this incredible and haunted twilight sea. The air in this underworld was warm and they were already drying off.

Turning inland, they saw a world of rocks, boulders, and ratty-looking gray scrub brush. Beyond this primordial landscape rose the barely visible, murky, shadowy outline of a horrifically shaped city.

Behind them, inside this eternally dark sea lived alien creatures that had never seen the light of day. Some had eyes, and many didn't. Most were albino-white, having no skin pigmentation because they had no sun. And in this eons-old haunted underworld they fought the never-ending battle to eat, and not be eaten.

Waves were now rippling just offshore as seven large, eyeless, ghostly pale things were quietly coasting toward the limestone beach. They sensed with their inbuilt radar three unsuspecting potential meals.

As the seven hungry amphibians approached, Citlalli turned in time to see them.

"Monsters!"

They all began moving quickly inland, away from these albino things.

Seconds later the creatures were hopping onto the beach on their four webbed and clawed feet, ready to give chase. However, at that precise moment Jamila and Gilad sailed out of the cave wall and slammed into the water with big splashes.

They both resurfaced, gasping for air with Jamila thrashing like a drowning person. As Gilad helped Jamila, he saw the carnivorous white things diving in after them.

"Quickly," said Gilad, "we're being chased." He helped Jamila dog-paddle frantically toward a more distant shore.

The many web-armed amphibians sensed this move and started to give chase. They were vastly superior swimmers and gaining rapidly. Gilad and Jamila didn't stand a chance.

Just then, flying out of the cave tube were the dozen star-eyed monsters that were chasing Jamila and Gilad. One after another they bombarded the seven swimming carnivores, and in seconds there was a frantic battle taking place between these two ancient underworld enemies.

By now Tarayon, Lupe, and Citlalli were far inland, happy they'd escaped whatever was crawling from the twilight sea. They were unaware of the life and death struggle going on back at the water.

Ahead of them lay the ruins of what must've been a vast alien city many millions of years ago. In the shadowy twilight of this unbelievably old and inhuman underworld everything seemed dark, sinister, and haunted.

"Can you sense anything?" whispered Tarayon.

"Whatever wishes us to be here lies ahead, inside this terrible place," said Citlalli.

They rounded a final jumble of rock and climbed carefully around the outside of an unstable rubble pile. Directly in front of them was a vertical city wall made of large interlocked stones. There seemed to be no way inside.

Back at the water, Jamila and Gilad finally staggered onto the shore, turning to see the desperate battle between Obaddon monsters. The dark, star-eyed beasts' numerical superiority had won out, killing all the albinos. However, only two survived and made it ashore, both bleeding bluish blood from multiple bite wounds. The white amphibians hadn't gone down without a fight.

Jamila and Gilad began moving inland, but their angle toward the city left them vulnerable, and within a minute they'd been boxed into a rock strewn corner, face-to-face with the two surviving monsters.

The things shrieked, windmilled their razor-sharp tentacles, and banzai charged, their way of striking fear into their enemy as they struck.

Desperate, Gilad and Jamila picked up rocks and began firing them, knowing they were futile weapons against these monsters. However, the confusion on the beasts' star-eyed sac-faces was priceless. They'd never experienced projectile weapons of any kind in this primordial world and came to a full stop, tentacles twitching in surprise. When more rocks were thrown they screeched and fled back toward the water.

Jamila and Gilad didn't wait to see if they changed their minds, and began running toward the distant city.

After a brief search of the ancient city's stone wall, Citlalli found a crack they could squeeze through.

Before their eyes was a cityscape of bizarre angles and warped shapes, totally alien and unsettling: mushroom statues, spiral platforms, upside-down structures, smashed debris, freakish doorways, cone shapes, slanted obelisks, and windows into dark murky interiors—a strange and frightening shadowed nightmare come to life.

And somewhere deep inside this unfathomably old and alien place they could see sickly jaundiced light crawling upward into the oppressive gray twilight. And occasionally, they heard distant sounds like the scurrying of rats in the walls.

Tarayon's senses were on full alert. This place oozed with menace.

Lupe could barely breathe. She'd thought things couldn't get any scarier, but now she wanted to scream and run away.

Citlalli felt terrified, yet strangely calm, knowing they were nearing their journey's end in this million-year-old hive.

Moving quietly toward the pale light, they discovered a well-worn narrow pathway between unnerving, oddly bent and twisted structures. Lupe and Citlalli huddled next to Tarayon as they walked these dark and menacing streets. Coming to a dead end, their only way forward was up. Bizarrely shaped grips in stuck out of a steep wall, perhaps used ages ago by tentacle beings. Halfway up, one of Citlalli's grips broke loose. Lupe extended her arm and held Citlalli, stopping her from falling. It was slow going, but they finally climbed onto another walkway. Looking down an empty corridor, they could see light filtering through an opening far up ahead. A nasty, horrid stench of rot rolled over them from whatever lay ahead.

They were getting close.

HORDES

History tells us that in 410 A.D. Alaric led his Visigoth armies in the sacking of Rome, unleashing Dark Ages across Earth. Now Commander Rooq's Doozy and mercenary hordes were moving toward the sacking of Earth and Mars. They planned on crushing the Humans and their friends, starting a Galactic Dark Age of their own.

Advance scouts brought news of their approach to Thrix and the allied defenders. Thrix relayed instructions for the defense of Mars. Whatever happened here around this red planet would determine the fate of both Human and allied galaxies.

Inside their locked room, David, Maddy, Mary, and Lucy heard Thrix on the ship's communications channel. They knew the first waves of attackers were expected in an hour. It was frustrating to sit here, helpless, but there seemed nothing else they could do.

With so much at stake, all Earth had a live multi-camera televised link to Thrix's bridge. Most of Earth's billions were watching. After so many false predictions of the Second Coming, global Armageddon, and other doomsday scenarios these past thousand years, the actual end of the world was really, finally, truly at hand.

TRANFORMATION

Back at the waterfall camp on Obaddon, Heather was coming in and out of delirium, the pain in her legs far beyond any soothing leaves Yore could find. Her breath was getting more and more ragged, and even to an alien like Yore, it was obvious Heather would die soon if something wasn't done. He was lizard-sick with worry for this gutsy Human friend he'd found on this lousy, miserable planet. He had to find an answer. There had to be some way to help Heather. Yore didn't know what he'd do if she died.

Waima sat next to Heather, wishing there was something she could do to help this suffering Human. Until now all she'd seen from Humans was compassion, determination, humor, bravery, and loyalty. These were traits her father had taught were important.

While Yore and Waima fretted, Theal lay quietly on the other side of Heather. She hadn't spoken in hours, eyes closed in intense concentration.

"Come," said Yore, "let's try to find something that will help us..." His tongue flicked in and out and he sighed. He was going to say *when we're removing her legs*, but couldn't get out the words.

He rose and Waima followed him into the surrounding forest. Waima had no idea what she was looking for, but this was better than sitting by that poor Human girl.

The moment Yore and Waima were out of sight, Theal's eyes bolted open, staring at the pinkish sky overhead. She'd been gathering her remaining strength, preparing for what needed to be done. Theal smiled, knowing her pathway was clear. It was time to transform from this life and use her lingering strength and power in one very special way.

Theal slowly sat up and gazed down at the delirious, sweating, and dying Heather. As she smiled again she could feel her Human eyes crinkle. What a strange physical sensation...to be inside a body. Being Human for a short time had given Theal an appreciation for the fragility of life and the bravery of these mortal beings.

She called upon her remaining Watcher powers.

It was time.

Several miles away, Einlen and Estrella waited at the hidden cave entrance. Estrella was happy Einlen was sleeping. Her terrible wound was healing, but it still amazed Estrella that Einlen had even survived after having her arm blown off. Even more incredible was how she'd swum one-armed in that terrible ocean filled with frenzied sea monsters, rescuing Estrella and getting them both safely to land.

Estrella gazed fondly at this ferocious-looking female Uppsalian. They'd been through much since being paired up in that tiny spaceship on Anubar.

A rustling noise in the forest brought Estrella's senses to full alert. She saw nothing, but could feel a presence. All she had was a wooden dagger. She held it tight and watched the surrounding woods.

During their short walk around the campsite, Yore and Waima found nothing to help Heather. Yore spent the time thinking about how to amputate Heather's legs. If she lived, they'd make something to pull her. Yore's species had yellow hearts and his was breaking.

Waima thought about the last day with her dad on the spacecraft. He'd talked about a new future for Doozies, and how proud he was of Waima. The road ahead would be incredibly hard, and now she faced it alone. Of course none of this would matter if she didn't make it back home.

They reentered the camp and glanced over at sleeping Heather, knowing the time to amputate both legs had come. Looking closer they noticed Theal was missing.

"Stay close beside me," whispered Yore.

He led Waima around the campfire, ready to spring on any intruders. The hillside was quiet but shadows were everywhere. Yore prayed there were no more waterfall beasts. After a brief look around they approached the sleeping Heather.

Something wasn't right.

"Do you smell...burning?" said Yore.

"Yes," said Waima, "like energy bolts."

Yore dropped to the ground where Theal had been. It was charred and he could feel lingering heat.

"I think Theal caused this," said Yore.

"Over here," said Waima. She held up some kind of recording device.

"What are you doing here?"

Yore and Waima spun around, seeing Heather aiming a rock with her pitching arm, murderous intent in her eyes as she glared at Waima.

"Step away from my friend, Doozy, or I smash your head!"

Heather was standing on two perfectly healthy legs.

Still sitting at the cave entrance, Estrella continued hearing movement in the surrounding forest, but whatever it was remained out of sight. She wanted to wake up Einlen, but knew her friend needed to sleep. Yawning, she sat her dagger down for a moment to stretch.

In that split second Estrella was yanked into the air and whisked away into the dark forest.

Einlen continued to sleep peacefully.

SPEARHEADS

A first glimpse of the massive Doozy war machine appeared on the allies' distant tracking screens. Their arrival into Mars space was imminent.

Thrix had a thousand allied battle cruisers in a helix formation in front of Mars. They would move in a five-thousand-mile-wide spiral attack, hoping to catch the Doozies by surprise.

Inside their locked room, David still fumed, while Maddy tried finding her inner calm, willing the room's alien lock to concede defeat. In seconds she won the battle, the lock tumbling and the door was sliding open.

Maddy beamed triumphantly at David, and he gave her a smile and high five in return.

Mary watched all this with quiet amazement, then awakened Lucy from her bone-burying dreams so they could follow the older kids.

On board Exterminator II, Oophak and his fellow Doozy suicide heroes were hidden behind the front wave of Doozy ships. In moments, Oophak would fly Exterminator II past the front lines. After locking in final instructions and accelerating toward Mars, Oophak would unleash Armageddon. Within seconds the entire allied space fleet would be incinerated, having no time to escape Exterminator II's awesome power. Moments later Mars would be overrun by the blast wave and scorched clean.

Now Rooq ordered Xox and his ten million mercenaries to take their strategic positions around Earth. The moment Mars was incinerated, they'd descend upon Humanity.

On board Thrix's command ship, David, Maddy, Mary, and Lucy had located the main bridge. Thrix saw them and nodded. They deserved to be here.

The kids had no idea a camera had spotted them and they were being watched worldwide. Even their families saw this amazing sight from the comfort of their homes. David and Maddy's parents had been released once the kids' location with Thrix was confirmed. The Earth TV director kept one camera on the kids, while several others focused on the approaching Doozies.

The end of the world was being broadcast live.

The Doozies began firing laser cannons, even though they were too far away. Thrix was concerned, wondering why they were wasting laser power.

"Something is coming from behind the defenders' front line," said the intercom.

"Magnify," said Thrix. "This must be the reason for the laser fire."

On the screen was a weaponless spacecraft sailing toward them at high speed. A terrible truth hit Thrix. This was their planet killer. If it had the power to work from this far away, their space fleet and Mars were doomed.

"Do we have anyone in striking range?" asked Thrix.

"Nothing closer than us," said his second.

"Entire fleet," said Thrix on the intercom, "top speed toward the approaching spacecraft. Stay in helix formation. Everyone go now!"

The entire armada began its synchronized helix attack, but this took time...time they didn't have.

Rooq watched this unfold, a Doozy sneer on his pasty face. These enemies had underestimated ol' Rooq. He admired the creative allied attack, but it wouldn't matter. In seconds Exterminator II would detonate. Nothing would survive.

Things had worked perfectly. After Mars was fried, he'd unleash Xox and his mercenary soldiers to finish off Humanity. The five hundred transports were already in place around Earth awaiting his go-ahead.

Across the globe people everywhere huddled together, seeing events unfold on Thrix's bridge, including the kids' wide-eyed stares. As a species it would be fair to say the entire Human race finally achieved the impossible task of considering themselves one family.

David, Maddy, and Mary also saw the tiny Exterminator II, a white smudge against black space. Lucy was paying more attention to colorful blinking lights off to one side and sniffing the stale spacecraft air.

"How long until they're in firing range," said Thrix.

"Four minutes," said his second.

"When we reach thirty seconds, I want dispersed firing from everyone. Maybe we'll get lucky."

On Exterminator II, Oophak and his copilots said final prayers, ready to head into Doozy history. Their glorious sacrifice would be legend forever.

All three Doozies looked at one another.

"It is time," said Oophak.

The others nodded and stared out at the distant red speck called Mars. Oophak pushed the final button.

Exterminator II would detonate in ten seconds.

HOOLOO

As the destruction of Mars began, the threesome of Tarayon, Lupe, and Citlalli had quietly reached a slanted balcony where light was shining. The awful smell was nearly overwhelming, but the only way to see the ground below was on this shaky-looking balcony.

"Wait for me," said Tarayon. He slowly slid onto it, wiggling and trying to make it move, but apparently it was stronger than it looked.

"There's a railing we can hide behind."

Tarayon moved forward, followed by the girls. They peeked over the railing, looking down at a sea of star-eyed creatures around a blasphemous black altar. These monstrous things kept whisper-chanting the word "Hooloo." It also seemed obvious the eye-watering stench must come from these degenerate beings.

Behind this ghastly scene of worship a stream of gray mist floated down from the darkness far above. Since there was no wind in this underworld, the water fell straight down, never drifting. The gentle mist landed in a tiny lake, its glistening water trickling out of sight toward the distant sea.

Citlalli saw someone seated on the altar, partly hidden by strangely shaped columns that supported a weird cone-shaped roof.

"I think that's Tyson."

Tarayon and Lupe peered close.

"Who else could it be in this place," said Tarayon.

"What can we do?" said Lupe.

"Come on," said Tarayon, "we'll find a way down."

Coming from the opposite direction were Gilad and Jamila. Each carried sharp weapons they'd found as they walked through the alien city. They'd wandered, searching for the others and reaching several dead-ends before finally stumbling on the altar stream. Cautiously they followed it uphill toward the distant light. They whispered back and forth, caught again in their eternal mutual anger.

"My two brothers and parents were killed by Mossad," said Jamila, "how do you expect me to feel?"

"Were they were innocent in shedding my people's blood?"

"You and your family never took the lives of my people?"

Getting closer to the light, they crept in silence.

"I'll make you a deal, Jamila."

"I don't make deals with my enemy, Mossad."

"Just hear me out, and please call me Gilad."

Jamila thought this over. Since they were probably about to die anyway, it wasn't unreasonable, but still...

"Don't push it Mossad. Go ahead; tell me of your...deal."

"When we get home, you and I will persuade our peoples to work out a peace. Stop the endless killing."

Jamila looked in the eyes of Gilad. An enemy she wanted dead when this crazy journey began. She could understand why he was a good Mossad leader.

"I think the odds of our surviving the next hour are slim, and the chance of our people's listening to us even slimmer, but I will consider your suggestion...uh, Gilad."

He smiled and she couldn't help but smile back.

"How in Allah's name did we end up here Mossad?"

"God must have a sense of humor after all."

Just ahead from the shadows walked a creature. Jamila and Gilad instantly attacked with their daggers, Jamila going for the things midsection, while Gilad sank his deep into its star-eye. Shrieking, the monster fled back into the dark building, Gilad's dagger buried inside its head.

"So much for the element of surprise," said Jamila.

They moved uphill faster, peering around debris at the thousands of chanting creatures. To their amazement, sitting in a daze on a twisted altar stone was a young man—a Human—that neither of them recognized.

GAMS

The last time Heather had seen a Doozy was in the Death Arena on Yerti—not the fondest of memories. The sight of this white Doozy that Yore called Waima was blood-curdling. Yore quickly explained Heather's delirious past two days, since nearly being killed by that waterfall monster, and how Waima came to Obaddon.

"Now," said Yore, "tell me if ya saw Theal."

"Who's Theal?"

"She was lying next to ya, a Watcher turned Human, and very sick. She's up and disappeared."

Heather looked around, confused.

Waima still hadn't spoken, shocked to see Heather's healthy legs. Those legs had been savagely broken and splintered.

"Somethin' happened," said Yore. "Yer legs were broken into pieces."

Heather's eyes opened wide, memories of being swung by the monster flooding back. She gasped, remembering mind-numbing pain, now looking down and marveling at her healthy legs. Her camo-suit had been neatly sheared mid-thigh, leaving Heather wearing white shorts.

"I...remember," said Heather.

"Theal was lyin' next to ya when we come back and the ground was warm, like an energy spike. And there ya are with two legs, good as new."

Waima was still fiddling with the device they'd found, and suddenly Theal's voice burst forth.

"Farewell, friends...my transformation is upon me. My mortal body is done. I willingly use my remaining energy to replace what's horribly broken with something very new. My only regret is not being able to stay and see how they're put to use."

They heard Theal chuckle.

"Watcher thoughts are with you; may universal energy and light watch over you; farewell, my friends, farewell. Always let the Light shine through you."

All three remained silent for a few moments.

"Did this...Theal—did she fix my legs?"

"I'm thinkin' she did."

Heather ran both hands over her new legs. They felt real. How had Theal...how had she done this?

She knelt to pick up her ragged softball cap and slapped it on her head.

Waima watched all this with intense concentration. These Humans never ceased to amaze her. She found enough courage to speak, "I'm honored to meet you." She extended her hand in the ritual she'd seen Humans do many times.

Heather looked at this tiny Doozy, finding it hard to think anything good about an alien race that tried to kill her and had murdered several of her friends.

"Tell me about the Supreme Doozy," said Heather.

"My father and I tried to kill him with a bomb on Yerti, but failed. We barely escaped to Mars."

Heather's mouth fell open with undisguised surprise. She slowly raised her hand and grasped Waima's.

"If what you say is true, I'm pleased to meet you."

Waima blushed a Doozy pale green and smiled.

"Okay, we're all frien's. Come on, gals, let's go find the others."

They started toward Theal's crash site. Yore led followed by Waima with Heather in the rear.

Heather noticed a peculiar feeling in her legs. It was all she could do to walk slowly. Her legs had the desire to break free and run like the wind. She noticed the scars and freckles that made her original legs unique were gone. Each leg was perfectly smooth with no marks, freckles, hairs, or anything other than sleek, pale skin. She didn't know who Theal was, but silently thanked her.

ARMAGEDDON

Everything had led to this instant in galactic time, with two mind-bogglingly huge space fleets facing off to determine the fate of Mars, Earth, and so much more.

The allied space fleet was still far away and directly in Exterminator II's line of fire. They'd be vaporized as its planet-killing pulse wave rolled toward Mars. There was no hope all the alien allies and every Human on Earth.

Oophak's timer hit 3...2...1...

Some people who'd lived through past atomic bombs on Earth were blinded by their intense brightness. As Exterminator II detonated it was even brighter.

On Thrix's spacecraft and the video link to Earth, everyone instinctively looked away.

On Thrix's bridge only one individual didn't know what was going on: Lucy. She flinched at the flash, her canine cranium spinning madly. This happened in a Basset hound nanosecond, causing an instantaneous and powerful telepathic request to speed forth, the instruction clear: BRIGHT LIGHT STOP!

A couple of seconds later the Exterminator II blast froze in space, an intense miniature star between both space fleets.

Everyone stared at this unbelievable sight—everyone except Lucy. The hurtful light was still there, so she turned away to find something more interesting, forgetting the brightness. Set free, the explosion continued, but now with no forward momentum, its immense lethal power and energy spreading outward as a massive deadly cloud.

The Doozy fleet had been following Exterminator II at top speed.

Rooq shrieked to stop, but his message was too late for hundreds of Doozy battle cruisers as they were incinerated by the remnants of Exterminator II.

Continuing to shout commands, Rooq led his decimated space fleet around the nightmare cloud. Thrix's armada continued their spiral helix attack run, and as both fleets intersected they began the largest space battle ever in the Milky Way galaxy.

INVASION

A furious Rooq spoke to Xox, whose spacecraft was stationed above Paris.

"Exterminator failed...attack Earth now. Deploy armies... begin slaughter. We'll join after Mars falls. Win battle like old times."

Xox's sharp teeth glistened in anticipation. The time for total Earth invasion had arrived.

His first order was a laser strike on every known Earth military site. As the five hundred Doozy transports descended, this devastating laser barrage wiped out nearly all Human air and ground defense. The Doozy ships also blasted many communications satellites into space junk. There was nothing left to fight back.

The extermination of the Human race had begun.

Amongst the mercenary soldiers, all forcibly taken from their home worlds, word spread fast about Exterminator II. As the army of ten million grumbled, they descended toward five hundred Earth landing sites. Each transport would unleash twenty thousand unstoppable killing soldiers.

However, on some transports there were a few brave mercenaries taking matters into their own feelers, wings, appendages, claws, tails, orifices, tentacles, and hands.

As the invasion began, millions of people were fleeing targeted locations.

Fourteen-year-old Oriel Dumont lived with her family in a suburban home east of Paris. Their neighborhood had watched an amazing light show as bright laser beams sliced out of the overcast night sky, causing distant explosions and fires as they decimated French military locations.

As the laser attack stopped, an enormous spacecraft descended rapidly over Paris. Oriel climbed atop a nearby fence for a better look. She saw the spacecraft vanish below the horizon into Paris. At that moment a second transport emerged from nearby clouds. It landed incredibly fast, on the ground in a heartbeat less than a kilometer away.

People in surrounding neighborhoods and throughout the area watched this landing in stunned amazement. Then screams and mass panic ensued.

Before Oriel knew what happened, people and cars were flying in every direction. She hopped down and started running to find her family, but was knocked down and hit her head on the sidewalk. Later, groggily opening her eyes, Oriel found she was all alone on the dark street.

Oriel pushed herself up, feeling the bump on her head where it had hit the cement. She slowly got to her feet, head throbbing, and saw a couple of figures moving toward her. With a growing sense of dread, she realized they were moving too fast for people.

In seconds Oriel stood before two very different alien creatures, petrified with fear and expecting to die.

One alien seemed to have three heads but no visible eyes or mouths. The second had one head that sort of looked like a frog, but with three eyes, six arms, and three legs, several holding weapons. The two aliens were jabbering and making bizarre sounds. Oriel was petrified, shaking uncontrollably and waiting to be killed.

Finally the frog thing raised one of its weapons and peered at her with three silver eyes. It rattled more alien gibberish and rolled a horrible green tongue around its enormous mouth. Oriel flinched as it reached out and grabbed her arm. She felt tingling all over her body, seeing everything around her fade to black.

On the other side of Earth, fourteen-year-old Anne McDonald had grown up in Darwin, Australia, always hearing about the surprise Japanese attack on Darwin Harbor, February 19, 1942.

Anne was tired of watching the depressing invasion news and wandered off to her favorite hillside spot overlooking Darwin harbor. She was the first to see two alien transports far away over the Pacific Ocean. Lasers shot out of one with deadly accuracy, tearing apart several naval vessels. Anne was horrified, thinking this must've been what it was like, seeing the Japanese fighters and dive bombers approaching Darwin.

As the transports arrived, one landed at the edge of Darwin, while to Anne's surprise the second continued and stopped directly overhead. Not sure if she should run or hide, Anne felt the same tingling and blackness that Oriel had experienced. As Anne vanished, the other ships mercenary soldiers were already on the streets of Darwin, killing anything that moved.

In Buenos Aires, Estrella's friend Salvador hadn't seen her since their brief reunion atop the Pyramid of the Moon at Teotihuacan.

On this day of Earth invasion he and his family were in one of Buenos Aires's oldest parks, Parque Tres de Febrero. Along with thousands of others, they saw three Doozy spaceships in a triangle formation surrounding the city. There was some panic, but mostly quiet praying and watching.

Salvador was terrified, but he could still marvel at the awesome sight of these spacecraft. The closest was spinning slowly as a bright laser beamed out toward the heavily populated Palermo neighborhood. Explosions and flames shot skyward. Now panic hit the crowd, people screaming and running in all directions.

Salvador's family didn't move from their spot by the lake, and thus saw something very strange. One of the other transports fired its laser at the spacecraft right above them. Internal explosions blasted shrapnel into the sky like shiny confetti and in horrific slow motion the huge saucer-shaped spacecraft fell straight toward the park's lake.

Most of the crowd, including Salvador's family, broke out of their trance and ran away from the lake. The gigantic spacecraft smashed into the water, tipping over upside-down, its upper half falling onto dozens of buildings, flattening them. Lake water turned into a mini-tsunami and hundreds still near the shoreline were swallowed up into the churning and steaming water.

Salvador and the horrified crowd looked toward the heavens to see what was next. Staring back was an empty blue sky. The other two spacecraft had vanished.

Cody Smithers had also survived the Teotihuacan battle with Salvador and Estrella. He was now with his parents, fleeing Tampa Bay after laser attacks on the many Air Force locations. All radio was silent and no one knew what was happening. The roads were jammed with unmoving vehicles.

Cody and his parents got out of their car and joined everyone else in watching tiny space fighters locked in an amazing dogfight. And then the larger transports began firing upon one another.

Watching from the ground, it was hard to figure out who was fighting who or what was going on. After a minute of intense fire, one transport exploded with tremendous violence, flaming debris spread across the sky. Seconds later the shock wave hit with a roar that knocked people to the ground, vibrating the earth like a Florida quake.

Somewhere over Russia, Xox's command ship was getting conflicting messages from around the globe. Mercenary armies were overrunning Los Angeles, Tokyo, Mumbai, and London, but he was losing contact with more and more transports. It couldn't be Human weapons and he detected no alien presence. A worried Xox began moving his command ship toward northern Europe.

An hour earlier, onboard spacecraft over Paris and Darwin, Oriel and Anne had been recruited by the rebels. Now wearing universal translators, they could understand every word and knew what they must do.

WHIPPERSNAPPERS

Lucy's innocent power had saved Mars, but the battle was still being lost. Thrix's skills had kept their flagship alive, but the Doozies' superior weapons and wartime experience were too much. Spacecraft were being blasted into pieces and thousands of aliens tossed like confetti across the blackness of space.

Rooq was trying to find the allied commander's vessel. As he destroyed a smaller Gelzian vessel, Rooq spotted Thrix's spacecraft. In moments he was in range, opening fire immediately.

Thrix had been saving three smaller vessels when Rooq sneak-attacked. Thrix returned fire, but a direct hit to the main bridge sliced a hole that began venting everyone into space and certain death.

Near the back, David, Maddy, and Mary barely had time to grasp a railing. Lucky Lucy had been snooping behind a console, and was now plastered against its far side as the deadly vacuum sucked everything out into space. Thrix was hanging on for dear life with his two remaining arms.

David could see Maddy and Mary's hands loosening, moments from letting go. Maddy's eyes were pleading as he saw her about to be ripped off the railing. David reacted on instinct.

Seconds later emergency repair drones stopped the venting with a sealant over the hole.

Thrix sadly noticed the kids were gone, suffering a gruesome space death. Only the tiny dog remained.

But Thrix was mistaken.

Rooq was lining up a final killing shot at the command spacecraft when three Humans appeared on his bridge.

David's instantaneous teleporting had saved Mary and Maddy as they materialized in front of Rooq's big view screen.

David had been tightly holding onto the wireless TV as it ripped off in the transfer. He dropped it to the floor where it amazingly still broadcast a skewed wide-screen image of the Doozy bridge and all three kids. Billions on Earth could see everything, while Thrix's bridge saw nothing and assumed the kids were dead.

Viewers saw Mary holding a ripped-off titanium railing in her hands, the bottom end torn and bent at an angle.

And everyone could see four Doozies.

Rooq detected no weapons or bombs, figuring these were harmless spawn from the other ship. He signaled an assistant to stun them. They would be his prisoners to toy with later. The aide fired a stun blast that slammed David against the wall.

Maddy focused her mind on wrecking weapons. Her mind ripped off alien knobs and controls from around the bridge, causing them to fall and scatter across the floor. Several rolled toward the young Humans.

Rooq was livid and pale green with anger, screaming at his subordinates. He turned and fired a stun blast that knocked Maddy to her knees, then turned back to eliminate Thrix's allied command vessel.

Wobbling on her knees, Maddy found an inner strength she never knew she had, and mentally sent electric bursts that dropped Rooq's subordinates to the ground, quivering and shaking uncontrollably. The mental power surge also sent Maddy into convulsions. By now David had managed to sit up, and he took the shivering Maddy into his arms.

Rooq turned back again, greener than ever. He'd had enough interruptions. He reset his weapon to kill, to incinerate these Humans.

David tried teleporting them, but the stun blast left him unable to focus. Maddy was incoherent and Mary still stood frozen and helpless with the metal railing in her hands. Everyone on Earth was riveted to their video screens, turning away as Rooq raised his blinger.

Heart speeding in her chest, Mary saw the cruelest of smiles stretch Rooq's scarred face. Ten-year-old rage broke her trance. With determination and backyard instinct she raised her metal railing as Rooq prepared to fire, and using the bent end like a hockey blade she drilled one of the rolling control knobs with a wicked slap shot. The hard projectile smashed off Rooq's forehead as he fired, causing his shot to incinerate a Doozy chair instead of Maddy. As Rooq staggered and tried to shoot again, Mary slid over to a second knob just like she did on her back lawn and ripped off a one-timer that ricocheted off Rooq's good eye, smashing his eye-bone and knocking him to the floor, twitching and senseless. For good measure Mary rifled a final knob toward Rooq's five-hole, scoring a direct hit between his legs. The effect on a male Doozy was full paralysis. Rooq jerked to rigid attention on the ground like a wooden plank.

The global Earth audience had seen it all.

On board Thrix's command vessel it was obvious they were sitting ducks awaiting a final Doozy killing blast. It was surprising they hadn't already been blown to pieces.

As Thrix and his crew watched, the view screen blinked back on. Staring back were David, Maddy, and Mary from the bridge of the Doozy command ship.

SYZYGY

As the fight for Earth and Mars continued, Yore, Waima, and Heather first found Tarayon's tree house spacecraft and then the cave entrance, where only Einlen remained.

Einlen had awoken to find Estrella gone, and by the time the others arrived knew something bad had happened.

They searched the area around the cave but found nothing. Einlen was happy to see Heather's miracle legs and privately hoped for a similar Estrella miracle. They decided to return to the waterfall campsite, hoping Estrella and the others would return there.

Einlen would never show emotion, but inside she was worried about Estrella in ways she never thought possible.

Thirty minutes after they left the cave entrance someone else arrived, but not Estrella.

Wizza, Summahon, and Sklizz had fought their way back to the surface, using their lone blinger to fight off the star-eyed beasts. They each had deep gashes caused by the monsters' razor-like tentacles, and as they emerged from the cave, Sklizz tried blasting the entrance closed. The monsters' piping was close as rocks started falling. They saw several monsters crushed as the entrance sealed shut, the piping screams of the underworld beasts echoing from within.

Summahon was hurt the worst. In fact, Wizza was surprised she'd had the strength to make it back to the surface. They built a stretcher out of branches and sturdy leaf material. She'd lost a lot of blood and might not survive. They tried cocooning her in very large leaves for warmth. An exhausted Wizza and Sklizz struggled as they carried Summahon toward the waterfall camp.

Far beneath Obaddon's surface, Tarayon, Lupe, and Citlalli had managed to sneak much closer to the star-eyed creatures and Tyson on the altar. They still weren't sure what to do, watching and listening to the incessant chanting.

On the opposite side, a mere hundred yards away, Jamila and Gilad had spotted and watched Sklizz and the kids move to their new hiding place. They could also see a couple of monsters moving in the trio's direction. The monsters hadn't seen them yet, but in a minute they'd be discovered.

"Is there any way we can signal?" said Gilad.

"I only have my dagger," said Jamila.

The monsters were getting closer.

"We have to distract them," said Jamila.

Gilad took a moment. Then he nodded resolutely, stood, and flung a rock at the mass of star-eyed monsters.

"Over here, you alien octopuses!"

Jamila stood and threw her dagger, pleased when it stabbed deep into one of them.

The monsters approaching Citlalli and the others saw Gilad and Jamila and ran back down. However, the entire mass of monsters had turned toward Gilad and Jamila, tentacles raised like unholy antennae.

"I'm not so sure we'll have that chance to create a peace between our peoples," said Jamila.

"It's enough for me that you were willing to try," said Gilad.

They both looked at one another and smiled.

"It was a nice idea," said Jamila as the monsters continued moving toward them. "But it doesn't matter now; it's time to fly Mossad."

"If it's our time to die, I will fight by your side."

"Well then, Mossad...Gilad...let's give these monsters a run for their money."

Jamila took the lead and Gilad followed, sprinting downhill alongside the underworld river.

Sklizz, Lupe, and Citlalli were shocked to see Jamila and Gilad. Their suicidal stunt happened so fast, and then they were gone with the entire mob of dark things in pursuit.

Just as surprising was seeing the altar now shimmer and disappear, followed by a flash of light from the top room of a tall, oddly shaped, pointy tower next to the misty waterfall lake.

"Follow me," said Tarayon, taking a roundabout path toward the tower. They moved stealthily through the shadows and lingering stench, the sound of monsters chasing Jamila and Gilad fading in the distance.

The closer they got the more Citlalli felt they were staring into something vile and beyond all understanding. "Great Quetzalcoatl," prayed Citlalli, "help me fight the evil presence in this terrible place."

Climbing a small, twisted snake-like ramp, they reached the entrance of the narrow cone-shaped tower. It seemed they'd made it undetected. Tarayon led the way inside, climbing winding stairs that were more like a slide, as though built for crawling things. There were no windows and no lights, except for whatever waited at the top floor, nearly two hundred feet up. The only sound was their shuffling feet on the strange spiral ramp.

Knowing the underworld ocean held monsters of its own, Jamila and Gilad ran along the shoreline, hoping to find an escape route. With screaming red-eyed madness chasing them, they came up against a dead-end wall of rock that stretched far out into the ocean. As experienced warriors they could see no escape and only a small ledge to climb upon. After scaling the wall, they stood on the tiny outcropping fifteen feet up, staring down at a stinking sea of writhing tentacles and star-eyes. The creatures were now deathly silent, just staring up at Jamila and Gilad. The two Humans gradually caught their breath, each grimly aware there was no way out.

"I always knew I'd die fighting an enemy, but I never thought I'd go to Allah beside my enemy," said Jamila.

"That makes two of us."

They watched the closest monsters start moving, tentacles grasping for holds on the cliff face.

"Tell me Gilad, our Gods both preach mercy and love, right?"

"Yes, mercy, love, and forgiveness."

Jamila looked at Gilad, tears running down her face.

"Then I ask your forgiveness, Gilad, for anything I've done in this Earthly life that has been wrong or sinful."

Gilad's own eyes brimmed with tears.

"Of course, Jamila, you have my absolute forgiveness."

Jamila smiled.

"I too forgive you…Gilad, for any sinful or wrong acts you have committed during your life."

A tentacle reached up for Gilad and he kicked it away, nearly losing his balance. Jamila reached over and grasped his hand. Once they were both sturdy, each looked down at their clasped hands, then back up at one another, ironic smiles on their faces.

The monsters were climbing and more tentacles were reaching upward, nearly upon them.

For two who'd spent their lives fighting and cheating death, no more words were needed. Jamila and Gilad each knew their time was finally up. They gave one another slight nods and smiles, once deadly enemies now two Human comrades at the end, turning back toward the sea of aliens. Still holding hands, Jamila and Gilad leaped into eternity.

GRAVITY-FALLS

As Tarayon, Lupe, and Citlalli climbed the strange and ever narrowing cone tower; it became obvious there was no escape from this building. They'd entered the only doorway and climbed around bizarre winding stairs until nearly reaching the lighted room. As it came into view, they saw a level entrance area in front of a large round opening. The light spilled out, beckoning them inside. The awful presence waiting for them was making Citlalli want to scream. They didn't hesitate, stepping into the room.

The room had one window with the hazy mist of the waterfall right outside. Next to the window and far wall was a tall liquid container with a fully clothed Tyson inside, eyes closed and floating. Citlalli and Lupe gasped, thinking Tyson was dead. However, a single heartbeat later Citlalli could feel incredible evil, whatever it was, residing inside Tyson. They all moved closer to the container.

Tyson opened his eyes.

Shocked, Tarayon and Lupe backed away, while Citlalli took one step closer.

After a moment both eyes focused on Citlalli and a slow smile spread across Tyson's face.

But it wasn't Tyson smiling.

"You are not Tyson," Citlalli said.

When Tyson replied, the voice was deep and loud, barely impacted by being underwater.

"Greetings, Citlalli. The task is completed, at last."

Tarayon and Lupe moved to Citlalli's side.

"Who are you? Where is Tyson?" said Citlalli.

"The Dark will extinguish the Light. The Watchers' gamble has failed."

"What are you saying?"

"They put such faith in Humans; in you, Citlalli. But they never discovered our glorious deceit, perfected these past millennia in the service of the Dark."

"We're here to stop you, to end your slowing of the zips," said Citlalli.

"Of course you are. Our illusion worked with galactic precision. Zip slowing has never been real; merely a way to distract the Watchers as we moved on other areas across the universe. One more glimmer of the Light crushed. One more doorway opened between the stars for the awakening of the one who has lain sleeping since the time before time."

Citlalli and the others were mortified.

"We did wonder about you Humans and your Earth; out of all the trillions of planets and life forms...and whatever misguided faith the Watchers saw in you. Clearly they were fools, their faith misplaced. At long last our need for this useless planet you call Obaddon and its mindless underworld spawn has ended."

"Wait," said Tarayon, "the zip vanishings, all the innocent beings teleported here to die—"

"Oh to be sure, zip fluxes are not our doing; just the universe showing its age. But enough! You've all served your purpose. You are now a waste of our time."

Tyson looked directly at Citlalli.

"Farewell, Citlalli of Earth. We leave you to face your own mortal doom; your failure is complete."

Inside the tank whatever had been inside Tyson left, leaving him limp for a moment, before he began madly thrashing, sloshing liquid over the top. Tarayon was barely tall enough to lean over and help out a gasping and gagging Tyson. Citlalli and Lupe helped keep him from falling hard to the ground. They propped him against the wall next to the window.

All three now saw a distant wave of degenerate darkness moving rapidly upriver toward the tower. Whatever fate had awaited Jamila and Gilad was history.

Now these underworld beings were coming for them.

Back on the surface, Sklizz and Wizza staggered into camp with Summahon. Yore, Einlen, and Waima helped with a special wrap around her badly gashed head. Then everyone shared the latest news from above and below the surface of Obaddon. Of course Sklizz and Wizza marveled at Heather's miraculous recovery.

"Do you think those underworld monsters took Estrella?" asked Wizza.

"I don't know," said Einlen, "many vicious creatures on planet."

"What about Citlalli?" said Heather.

"I don't see how Citlalli can survive what's down below and return," said Sklizz, "but Theal's gone and the Watchers made it clear Citlalli is our only ticket home."

"Ya think we should try goin' underground?" said Yore.

No one answered for a few moments.

"Only as our last resort," said Sklizz. "For now, we recuperate and hope."

Far below them in the cone-tower, Citlalli could hear the sound of star-eyed monsters climbing the spiral stairs, growing ever closer.

"Help me push this over," said Tarayon. Lupe and Citlalli got behind Tyson's tank and after a couple of rocking motions they toppled it over, and the entire liquid contents went rushing down the winding stairwell. New sounds of screeching came from below as the liquid flash flood surprised the climbers.

"We're still trapped," said Lupe.

Tarayon looked out at the two-hundred-foot drop. A good leap might make the lake below, but how deep was it? And besides, there were thousands of these dark things waiting below. They were truly trapped, with no escape.

"How did you guys find me down here?"

Tyson's voice surprised everyone. As he struggled to stand, Lupe and Citlalli each took an arm and helped him up. He could feel his strength slowly returning.

"That horrible flying thing had you," said Lupe.

"Yeah, it flew me here, but I don't remember much since."

"We found a cave entrance and traveled here," said Tarayon, "much of the way by an underground river."

The sound from below was growing again as the monsters struggled up the wet tower stairs.

"How'd you expect to get back to the surface?"

No one had an answer. Finally Citlalli spoke, "We had to stop the zip slowing, but it seems the entire trip was an illusion."

"There has to be a way to the surface," said Tarayon, moving back to the window and wracking his Trixian brain for a way to escape.

"They showed me visions," said Tyson, "worlds throughout the universe, stars exploding, galaxies forming, unbelievable power."

"But what are they," asked Tarayon.

"Galaxy Wraiths," said Citlalli. "I could feel them. They serve the Dark. They want to destroy the Light, to make all time and space theirs. The Watchers helped protect of our tiny part of the universe."

"None of this will matter once they get their tentacles on us," said Tarayon.

The monsters were nearly upon them, the loud piping and screeching echoing from very close.

Tyson still couldn't believe his friends had found him. He'd long ago given up hope. And now the monsters were about to kill them all.

"I saw them use the gravity-falls," he said.

"The what?" said Tarayon.

The monsters would be appearing any second.

"Gravity-falls...There's no time, I'll show you."

To everyone's amazement, Tyson took one big step onto the window ledge and leaped out as far as he could toward the waterfall mist. They saw Tyson plummeting down to certain death, when miraculously the mist seemed to catch him, and in a heartbeat he was whizzing past them, straight up inside the waterfall.

At that moment the first dark thing reached the doorway, stopped by the liquid tank blocking the entrance. It started squeezing over the top, allowing Tarayon to take his last dagger and drive it deep into the things head.

"Quickly, each of you must go," said Tarayon, pushing with all his strength against the container, holding the monsters at bay for a few more moments.

Lupe didn't hesitate. She hopped on the ledge like Tyson and leaped, flying past seconds later.

Citlalli hesitated, not wanting to leave Tarayon.

"Go, girl," the Trixian cried, "go now!"

Citlalli ran, leaped, fell toward the ground, and then sailed skyward. She had only a glance back inside the tower room, glimpsing monsters swarming around and over the container. She didn't see Tarayon.

And then she continued skyward, staring down upon a haunted cityscape that stretched as far as she could see, until it finally blurred into the distant twilight gray.

She continued to squint into the blurry mist below for Tarayon, desperately hoping he'd made it out alive. All she could see was the water mist and vapor.

After Citlalli's exit, Tarayon had slammed into the container one last time, slowing the monsters. He knew there was one chance to escape and ran for the window. The pursuers were able to spin the container, knocking him sideways against the wall. Several started scrambling onto the top, with one making it over and rolling off. Tarayon darted cat-like, grabbing a couple of its tentacles and swinging it hard into the container. Then, using his momentum, he took two steps and leaped out the window.

RETRIBUTION

The battle for Mars continued...with an amazed Earth audience watching the miraculous takeover of Rooq's command cruiser by David, Maddy, and Mary. With Rooq and his subordinates still down, Maddy mentally locked the bridge door to keep other Doozies from entering. For the moment, the Doozies didn't know their command spacecraft had been taken over by three Earth kids. The allies helped David broadcast surrender orders to the entire Doozy fleet. Most surrendered immediately, and those that resisted were easily eliminated.

Thanks to the kids and Lucy, against incredible odds, the battle for Mars had been won.

However, Thrix's space fleet had been devastated, and would be little help in saving Earth from the Doozy mercenary armies. But they had to try.

He gathered the remaining ragtag fleet, including captured spacecraft, and began the trip to Earth.

By now things were turning topsy-turvy on and around Earth.

"What do you think you're doing!" shouted Xox at the rebel commanders of twelve transports now hovering over northern Europe.

"We've come from the Human hive called London," said Arrik, one of the mercenary rebel leaders. "We destroyed all Doozy spacecraft that wouldn't stop the Earth invasion. The star tide has turned, Xox."

"Why? You traitorous scum, why?" shrieked Xox.

"You know all too well our Doozy masters have an unspeakable weapon. If they would use Exterminator here, they would use it against our own worlds," said Arrik. He then brought Oriel into view.

"A Human! A Human? What is your game, Arrik?"

"This is Oriel, and she's about to broadcast a message to her fellow Humans. To let them know we are no longer their enemy. That we—"

"NO! This is treason of the highest order!"

Arrik just smiled into the view screen. He could see three fellow rebels moving behind Xox. Apparently they'd been successful in subduing the crew. He would give Xox one final chance, though he already knew Xox's answer.

"Will you listen to reason, Xox? Will you help us return to Yerti and free our peoples?"

As Xox answered, Arrik moved Oriel away. He didn't want her to see what was about to happen.

"NO! NEVER! We'll begin hunting you down and—"

Without warning one of those standing behind Xox quickly and cleanly severed his ranting head from his body. Holding it up by one of the devil horns, the surprise in Xox's eyes was enjoyed by all those who'd survived his ruthless killing all these years.

Moments later Arrik had Oriel speaking to the people of Earth. On the other side of the planet a similar message was being delivered by Anne from over Darwin.

Oriel and Anne were broadcasting the salvation of Humanity. They told Earth that the mercenary rebels would gather their remaining army and return to Yerti, where they would enact revenge upon their Doozy masters. It wouldn't be easy, but they hoped to regain freedom for their peoples, planets, and civilizations.

By the time Thrix and his fleet reached Earth, the worldwide killing had stopped. The mercenary fleet had regrouped and initial alliance talks already begun.

David, Maddy, and now Mary were returning as heroic superstars to an Earth that was more united than at any time in Human history.

It was truly miraculous.

One perplexing mystery remained unsolved with no logical explanation: the question of how or why the unstoppable energy of Exterminator II had frozen in space, then turned the tide of battle in favor of the allies.

Of course Lucy, who'd set all this in motion with a single innocent Basset hound thought, was mostly thinking about her next meal and a nice nap.

CONVERGENCE

Since the ancient Obaddon sun had renewed his strength, Jak-toll had wandered in the forests searching for Heather, Yore, and the others. Several times he'd had the feeling of being tracked, of invisible eyes watching from deep in the forest, but he never saw a thing. Jak-toll was getting closer to the waterfall campsite, climbing the hills that rose above the cave and pathway into the underworld.

After escaping from the cone tower, Tyson sailed ever higher through the waterfall mist. He spotted one of the girls below, but couldn't tell which one. It was hard to see as the mist became more like a real waterfall, and he figured they must be getting nearer the surface.

He couldn't believe they'd rescued him. As a foster child Tyson had always found it hard to accept kindness from anyone. He was soaking wet and strangely happy. He couldn't wait to reach the surface. Of course they'd all have to run for their lives, but he'd be among friends.

After the waterslide ride into the underworld, Lupe didn't think she'd ever experience a greater thrill ride. Well, she was wrong. The gravity-falls were spectacular. Nothing on Earth could compare to this sensation of flying.

Lupe was worried about Citlalli and Tarayon. She could barely make out the silhouette of Tyson above, and there was no sign of Citlalli below.

Citlalli was there, still searching in vain for Tarayon. She was focusing on everything the Galaxy Wraiths had said through Tyson. Incredibly powerful forces seemed to be locked in an eternal struggle. To Citlalli, this all sounded too familiar.

As a child, she'd learned all the ancient stories. Anahuac legends said the Mother of all Gods, Coatlique, first brought Light to the cosmos, giving birth to the Goddess of the Moon, Coyolxanuhqui, as well as many male Gods who became the stars. When Coatlique learned her children were plotting to kill her, she brought Dark to the cosmos, giving birth to the God of War, Huitzilopochtli. He destroyed his brothers and sister. In Citlalli's world, the Anahuac universe was born of Light and Dark with the heavens crumbled to pieces.

To Citlalli it seemed clear that Light and Dark were still battling and the very fabric of the universe hung in the balance.

Below Citlalli in the gravity-falls another battle was taking place as Tarayon fought for his life. He was soaked again, but quickly forgot his wet misery with two monsters gaining on him. Somehow they knew how to float faster, sailing next to one another and closing the gap. Their razor-sharp tentacles clawed through the mist for Tarayon's feet. He had no weapons and was at the mercy of these unholy monsters. He could see the light far above. They were nearing the surface and the rocky walls were narrowing.

He felt a tentacle brush his toe and yanked both feet out of reach. The monsters would grasp him in seconds.

Reacting instinctively like a cat, Tarayon curled up and dived downward in the mist, spinning behind the surprised monsters. He kicked out hard with both feet, driving the black things partly outside the gravity-slide. His timing was perfect as a rocky overhang was speeding past, colliding with and pulverizing the octoskulls of each monster. They were killed instantly, their corpses rotating slowly in the mist.

Tarayon managed to climb atop one floating dead monster and pushed off hard, moving up the gravity-falls ahead of the monster bodies.

Soon they would reach the surface of Obaddon.

At the waterfall campsite everyone waited, unsure what to do next.

In the shade of a large boulder, Waima and Heather were sitting quietly. Curiosity finally got the better of Waima as she looked at Heather in her powder-blue cap.

"What is your head covering for?"

"It's my team's softball cap." She took it off and handed it to Waima.

Waima held the cap reverently, as though it was a fragile piece of art. Heather chuckled and smiled.

"Citlalli was just the same. Go ahead and put it on."

Waima slowly slid the cap over her hairless white head, as though expecting something to happen. It was too big and slid down, nearly hiding her large black eyes.

"You look cool," said Heather.

"Cool?" said Waima, handing the cap back.

"Uh, yeah, cool, good. You looked really good."

Meanwhile, Einlen sat by herself, worried sick about Estrella. She'd never felt this way about another living being. It was tying her three Uppsalian stomachs in knots.

Wizza sat next to an unconscious and tightly wrapped Summahon. Yore was down at the river getting a drink and the others were scattered about.

Sklizz rose from his shady spot and started walking toward Wizza. He remembered how his sister Arizza had loved old Human phrases, and this quiet waiting seemed like "the calm before the storm." Sklizz could sense something coming.

At another time on another planet it would've been a great day and beautiful location for a relaxing picnic.

Into this idyllic pastoral scene flew a windmilling Tyson, arms and legs flailing as he shot out of the waterfall entrance at least twenty feet into the air, arcing toward a soft mossy area where he landed on his back with a thud.

After everyone's moment of stunned amazement, Heather jumped eight feet into the air, not even noticing this impossible leap as she sped to Tyson in a blur, her legs showing off their speed for the first time.

Tyson lay gasping, the wind knocked out from the hard landing. He tried conveying the coming danger, but before he could catch his breath, Lupe sailed out the waterfall entrance. She didn't sail as high as Tyson and landed feet first, doing a somersault to break the fall. Her gymnastics classes had finally paid off. Seeing everyone together she shouted, "We're being chased. Get ready to run. *Vamos!*"

Before the group could react, Citlalli was flying out the hole and landing nimbly on her feet. By now Tyson was up and waving everyone downriver, away from the waterfall.

"Quickly," yelled Tyson, starting to run, "follow me. There are hundreds of them." Obviously any questions about everyone's miraculous return would have to wait.

Sklizz and Wizza picked up Summahon's stretcher and led the way. At that moment Tarayon was also landing on his feet after spouting out the waterfall exit. He dodged the flying corpses of both tentacle monsters as they hit the ground with sickening splats.

"Run fast," he shouted, sprinting after everyone.

The first star-eyed monsters shot out of the underworld with piping shrieks. At this noise the group glanced back and saw Yore still at the waterfall. Darting forward, Yore clamped his teeth on the first live monster's octo-head, crushing it and then flinging the corpse with a shake of his lizard head back toward the waterfall.

Heather was mortified at the sight of her friend about to be overrun by these terrible creatures and ran back to help. Heather was a blur: a Human girl running at cheetah-speed.

The second monster had already grabbed Yore with its sharp tentacles, but let go with a shriek as the speeding and out-of-control Heather slammed into it from behind. It stumbled and fell face first into the waterfall, only to get slammed into with a sickening wet thud by another flying monster, both spinning wildly into the jungle. In one smooth move, Yore tossed dazed Heather onto his back, where she could grab hold tightly as he turned to run after the others.

By now there was a steady stream of hideous dark monsters spewing out of the waterfall and into the light. The insane mob of berserk pursuers was growing by the second.

High above on the hill overlooking the waterfall river valley a tall blue leafy figure had just arrived. Jak-toll stared down at the unfolding madness below. He could see his friends in the distance and that they were in dire straits. The dark things were multiplying and gaining rapidly. Moving as fast as a ten-foot-tall, two-legged plant can run, Jak-toll cut across the hill, taking a shortcut toward a rocky valley up ahead.

Into this valley, following the river path, Tyson led the way. Sklizz and Wizza were right behind, carrying Summahon but tiring fast. The entire group was in the valley and heading up a small hill next to the river. The dark horde had grown to several hundred strong and already entered the valley behind them. They didn't stand a chance. The chase would be over in moments.

Jak-toll used his remaining arms to push a couple of small boulders. They plowed into the front wave of monsters, slowing them and killing a couple, but then a small swarm broke free and began charging up toward Jak-toll. He turned and ran, the crazed things screaming and following.

Down below, reaching the top of the small hill, Sklizz and Tarayon shouted to stop. The monsters were already surrounding the hill and there was no escape. At least they'd have the advantage of high ground for a final stand.

Heather remembered a driving vacation to Yellowstone National Park. On their way back home, her dad took them to a place called Little Big Horn. There she had learned all about

Custer's Last Stand. She wondered if General Custer had felt this way, surrounded by the Sioux on that final hilltop.

The mob of creatures halted at the base of the hill, surprised that their prey had also stopped. They peered up eerily with their piercing red star-eyes, tentacles waving in anticipation of a slaughter.

Heather leaped off Yore, finding it hard to accept that after all they'd been through, this was finally the end. Similar feelings were running through everyone's head.

"Quickly, kids," said Tarayon, "make a leap for the water. Try and swim to safety."

Everyone peered at the wrongly flowing river.

"I'm not leaving," said Citlalli.

"Me neither," echoed Lupe, Heather and Tyson.

At that moment the deranged monsters began windmilling their sharp tentacles, letting loose with their piping shriek and starting another banzai charge up the slope. The adventurers backed into a defensive circle, ready to fight to the death.

In the span of a heartbeat, the charging tsunami of monsters stopped, windmilling arms splayed in every direction like a sea of frozen calamari. Absolute silence fell over the valley. Out of the tense quiet came a new sound, a trumpeting roar that echoed from every direction. Blinking into view from out of thin air appeared the incredible sight of hundreds of Fantasmas with their twin trunks and seemingly headless bodies. And most surprising of all was seeing Estrella riding the largest Fantasma, her red hair flying behind her and screaming like a raging Amazon warrior princess as they charged into the monsters, using their trunks as weapons. It was hard to tell how they did it, but these trunks were killing the dark things. They fought back and many a Fantasma fell under their razor tentacles, but in less than a minute the surviving monsters were shrieking and fleeing back downriver toward the waterfall, a group of Fantasmas in pursuit.

Stunned at this miraculous rescue, Einlen and the others watched the mightiest Fantasma kneel down, allowing Estrella to leap off. Einlen was quivering from snout to foot, bubbling over with feelings she couldn't understand.

Estrella turned to the wall of enormous Fantasmas, now fading to their opaque state, everyone amazed to be seeing through their shimmering translucent bodies. The leader intertwined both long trunks as one and gently tapped each of Estrella's shoulders, like King Arthur using a sword to welcome a new knight to his round table. And with that they completely disappeared, the underbrush moving as they headed back into the jungle. A final triumphant trumpet call echoed throughout the valley.

Before anyone could say a word they heard a distant screech, and then saw the gigantic flying octo-monster that had carried Tyson across the sea. And it was headed straight toward them.

"Into the trees," yelled Tarayon. Everyone ran down the hillside toward Estrella and into the forest edge.

"Let's keep moving toward the sea," said Sklizz, still carrying Summahon under her wrappings. Tarayon wondered briefly who was on the stretcher, but then they were all moving again. They heard continued screeching as the angry creature circled above.

Jak-toll had a head start on his pursuers, but the monsters were faster. They were a minute or two from catching him when they stopped, as though listening to something, then continued their shrieking but headed back toward the waterfall.

A relieved Jak-toll was once again lost. Since the others were probably going to the sea, he headed that direction too.

After hiking through dense jungle, the group emerged onto the black sand shoreline. The ocean was still infested with sea monsters now angrier than ever, swarming and snarling at sight of their enemy. Far up in the sky the terrible monstrosity was still flying, all wings and tentacles. Lupe thought the flying monster looked like a gigantic dragonfly.

Glaring down at the puny prey far below, the demented mind of the hovering beast called for its brothers and sisters. They would arrive soon.

Sitting on the beach, everyone was at a loss. Heading back inland was out of the question, but sailing across the sea was suicidal. And yet their only hope seemed to be getting their one surviving spacecraft fully operational again. But it was located on that plateau far back across the serpent-filled sea.

Things seemed hopeless.

Citlalli sat by herself at the jungle's edge, deep in thought. Others were scattered here and there, mostly staring out at the sea.

Wizza sat next to Summahon who was now awake, feeling much better and wanting to get up. Wizza carefully unwrapped the covering from all around her, allowing Summahon to gingerly sit up.

Tarayon was looking out at the sea, wracking his brain for a plan of escape. He figured the beasts must be patrolling the sea in shifts, while the others hunted. It was the only explanation. He turned to discuss strategy with Sklizz.

At that moment, for the first time Tarayon saw who was on the stretcher. He could not believe his eyes. He stood frozen with mind-spinning confusion, seeing his long-lost life partner.

Summahon continued gazing in the other direction as Tarayon staggered over, falling to his knees next to her. She turned, seeing the tear-streaked face of her life partner. Lightning bolts shot up her Trixian spine, and moments later they were hugging for joy.

Neither Summahon nor Tarayon had ever expected to see one another again. In more than a billion years of zip vanishings, they were the first two beings to ever be reunited.

Eventually they all shared their stories, filling in the cosmic puzzle as to how and why they'd ended up on this miserable planet at the back-end of the universe. This included the Wraiths' elaborate plan to trick the Watchers. The only question was why the Wraiths did this.

Unfortunately these stories and putting the puzzle together still left them with no hope of escape.

During the talks, Citlalli had been thinking. She excused herself and walked a little ways down the beach to the jungle edge, sitting quietly and looking out to sea.

From the opposite direction, far down the beach, Jak-toll was approaching. He'd found a good spear-shaped tree branch and carried it as a weapon in one of his remaining arms. He couldn't yell, so no one saw him. And then to make matters worse, from the other direction came three new flying octo-monsters. They were already diving toward their prey along the beach. Like their underworld brethren, they let loose with a banzai shriek of their own, zeroing in on the jungle below.

Like many species throughout the universe, they could create extreme heat from a specialized internal organ and release it through shielded nasal passages. This is a fancy description for fire-breathing dragons. Thus the kids saw these fire-breathing octo-dragons shoot flames across the jungle, starting a raging fire that trapped everyone at the water's edge. Thankfully these creature's fire-producing organs needed an hour to recharge, so the monsters would have to kill with their tentacles and teeth.

Seeing the flames and danger, Jak-toll began running toward his friends. They were scattering around the beach trapped between flames and water.

The first beast circled and dived, zeroing in on a red lizard and small alien with a blue head covering.

Yore and Heather saw the approaching monster, and with nowhere to hide they turned to face their attacker. It swooped down, tentacles flying behind like streamers, its horrid octo-mouth stretched open to kill. Yore dropped spread-eagle on the sand as Heather leaped incredibly high in the air. The monster missed both and slammed face first onto the beach. Heather landed on its back and bounced off with another powerful jump, landing and rolling toward a trancelike Citlalli.

Jak-toll now arrived at full charge, driving his spear deep into the stunned eye of the crashed monster. Heather and Yore had time to shout Jak-toll's name once as the monster snapped him in its jaws, staggering blindly to its feet and starting to fly out over the sea. Before getting far, two sea monsters with their four heads exploded out of the water and chomped into the flying thing. With a tremendous splash, the monster and Jak-toll were dragged under. Jak-toll's final thought was a happy one. Hearing his friends calling his name, Jak-toll knew he'd died with honor fighting for them.

The other two octo-monsters were furious at their brother's demise and wanted revenge, immediately zooming down toward the beach. One of them targeted a shiny-haired alien and long-snouted beast that had been running toward the leafy creature before it was gobbled up.

Estrella and Einlen and had seen Jak-toll's valiant sacrifice, and now the other monster was seconds away, red eye raging and mouth filled with sharp teeth.

Einlen used her lone arm to grab Estrella and toss her sideways, then turning to face the attacker head-on, to die with Uppsalian honor. To Einlen's dismay it veered sharply toward Estrella.

As Einlen cringed, Estrella disappeared. The shocked monster closed its jaws on empty air then smashed face first into the sand. Its sharp turn sideways toward Estrella caused its neck to snap as it drove itself into the ground. The beast's massive torso crashed violently onto the beach, its body bouncing once and careening into the jungle. Its momentum carried it far enough to reach the raging fire, and the beast roared with death shrieks as flames consumed it alive.

By now the third monster stared down from far above in stunned disbelief. No one ever killed the brothers of the sky. They reigned supreme on this planet, and these miserable tiny things had killed his two siblings. Filled with grief and rage, it would not make the same mistake. Better to move slowly, while trapping and devouring these things. However, he also sent a message to the underworld creatures to return.

Either way these ridiculous tiny creatures would all be killed.

By now the group was clustered on the beach, except for Citlalli. To everyone's dismay she sat a little ways up the beach and seemed to be asleep, an easy target for the monster.

The third beast had landed on the black sand near Citlalli and began moving toward them.

Even worse, they all spotted another flying thing approaching from far over the horizon.

The monster on the beach turned toward the trancelike Citlalli. It could sense the tiny white-haired thing was still alive. Perhaps it was injured. Either way it was going to be dead.

The monster sent a single powerful tentacle to drag Citlalli into its hungry mouth.

Everyone watched the nightmare scene unfold in slow motion, unable to help the brave Anahuac girl.

Heather reacted on instinct, grabbing a piece of sharp driftwood and running like a blur toward the thing. She remembered Citlalli's leap onto the eye of that beast inside the death arena. It was time to return the favor.

The tentacle yanked Citlalli into the air and moved her quickly toward the razor-toothed mouth. Even Heather would be too late.

At that instant a mysterious laser shot from the sky, slicing through the monster's octo-head and torso, killing it instantly.

The lifeless tentacle released Citlalli as it flopped to the beach. Heather skidded to a stop, sending sand flying.

Following the laser's shooting path, everyone saw the lone surviving saucer spacecraft that Einlen had landed on that distant Obaddon plateau.

Heather scooted over to Citlalli so the spacecraft wouldn't land on her.

"Who is flying this spacecraft and firing lasers?" was the question on everyone's mind—everyone except Citlalli. Citlalli was the pilot and laser shooter.

As the group ran forward they were all relieved to see Citlalli now standing side by side with her friend Heather.

REMEMBRANCE

Back on Earth and Mars things were moving fast, but the battle's damage was terrible. Several million people had been killed before the alien mercenaries gained control from the Doozies. Several cities were nothing but smoking ruins.

After meetings between the mercenary and allied leaders, the entire armada headed back toward planet Yerti to teach their Doozy conquerors a lesson. They took along thousands of Doozy survivors as prisoners, including Commander Rooq.

The allied space fleet regrouped, most heading home to their neighboring galaxies to begin preparations for a more secure future.

The terraforming continued on Mars with Thrix back in charge of the Fiberian colony and welcoming hundreds of Earth's first ever off-world colonists.

And finally there were the Human heroes, the three kids who'd miraculously escaped death with David's teleporting power, eliminated Rooq's Doozies with Maddy's telekinetic mental power, and ensured victory with the three most amazing slap shots anyone had ever seen from Mary.

On this beautiful sunny day all three kids were part of a globally televised awards ceremony from the Los Angeles Coliseum. Southern California had been hard hit by the Doozy attack, with downtown leveled and hundreds of thousands killed. On this day of rebirth, remembrance, and celebration, there were more than a hundred thousand people in the stadium and a record-setting global audience of billions watching on TV. Simultaneous events were taking place in cities around the world. Oriel and Anne were part of the Paris and Sydney gatherings.

The whole world was thinking as one.

DESTINIES

Back on Obaddon the group stood around their long-lost space-craft, marveling at the power it must have taken for Citlalli to fly it from that distant plateau across the sea.

Looking inside the vessel, it seemed to be in perfect working order. If they could get it off this planet at least they'd have a chance, assuming the Watchers could communicate with Citlalli and had the power to bring them back home.

After everyone peered inside the spacecraft and gathered around Citlalli, a subtle nod of understanding passed between Yore and Einlen. Without anyone noticing they slipped quietly into the surrounding foliage, finding a pathway through the dwindling flames.

"How did you know you could fly it?" asked Estrella.

"I didn't know," said Citlalli. "Something guided me—a spirit voice, a light inside me. I had to focus, to concentrate all my thoughts. Eventually it got easier, just in time for me to use the laser."

"Can you get us outside the planet's atmosphere, into space?" asked Sklizz.

Citlalli gave a typical fourteen-year-old's shrug, "I don't know."

Tarayon had been pondering what to say next, speaking the dreaded words that everyone had been thinking.

"What do we do about passengers? The kids can double up, but that leaves six of us for four seats."

It was only now that Heather noticed her friend Yore was missing, and then Estrella realized Einlen had disappeared too. Everyone scanned the area. Gradually the sacrifice made by Yore and Einlen became obvious.

"No, no," said Heather, shaking her head, tears bursting out. "He saved me. Yore saved my life. He deserves to go. We can't just leave him."

Estrella couldn't say a word, as she was shedding tears of her own. She'd gotten to know Einlen so well; this act of sacrifice made perfect sense. It was exactly what Einlen would do.

Yore and Einlen had made the decision easy as to who would stay behind. Moments later none of this mattered.

The distant rumble of underworld dwellers came from down the beach. Everyone recognized the hooting and piping and knew they'd better get off this beach fast.

"Inside now," said Tarayon. He led the way, climbing into the pilot's seat. Seconds later everyone was on board and the hatch locked tight. The kids doubled up: Citlalli on Tyson, Lupe on Heather, and Waima on Estrella, harnesses protecting everyone in their seats.

Sitting on Tyson's lap, Citlalli found it hard to concentrate on flying the spacecraft.

Out the side windows they could see a massive black wall of death moving toward them.

"Citlalli..." said Tarayon with urgency.

Citlalli tried to shut out all thought, all outside senses, focusing entirely on her spirit center, concentrating on the Light. Citlalli breathed deeply, summoning the vision of her honored grandmother Analalli, remembering sitting with her around the fire on her spirit quest. It was Analalli who taught Citlalli about her own special place—a place deep inside that held tremendous spiritual power, a strength and energy only women could find. A true spiritual center of the soul.

Yore and Einlen had scaled a small hill and could see the entire beach. They saw the unstoppable wave of black moving toward the spacecraft. The dark swarm of death was seconds away from enveloping their friends.

"Go," growled Einlen under her breath. Then louder she rasped, "GO!"

As Yore and Einlen watched with gut-wrenching alien emotion, the wall of monsters rolled over the saucer, burying it under a sea of waving tentacles.

Also watching this horrible sight was a phosphorescent shimmering presence that floated behind the two loyal alien friends.

Inside the spacecraft all eyes were on Citlalli as everything went dark. The sound from outside had reached an ear-shattering crescendo of horrifying piping and chanting. The spacecraft was starting to wobble under hundreds of sharp-tentacle monsters. Their razor tentacles were scratching everywhere, frantically trying to get in.

Attaining one's spirit center was hard, but as Citlalli relaxed more and more she could hear the voice of her ancestors, and especially her revered Analalli. She could feel the touch of her grandmother's hand on her hair, gently brushing the white streak that they each shared. She was so happy to be with her grandmother again.

In the murky darkness of the spacecraft, all those who could see Citlalli saw a face filled with focused determination suddenly relax into a gentle smile.

On the distant hillside, Yore and Einlen could see the spacecraft start to wobble and rock. The sea breeze carried the faraway maniacal piping and screeching of the monsters. The horrible things must've found a way in and were killing everyone. They each sat back, devastated.

But as they watched, it became apparent the rocking motion was actually the spacecraft starting to levitate, struggling to rise into the air. In seconds the saucer was airborne, rising slowly above the boiling, seething blackness. The spacecraft was still covered with dark creatures, looking like a messy flying pie with blackberry topping; except this topping moved and writhed like a nest of black ants. Many of the dark monsters dangled off the edges, hanging on desperately by their tentacles.

Yore and Einlen watched this awesome sight with open-mouthed wonder. As the craft picked up speed, rising ever higher, distant black specs continued to fall off like freshly baked berry drippings. And then the ship was gone, vanishing into scattered clouds and off to whatever destiny awaited.

Yore and Einlen kept staring at the spot in the sky where their friends had disappeared.

Behind them the phosphorescent cloud shimmered for a moment, and then began moving toward them.

As the passengers peered out, they could see frantic monsters gradually letting go one by one as Citlalli accelerated the spacecraft ever higher. By the time they completely exited the planet's atmosphere, entering the deadly vacuum of space, the few remaining monsters could be seen drifting away into frozen eternity.

All this time Tyson had sat motionless in his seat, afraid to jostle or distract Citlalli in any way. And now as everyone looked over, they could see a sweating Citlalli opening her eyes. Somehow, with her unexplainable and remarkable power, she'd done it!

Catching their breath, hardly believing they'd escaped Obaddon, the passengers all sat quietly.

In this brief moment and without even realizing it, Citlalli sent a message to the Watchers. It was received and the Watchers wasted no time in reaching across the universe to capture this lone surviving spacecraft, with just enough energy remaining to bring them home.

LIGHT

Having seen the nerve-wracking escape of their friends off the beach, Yore and Einlen sat quietly. They would evaluate their next Obaddon survival moves later.

And then the twinkling luminescence moved through and in front of them, floating a few feet away. They each tensed, ready to fight.

The shimmering cloud flickered as they heard the voice of Theal inside their heads.

"Hello, my friends, it's good to see you. The selfless sacrifice you made for your friends and the loyalty you have shown them is wonderful. Your kinds are too few across this uncaring universe."

Yore and Einlen thought they'd seen and heard everything, but this reincarnation of Theal had each of them speechless.

"We'll have need of this special devotion in the time to come. A terrible Dark threatens the entire universe. This battle on Obaddon was just a skirmish."

The shimmering vapor moved higher in the sky.

"My kind has known of this coming war, foretold for thousands of years. This contact with the enemy on Obaddon was necessary. They've already swept across other regions of space. The universal Light is looking to us. All this time we've been chasing time. Well, the time is here and the time is now. We're looking to you—you and many others—to help push back the Dark."

The translucent cloud descended, enveloping them in its shimmering mist, feeling comforting like a snug blanket.

"I cannot say more. I do not know more. Time is rippling. Equilibrium is unbalanced. Darkness and Light push against one another. Your own journeys are just beginning. Where or when you arrive, no one can tell."

They felt themselves tingling.

"I wish I could share more, but you'll have to work things out wherever, or whenever, you arrive. Much danger awaits and your journeys are far from over. My thoughts will be with you."

Darkness washed over Yore and Einlen as they vanished off the surface of Obaddon. Their last coherent thought was the fading voice of Theal, whispering in their minds.

"Let the Light shine through you."

PREDESTINATION

The Watchers knew their eternal battle against the universal forces of the Dark had entered its final phase. Most of the intergalactic chess pieces were in place.

"Were you able to place all the triggers?" said one Watcher to many.

Every surviving Watcher confirmed success.

"It is time for each of us to disappear and hope for the reemergence of the Light."

"So much can go wrong, leaving ultimate destiny with these few mortal life forms. How can this be?"

"All fate is beyond our control. To remain would mean our extinction. These transient mortals with their finite lifespans are our last chance to turn back the Dark."

"But if they do not—"

"Enough! Fate's axis wobbles. We must disappear and observe. The triggers we've planted and enchantments we've hidden must work as planned. It's up to Citlalli and the others now. May the Light shine through these mortals."

The Watchers quietly vanished to their individual secret places, the cracks and fractures between galaxies, to wait, watch, and hope for a miracle.

One of these Watchers was Theal, or what was once the Human known as Theal. Theal had sent Yore and Einlen on their own journeys, then hitched a ride on their trans-time coattails to make it home to Watcher space.

Theal's brief time as a Human had given her a tiny piece of Humanity all her own. She now worried for these brave mortals as they headed toward the incredible challenges ahead.

GAIA

When considering where to deliver the teleported spacecraft, the Watchers decided on somewhere safe and logical for all its passengers. The location selected needed to reconnect the Blue Third kids to Earth with a quick return home for all non-Humans. Thus they pinpointed David and Maddy's life signatures on planet Earth as the place to deliver the spacecraft.

The global remembrance had been taking place in Southern California, the huge Coliseum filled with people honoring the intergalactic victims and heroes. On the stage located at one end of the field were Thrix, Vorwin, David, Maddy, Mary, Lucy, and many others.

Allied spacecraft circled the planet, eliminating concern about any award ceremony surprises like the Doozies had brought to the United Nations. However, no defense could've prepared for a spacecraft materializing from the far side of the universe.

Speeches, awards, and performances had been going on for hours when the battered saucer spacecraft shimmered into existence out of thin air, floating ten feet off the ground in front of the main stage.

Mayhem erupted as people underneath and near the mysterious craft stampeded toward the exits. Many formed a ring of thousands staring up at this unknown alien saucer. No one watching worldwide recognized its Trixian design, except for Vorwin, and even he didn't know who or what might be inside. Security personnel had weapons drawn and allied spacecraft moved toward the West Coast of North America.

Whoever these surprise visitors were, there would be no escape.

Inside the party-crashing spacecraft were eight dizzy passengers. Their last memory was the miraculous escape and then floating in space around Obaddon, before suddenly materializing here. As they regained their senses, each had a momentary buzzing in their brain as Watcher implants and triggers settled in to await their time.

Everyone first noticed that Tyson was alone and Sklizz's seat was empty.

"Where are we?" said Summahon.

Peering out the windows they saw endless people stretching in every direction. From their angle above the floor of the large arena, it was hard to tell where they were.

"What happened to Sklizz and Citlalli?" said Heather.

No one had an answer.

"She was here..." said Tyson, "just a second ago."

Sklizz's empty chair and Tyson's empty lap stared back at everyone.

"This must have something to do with the Watchers. They probably have their reasons," said Tarayon. "So it's probably best if we say nothing about their disappearance, at least not immediately."

Waima was staring wide-eyed at the mass of Humanity surrounding their spacecraft. "Are we on your Earth?"

"It would appear so," said Tarayon.

Estrella noticed Waima's nervousness. "Don't worry," she said, "we won't let anyone hurt you."

Waima tried to give Estrella a brave smile, but it was hard. She was shaking from Doozy head to toe.

Heather could see the main stage out her window and spotted an old friend. "I see Maddy!"

Estrella and Lupe strained to get a better look.

"I see David next to her!" said Lupe.

"One last thing," said Tarayon, "say nothing about your special talents...your powers."

"Well, except you, Heather," said Summahon, "you won't be able to hide those amazing legs."

Everyone stared back out the windows at the sea of expectant faces.

"I think we'd better step out and greet these people," said Wizza, "before they decide to start shooting."

The whole world watched a door slowly open from the alien spacecraft and drop down to form a ramp to the ground. All eyes strained to see who or what would emerge from the murky doorway. Billions held their collective breath. In moments they were witness to the miraculous return of Heather, Estrella, Tyson, Lupe, Wizza, and three new aliens: Tarayon, Summahon, and Waima.

JUSTICE

Of course Tarayon, Summahon, and Waima caused quite a sensation. After quarantines and extensive debriefing for everyone, they were introduced to the entire planet.

There were meetings with Earth's leaders and soon everyone learned about Trixians and the good Doozies. The full story of their unbelievable journeys was shared, and after a couple of weeks Vorwin arrived with a second spaceship for Tarayon and Summahon. They would personally escort Waima back to Yerti.

The group did share the mystery of vanishing Sklizz and Citlalli. The question would always remain: What happened to these two Earth saviors?

These few weeks went by in a blur, whizzing past in the blink of a Trixian, Doozy, Gelzian, or Human eye. And then it was time for aliens and Humans to return to their homes.

Wizza was on her own spacecraft returning to Gelz. She'd really hoped to get to know Sklizz better, but with his second disappearance she was very upset and didn't want to stick around.

Meanwhile, Tarayon, Summahon, and their Uppsalian escort were delivering Waima back to Yerti. The outcome of the returning mercenary armies to Yerti was not known, so they proceeded with caution.

Arriving at Yerti, they discovered that the united mercenary armies were so overwhelming they got the complete surrender of planet Yerti and the Doozy Empire without firing a shot or losing a single life.

The Doozy civilization had been reduced to lesser planet status, while the Supreme Doozy and hundreds of other former leaders had been taken away to face their accusers as war criminals.

The mercenaries had begun removing all Doozy presence from their home planets and solar systems, and everywhere they began a complete dismantling of the Doozy war machine.

On Yerti things had changed for Waima. The long-suffering Doozy population welcomed Waima with open arms. She was the lone survivor of the brave attempt to eliminate their evil Supreme Doozy. Waima had become a symbol to rally around as Doozies tried to recover their honor and pride as a civilization.

Waima was a true Doozy hero.

Young as Waima was, there were already talks about her being a future leader of the Doozy Empire. She carried Stauffa's green blood, had proved her bravery on this incredible journey to the ends of the universe, and would help Doozies regain their honor.

As things turned out, Waima would indeed take on this kind of leadership position, but the nature of this role and the challenges ahead wouldn't quite turn out as planned.

AFTERMATH

Having survived an attack by the largest army and most destructive weapon the Milky Way Galaxy had ever seen, Earth was ready to enjoy peace and a first step into the universe of space traveling civilizations and cocoa trading profits.

At the same time, Earth's intergalactic heroes had survived incredible odds to return home. For some of the kids, their special powers were now public knowledge. Nevertheless, they were allowed to go back to their "normal" lives.

As a group they decided to try and downplay their special powers. The less people knew or thought about them the better, and no one mentioned Estrella's ability to disappear.

Reunited with their families, including Tyson with his foster parents, the kids were soon in school and life was sort of back to normal. They all kept in close contact with one another, able to share their unique experiences in returning to their former lives.

Back in Houston, Heather was a hero, but of course she could no longer play any sports where her legs would be an advantage. For Heather this was devastating, especially given her love of softball.

And then there was the way people looked at her, like she wasn't quite Human. Even her closest friends seemed distant.

She was the fastest Human on Earth, but hated her new legs. She was a worldwide hero, but unhappy and miserable.

David had lived in his cave-room before, online gaming all the time. Now he no longer enjoyed spending his time in a make-believe world, staring at a computer screen. He found it boring and couldn't help feeling he was wasting his time.

David had originally left Earth as a very shy teenager, barely able to speak with girls. Now that he wasn't shy, David had girls interested in him all around the world, but he could only think about Maddy. He often got the same kind of looks as Heather, feeling like an outsider even among friends.

However, David secretly practiced his teleporting, doing it mostly at night or when he was certain there could be no one watching. He'd even met recently with Maddy a couple of times, but doing this was very risky and they had to be ultra-careful.

Maddy found the endless social gossip and typical teenage girl stuff that had been her entire life before seemed remarkably trivial and unimportant now. Her feelings about boys hadn't changed, but for some reason she couldn't get David out of her head. They continued their long-distance friendship at first, and then had their secret meetings. She cherished their rendezvous, one to a park and the other in her own backyard, both at the witching hour of 3:00 a.m.

Like David she kept her special telekinetic power private, using it when no one else was around. She told everyone the power they'd seen had left her. However, over time she could feel her abilities growing stronger and stronger.

Lupe was already the hero of Costa Rica, so her amazing and heroic return raised her status even higher. As the only returnee other than Mary and Tyson who didn't have any apparent powers, Lupe tried hard to regain her normal life. Of course this was completely impossible.

And then the strange visions began.

Sitting with her mom, she'd see things in her mind, and then moments later her mom would talk about whatever Lupe had seen. It was as though she could see into other people's thoughts. She was afraid to tell anyone. After what went on before, she thought they might take her away.

Lupe had no idea this telepathic power had been triggered by the Watchers, using the lingering residue of the original amulet that she'd worn against the Destroyer. It was one of many things awaiting the entire group.

As the weeks passed, Lupe felt this skill become stronger and stronger, and eventually she began gaining powerful control over this ability.

You might think reading other people's minds would be fun, but Lupe hated seeing these thoughts. She worked hard to gain control over switching off this growing power, allowing her to remain sane.

Lupe told no one, not even her mother.

Back up in Canada, Lucy's Basset hound heroics had been the star in Mary's family, but now Mary was an overnight legend around the world and especially in the hockey-mad Great White North after taking out Rooq with those amazing slap shots.

Unknown to Mary at the time, her closeness to Lucy made her the obvious recipient of Lucy's mighty freezing powers. It wasn't time yet, but eventually as Lucy passed on—as all four-legged friends must—Mary would inherit the shower of Lucy's lingering amulet power.

As a foster child, Tyson finally understood that his foster parents really did care, and for the first time everything became easier for him. He was able to enjoy his hero status, no longer shunned at school, while also enjoying good times with his foster mom and dad.

For Tyson, his life had actually gotten better.

But there was a Dark side, and it was growing. Dreams of unspeakable things began to haunt him. Nightmares of terrifying destruction and things he didn't understand. Like Lupe, Tyson was scared to tell anyone about these horrifying visions. They showed him a devastated future Earth and other worlds that looked like smoking ruins. And all was enveloped in ever growing Darkness.

As the Blue Third heroes struggled to regain their normal lives, with problems that most of us can only imagine, progress continued for Earth and her allies.

Thrix returned to Mars and helped his Fiberian people blend with the new Earth settlers. In no time he'd begun the much more challenging terraforming of Venus.

Among the first settlers on Mars were many children, including Cody and his family from Florida, as well as Anne and her family from Australia. These were life-changing decisions by families like theirs from around the world, and in no time there was a thriving group of communities on the Red Planet.

Somewhere Ray Bradbury, the grand master of all things Martian, was smiling.

Life had forever changed for the heroes of the Blue Third. Some of these changes were good, and some of them were not so good. But soon all these changes and everything they'd experienced would be put to the ultimate test. Their journeys and the incredible things that had happened to them held part of the key to the future.

Darkness was about to swarm across the universe.

WEEVILS

The auditorium was dingy, torn up, and dark. On one side of the stage sat an elderly man, seated on a chair and tied up tightly, unable to move. Over his mouth was electrician's tape.

He was overwhelmed with despair, but not for himself. In a few minutes he'd be witnessing the assassination of two former friends, both having traveled a great distance across space and time to be here, only to be killed upon arrival.

The vicious Weevil overlords weren't talking, but he knew they had used him. Somehow the Weevils and their Dark masters had arranged this murderous ambush, extracting some knowledge planted deep inside his brain. He didn't understand how they did it, but instinctively he knew it was true.

The old man had traveled here in secret. He was going to meet the two most wanted underground rebel leaders in the galaxy. Then he and these rebel leaders were to meet their returning friends. It was vital to the Human race's struggle for survival that these meetings take place.

And now the old-timer was certain the Weevils had learned of this clandestine meeting from his brain. The Weevils had sprung from the shadows, easily capturing the rebel leaders and taking them away an hour ago.

The man struggled uselessly against his bindings. They were too tight, he was too old, and the silver tape had him totally gagged. There was no way he could warn his other friends who were due to reappear in minutes. He slumped in his seat.

Around the room were other Humans. However, these traitors to Humanity were the Global Earth Council: Human leaders who had sold their souls to the Weevil overlords. And now, to his disgust, these excuses for Human beings were talking and

laughing with the hideous Weevils, waiting to murder the returning travelers—his long-lost friends.

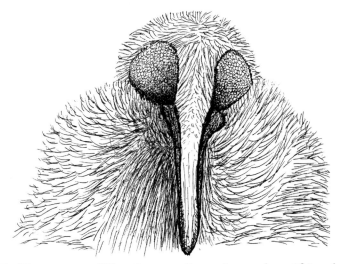

To Human eyes, Weevils were disgusting and terrifying looking creatures. They walked on six legs, sharp brown quills covering their bloated bodies with four opaque wings on their backs.
A long sharp snout jutted far out like a gasoline nozzle from
between two black checkerboard bug eyes. These alien Weevils
could tear a Human apart in seconds, and then use that long
snout to feast on their insides.

The old man remembered well the Weevils' first arrival, flying
in swarms numbering in the billions to conquer the Earth. And
it wasn't just Earth. All the allied civilizations throughout the
galaxy had surrendered in a few days.

However, the final gut-wrenching betrayal was worst of all,
seeing one of his old friends speaking closely with the Weevils.
She was obviously helping them by personally escorting their
friends to this ambush.

Looking out the open window at the dimly lit street, Tyson
thought back to the amazing adventures he'd had with Citlalli,

Lupe, David, Estrella, Maddy, and Heather. It was hard to believe so much had changed.

Somewhere in the distance, lightning flickered once.

FANTASY

It was early evening and a hot dry wind was blowing steadily off the ocean, a regular late fall visitor to this devastated city. The dust and debris of fighting and destruction swirled in the strong breeze, the only sounds in this haunted place.

Into this deserted city two travelers materialized in the shadows of an old building whose roof had been blasted off years before.

Sklizz and Citlalli stood motionless, confused and shocked at what just happened and where they'd arrived. Moments ago they'd been on board the spacecraft having escaped Obaddon and wondering if the Watchers would receive their message to teleport them home.

And then they blacked out and appeared here.

"Citlalli, do you have any idea...what just happened?" Sklizz asked.

Citlalli shook her head slowly. "Where are all the others? What have the Watchers done?"

The street and architecture reminded them of New York, but much smaller. There were no lights in any of the buildings, and everything seemed uninhabited.

"This place does not feel good," said Citlalli. "We were on the spacecraft, and now we are here."

"Let's stay out of sight and look around," said Sklizz. "We need to figure out what happened and where we are."

He led the way as they moved carefully along the edge of a wide street. There had obviously been serious fighting here as buildings were smashed and wreckage was everywhere. In a few minutes they reached a larger street and open area. Off to the left was what looked like a castle or bombed-out fortress of some kind. They started walking toward it when a distant flashlight caught their attention.

Citlalli ducked behind a broken statue, peering down a long street at the approaching light. Sklizz joined her, kneeling and looking closer at this unusual statue. It seemed to represent a man, but strangely he was holding hands with a much smaller alien with large ears. One of the ears was riddled with bullet holes.

The flashlight was growing closer. Carefully peeking around the statue, they saw a single silhouette. It was hard to see through the bright light. Whoever it was seemed to be the right size for a Human.

And now this individual, whether Human or not, walked around the statue looking for something, causing Sklizz and Citlalli to move around the statue too, staying quiet and out of sight.

As the searcher shifted the flashlight toward another building, Citlalli had a better look, seeing someone with long white hair, like hers.

Sklizz was trying to read the inscription on the alien statue, but most was scorched and worn off. He could make out a smattering of Human letters. "D-s--y---- -- -- -s - h-pp- -----."

When Citlalli saw the flashlight carrier wearing a dull-colored cap with the letter "R" on its front, her heart skipped a beat.

And then before Sklizz could stop her, Citlalli stood and whispered loudly, "Heather?"

Heather turned the flashlight on the squinting eyes of Citlalli and Sklizz, and a great big smile across her old and wrinkled face. "Oh my, you both look exactly as I remember."

As Heather walked over to a stunned Citlalli and Sklizz, she wiped her teary eyes. Seeing open-mouthed confusion on both their faces she said, "Things will become clear. You see, much has changed. You've been missing for seventy-five years. The Watchers gave us the knowledge of exactly where and when you'd arrive and here I am."

"But what...how..." said Sklizz.

"I'm sorry," said Heather, waving them on as she started to walk quickly, "You must follow me. We need to hurry. Time is very short."

Citlalli and Sklizz had to move fast to keep up with Heather and her much older miracle legs.

"I'm taking you to meet some friends."

The three shadowed figures moved rapidly down a shattered and deserted Main Street toward destiny.